LEAVING
DISNEYLAND

LEAVING
DISNEYLAND

alexander
parsons

thomas dunne books

st. martin's press ⨳ new york

Leaving Disneyland is a work of fiction. All the characters, places, and events portrayed in this novel are either products of the author's imagination or are used fictitiously.

This is a novel about a prisoner who is released from prison. In the novel, "Disneyland" is the name the inmates give to the prison. The novel is not about Disneyland, and the Walt Disney Company has in no way authorized or endorsed the book or any of its contents.

THOMAS DUNNE BOOKS.
An imprint of St. Martin's Press.

www.stmartins.com

DESIGNED BY LORELLE GRAFFEO

ISBN 0-312-27855-1

First Edition: October 2001

10 9 8 7 6 5 4 3 2 1

for stephanie

Prologue

Dead Earl beckons to Doc. His thumbless hand, like his face, is faintly luminescent, as if the bones glow through.

"Time to walk the road home," Dead Earl says.

Doc nods but makes no effort to rise from his bunk. There are debts to be paid and Dead Earl would be right to claim his due. But the apparition looks solemn, not vengeful, his voice weighted with duty—as if he, too, would rather be elsewhere.

Dead Earl exits the cell, bobbing down the tier walkway like a phantom swamp light or ignis fatuus. Doc stands, hesitant, naked but for a pair of sweat-soaked boxer shorts. The cell is as black as a mine shaft and saturated with heat, as if the stone and metal of the prison had absorbed a century of desert burn and moonless night.

His bare soles scuff against the concrete as he moves along the cellblock tier, the sibilant hiss of the quiescent inmates like the slow release of pressure. Twelve hundred men unshackled by sleep, all imagining futures in which they range free of the confinement of the prison, of circumstance, of their own character.

Doc descends to the cellblock exit, eyes fixed on Dead Earl's light. He emerges to a sky luminous with starlight, the Nevada desert pale beneath this. Dead Earl waits here, holding the reins of a kneeling camel. Doc has heard them mentioned in the oldest stories of the penitentiary lore, feral animals seen from the prison walls, part of a failed army experiment from before the Civil War.

"Ain't you heard of horses?" Doc asks. "Or cars? How about taxis?"

But Dead Earl's humor seems to have died with him. He motions for Doc to climb on. The animal rises, almost pitching Doc over its head. Soon, though, Doc settles into the rhythm of its steady and ungainly stride. He does not look back, knowing that to do so would compromise his escape; the bulked threat of Tyburn Penitentiary is enough to startle any man from sleep. The ground slopes upward, as if the weight of the prison has created a vast sink. The camel labors out of this, its chest heaving, its hide damp and hot. Dead Earl drifts ahead, a polestar that the beast knows to follow.

Through drifts of sand, over plains of hardened caliche, into the face of an unrelenting wind. The journey feels endless. Dawn breaks, a pale band of gray hazing to pink. Doc sees he has been riding through a wide river channel, the ground here dry clay. The sides of the winding channel are lined with the husks of trees— oak, maple, beech—their windstripped branches rattling like bones.

It is when he passes beneath a bridge—the structure eerily intact and in good repair—that he sights the white tip of the Washington Monument.

The camel's unshod hooves clop dully on the pavement as Dead Earl leads Doc through the abandoned city, winding down streets hemmed by brownstones and apartment buildings, no window of which reveals movement. It is only the knowledge of what he has left that has allowed Doc to endure this journey. Now, facing the neighborhood in which he grew up, he wonders if he should have remained in his cell. These surroundings hold no promise of escape. They are like painted facades, a cruel imitation of the refuge he has longed to reach during his sixteen years of imprisonment.

"I ain't going in," he says to Dead Earl. But Earl seems not to hear. He steps into Doc's childhood home, the home where Doc's grandmother had rocked on the porch, where Doc had lived with his wife and children between his sentences.

Indoors, the house is gutted, the air fetid and surprisingly cool, like freshly turned earth. He walks into what was once the living room, the light filtering through the empty window casings, the floor scabbed with rotting clothing, the walls covered with ragged strips of vaguely familiar wallpaper. He nudges a fire-blackened wastebasket with his foot. The parquet floor beneath is charred, the ceiling dark with soot. Upstairs is his bedroom. The floor is hidden by the detritus of a decade or more: old newspaper, empty packs of cigarettes, used condoms, broken bottles, discarded lighters, small glass vials and Ziploc bags, a scrawl of graffiti on the walls—*bitch suck me off, stay tru*—this accretion like an indictment for his long absence.

A long-armed doll is tied to the listing radiator, its arms and legs twisted into tight knots, its upturned, grimacing clown's face half-eaten by yellow mold. In the shifting light the doll seems to move. Doc recognizes it as the one he bought his son just before committing the murder that banished him to Tyburn. He shivers and turns from the room. A shadow passes by the door and he realizes he is terrified, his breath coming in quick, shallow gasps. He wants only to get out and begins to run down the hall, stumbling down the stairs, heedless of the glass vials that crunch underfoot and gash his feet so that he leaves a trail of bloody footprints in his rush from the house.

On the porch he stops. Dead Earl stands below, as substantial as a shadow at twilight. "We got other places we got to go," he says.

"Where are they?" Doc yells. "What did you do?" He wants his son, his daughter, wants to see his grandmother on her porch chair. He descends the steps to the sidewalk, almost slipping on the blood seeping from his feet.

Dead Earl turns, gesturing for Doc to follow. Doc leaps at him, the pair falling to the ground, where Doc fixes his thick-fingered hands around Earl's neck. "This ain't the right place," he shouts, tightening his grip as Dead Earl struggles weakly beneath him. The violence is a gift, a momentary release from fear. He pushes his thumbs hard into Dead Earl's windpipe, feeling the cartilage give, hearing an anguished cry that pairs with his own.

And then Dead Earl vanishes, leaving only his stained overcoat in Doc's grip. Doc stands in this abandoned dreamscape and hears only the rasp of his own breath and the wind that flows past these untenanted houses.

He looks down the street. The light is failing, and with it any landmarks from which to take his bearing.

He holds Dead Earl's overcoat before him like an offering and calls for his ghost again and again as the wind rises, leafless branches rattling, signs shuddering against their posts, a screen door knocking against its frame.

PART ONE
The Tyburn Cross

"The [burn] victims' actual pose, however, is often not
revealing. This is because heat dries out muscles,
which then contract and draw the body into what's
known as the 'pugilistic position'—a crouched stance
with arms out front like that of a boxer."

—*The Washington Post*, "Bodies, Debris at Ranch Apocalypse May
Hold Many Clues, Experts Say," April 24, 1993

The nights snapped out of sight like a lizard's eyelid:
A world of bald white days in a shadeless socket.

—Sylvia Plath, "The Hanging Man"

1

wasn't put out of the house. I left when I was fourteen. When my granddaddy died I went to living with a lady named Odessa. She was a queen of the whores, ran a gambling joint. I go to school, I come back, I got to clean up her place. I make sure the potatoes are peeled, mop the floors, any work she needs for my room and board.

"My father come past one time to bet, gave me a pair of white buck shoes. Only thing he ever gave me, and I cherished them.

"One day there was a fella in Odessa's who had gotten broke. He was drunk, and he wanted to tear up."

In Cellblock B, Doc sits in the recesses of his third-tier bunk, watching his new cellmate and thinking about parole. He studies the kid, who leans against the barred cell door. "Bouncer tried to put him out," Doc continues. "He turns around, knocks the bouncer out. Odessa tried to get around the bar to her gun. He grabs her and shakes her. I'm standing in the doorway peeling potatoes with a knife. When I seen him shake her I jump on his back and start hitting and hitting."

In his mind's eye a series of images shutter past: the broad back of a man in a cream-colored shirt, the fabric taut over the muscled shoulders; a knife blade driving into the meat of a deltoid; the white roll of a backward-glancing eye. Doc has told this story so often that at times it seems a recitation devoid of all association, abstract words linked to an abstract past. But tonight he pauses, waiting for the unsettling, vivid images to sink from view before continuing. He clears his throat.

"When all of this confusion's over they say, 'Hey man, you worked him like a doctor.' Got blood on my white shoes. Potato knife's still in my hand. That's where my name come from. I wasn't no Billy after that. Just Doc. Doc didn't have no feelings, no sympathy, no fear. Doc was, 'Hey, I'm not no sucker, no punk, no weakling.' Doc was, 'So what they gave me twenty years, so what.'"

The kid's lanky arms are looped loosely through the cell door's crossbars, stretched to either side, the long-fingered hands hanging like broken wings. His head is shaved, the effect that of an eggshell delicacy that belies the cultivated hardness to his expression. Doc wonders how the kid expects to get by now that he is no longer in the D.C. jail, now that his reputation counts for less than nothing. Good looks and naiveté smell like blood in the waters of the prison. The sharks are near and neither Doc nor the cellbars will keep them at bay.

"Started jumping out after that," Doc says. "Reform school at sixteen. Served four of a six-year bit for armed robbery at twenty-four. Been almost thirty years in prisons." He kneads the skin around the joints of his fingers. "I got respect," he says. "Spend thirty years fighting for who you is and not getting beat and you get that. But you—you a mark and fellas is gonna move on you. Come into Bone Hill and you got to know who you is. Got to have *certainty* of who you is and what you stand for." He tilts his head right and left, feeling the vertebrae pop and loosen beneath the thick cords of his neck. "I'm Doc. No sucker, no punk, no weakling. And if you here to fuck up my shit you best think twice."

The kid drops his arms. "I ain't want nothing to do with you." He gestures around him dismissively. "With none of this."

Maybe it don't matter what you want, Doc thinks. He has never been so anxious over a parole hearing, never been so close to getting out, not in sixteen years. He stares at the kid. *Been here almost as long as you been alive, boy.*

The kid turns to look out past the walkway. Doc rubs his sweat-slicked face, the outlines of the kid's view from the cell long etched in his own memory. The outer cellblock wall rises seventy feet, set twenty feet out from the fenced-in walkways of the tiers. The stone is scored with narrow windows, each revealing a vertical strip of sky now tinged with red, the sun's furnace heat and color spilling across the flat of the land to wash against the prison and soak into its mortared stone. Indoors, dust motes caught in the cellblock's convection currents spiral past the five tiers where prisoners lie varnished with sweat, and swirl lazily in the air trapped beneath the ceiling.

The temperature has built all day, and as Doc looks into the cool shadow of his cupped palms he notes that the heat has silenced most of the cons. The clatter and echo of the inmates has slowed, the white noise of the prison separating out into a spectrum: shouts, the wet rumble of plumbing, the whir of fans, muted conversations, and behind each a deep desert silence. He hears a screw walking the tier, checking each locked cell for Four Count. The slap of boots is loud enough that Doc knows it's one of the overweight hacks, Bayler or Grippe. In a few moments his guess is borne out. Grippe appears, a flush of red in his dark face, as if it is anger and not the heat that bothers him. Cell count is not a job many of the sergeants perform, but Grippe makes a habit of it. He clicks his counter twice and pauses. "Stand up for count," he says, looking past the kid's shoulder to Doc.

"You the one responsible for this?" Doc says with a nod to the kid.

"World works in mysterious ways, Kane. Stand for count." Grippe's voice is cigarette-raspy.

Doc withdraws into the shadows of the bunk. "Can see me fine, 'less you going blind." Irritated by the heat, he adds, "Maybe you ought to think 'bout *retiring*, your eyes getting so bad." Standing for cell count is a regulation usually overlooked by the guards; in this heat any movement seems a great imposition.

"I ain't the one that's too old to get up off my ass. Ain't too old to beat yours, neither."

Doc fixes Grippe with a look. "We can step outside the walls to clear up that misconception. You and me on neutral ground."

Grippe's laugh is a guttural bark. "Don't never give up, do you? Just another nigger angling to get out."

"Angling to kick your Uncle Tom ass," Doc says. "Just happens to be I want to do it outdoors."

"You going to stand for count?" Grippe shifts forward, his stolid form blocking the light lancing into the cell. He has the dense mass of a bulldog; his legs are short and slightly bowed from carrying the weight of his thick torso.

"Can see I ain't escaped," Doc says. He points to Grippe's counter. "Anyway, you already counted us."

"I can just write up a conduct report, Kane. Put you on punishment, cut your good time—ain't going to be much for the Parole Commission to reconsider."

Doc flushes. Grippe has attended his previous parole hearings, testified, and in each Doc's character has been classed deficient, wanting, unrehabilitated.

Grippe reaches an arm through the cell door and grabs the kid by the front of his shirt in a startlingly swift and accurate motion. He yanks him forward hard enough that the kid's forehead strikes the metal with a bony knock before lodging in the gap between two bars. "Stand and count off," Grippe says to Doc. The kid works at Grippe's hand, trying to loosen the fingers clamped to his collar, the fabric cutting into his thin neck.

"125630," Doc says, standing.

Grippe grimaces against the weight of his jowls, his teeth the nicotine yellow of old bone. He is breathing heavily. "Ain't so bad, is it? Just got to follow the rules. Sixteen years and you still can't follow routine."

"No point you hearing it every night," Doc says.

"Count off," Grippe says to the kid.

"36—366633," the kid grunts, the tendons of his neck rigid as he strains against Grippe. The guard unclenches his hand, the release sending the kid sprawling back into the center of the cell.

"That's your God-given name, understand?"

The kid coughs. "Ain't no God give me it." He massages his neck.

"Bureau of Prisons, shitbird. We give you six numbers that'll last longer than any name you had before. We name you and make you. *That* is God." He shifts his gaze to Doc. "Six numbers—only name you'll ever know or ever have."

"Ain't no number following me outside," Doc says quietly.

"Closest you get to the outside is the parole hearing room, Kane."

"You ain't the board," Doc says.

Grippe smiles wider. "Only one God in here." He turns away. "Forgetting it just makes life harder."

Doc sits back on his bunk, eyes fixed on a white piece of stuffing hanging from the underside of the top mattress. He pinches the bridge of his nose and breathes deeply, slowly, willing the muscles of his back to soften.

The kid stands looking out at the tier, rubbing distractedly at his neck. He turns to climb into the upper bunk.

"Shake the sheets."

"What?"

"Scorpions," Doc says. "They curl up where they can."

"Damn." The kid pulls the top sheet from his bed and snaps it in the air. "You die if you get bit?"

"Just dizzy. Bite you on the toe and it gets all swole up. Remember that when you go to put on your shoes."

The kid gingerly climbs into his bed. "Can't they call no exterminators?"

"Just as soon as they finish the Olympic-size pool."

"They got a pool?"

"What the fuck you think? And stand back from the bars when the hacks is around, like you got to with the monkeys at the zoo. Especially with that nigger Grippe. He'll fuck you up."

"He don't pump no fear," the kid says.

"Only 'cause you stupid."

"I ain't stupid."

"Whyn't you quiet down? Go back to dreaming 'bout that swimming pool," Doc says.

The last of the evening light fades as the cells are reopened following the completed Four Count and the ring of the Quiet Bell. The convicts are free to roam within their own cellblocks until ten, when the cells are locked down for the night at Five Count. Through the night they will be counted at midnight, three A.M., and five-thirty A.M., when the cells will again be unlocked. Doc doesn't have the energy to rise and make his way to the TV room; nor does he feel like visiting others on the tier.

The kid stays in the cell with Doc, perhaps afraid to wander. The first weeks spent in the prison's receiving unit are difficult. The guards haze the arrivals, looking for a chance to abuse their disoriented prey, intent on establishing a respect for the Byzantine rules governing the prison's hierarchy.

The kid shifts, the sagging springs above Doc's head creaking. Has he realized that this cell will be home for the rest of his life? Doc thinks it unlikely. There are facts, monolithic and unforgiving, that eclipse the light of hope if acknowledged. Facts best ignored in the manner that a child hides: covering the eyes in the belief that what is not seen does not exist.

Old Man Ellis warned Doc of the cell transfer two days earlier, revealing bits from his new cellmate's file. Byron Cripps. Twenty-one. Prisoner number 366633, to serve a life sentence without possibility of parole.

Ellis had visited him early in the morning, finding Doc alone in the cafeteria. His stiff, thin body was suggestiv weather-bleached tree, the kind that endures decades clinging to a barren ledge, its limbs hardened and gnarled by sun and wind. "You know you due for a move," he'd said.

Doc hadn't, though in a couple of hours the guards would come and wait for him to pack his possessions in two cardboard boxes and escort him to the new cell.

"It don't fit," Doc had said.

Ellis twisted a wiry forefinger into his ear like an auger, wiped it on his pantleg and continued, his eyes roving. More on Byron: that he ran a D.C.-based drug crew, fought violent turf wars, that he ordered the deaths of witnesses subpoenaed for his trial.

Doc had shrugged, more concerned with the location of his new cell. "They going to put me up on a higher tier? Can't take that heat."

"Ain't you listening?"

"He ain't nothing new here," Doc said. "Just another punk full of himself. He was so smooth and he wouldn't be coming here for a life jolt."

"That ain't what I'm talking about." Ellis tapped the table with a carefully manicured nail. "How you think I got this information?"

"Shit, Ellis, I don't know. You always nosing around."

"You keep your eyes open, Doc. That folder was on Raven's desk when I was due to clean. Raven ain't careless." He'd stood to leave. "And those witnesses that boy had killed? One was a D.C. Black. Cornelius's little brother."

"Ahh fuck," Doc said. *I don't deserve this shit.*

Now, with the kid ensconced in his cell, Doc's thoughts circle this exchange. He wonders, too, whether the kid has any idea of how tenuous his position is. What will he do when he realizes that he's bunking with a member of the D.C. Blacks? The law of escalating retribution is not to be denied, not by Doc, not by the kid.

Doc sighs, feeling as if the burden of his experience is pressing the air from his lungs. To have a young punk foisted on him reads like a sign declaring the administration's displeasure. Yet as best Doc can recall, he's given no offense. *Coincidence,* he thinks. *Or habit. They just in the habit of fucking with you. Motherfuckers don't give it no thought. Do it as natural as breathing or shitting.*

The heat lingers, intense, enervating. After dinner, Doc drifts in and out of sleep before waking fully for Five Count and the night's final lockup. From below he hears the electric buzz as the cellblock gate lurches into motion, a deep rumbling audible through the concrete, the hammer-strike of the gate locking into place, punctuating the arrival of night.

The closing of the gate has never lost its note of finality. It has marked his every day in prison as today it marks the kid's. The reverberations of the gate loom like something physical, crowding the air with their heavy black geometry. Doc listens, the sound bookending sixteen years. It surprises him that such a slight lull in the noise level of the cellblock is so apparent, makes him momentarily aware of how utterly connected he is to the rhythms of the prison. So many years in the crucible of the desert have fused him with the penitentiary, binding them at some basic level. A disquieting observation, more so because the same fate awaits this new arrival—a kid almost twenty years younger than Doc was when he arrived at Bone Hill.

He has spent sixteen years inside, but the details of riding the chain, of arrival, are fresh: the wire mesh crushed into the windows of the transport bus, the silence of the other cons catching their last glimpses of the outside world as the bus rocked over the buckled access road. Through the warped lens of desert air, Tyburn was, at first, indistinguishable from the desertscape. The sun had bleached the ground and bushes a sere spectrum of bone and ivory and potsherd brown, and in the midst of this, the coloring of the prison was no different: a trembling mass of granite, yellowed lime-stone, and burnt brick, a mirage as yet indistinct. He'd had the impossible hope that the B-More Crew would flash into sight, firing into the tires of the bus, the world suddenly full of possibility as he and Jake and Rebo escaped into the backdrop of the horizon in Jake's burgundy Impala.

But the bus continued its approach. The prison's silver dome glinted dully in the uncertain light, and the structure beneath firmed into a version of the Capitol, as if in the wake of some apocalyptic occurrence the landmark building now crowned an empty waste-land. Closer and the forbidding mass of the building was apparent in the heavy limestone blocks of the facade, in the deep shadows of recessed windows.

Doc can still picture the ornate lettering above the gaping en-trance, the name spelled out in rust-fuzzed iron set into the massive lintel stone. Tyburn Federal Penitentiary.

Doc's hands and feet were deadened by the shackles long before arrival. In the bus each con was chained to a partner and each pair of seats was separately caged, a taste of the awaiting confinement. He'd been lucky; Stirling Bison had been paired with him. Stirling—his first friend, and still his best. The bus passed the front entrance to the prison, pulling to a side wall, where a shuttered metal gate opened to admit it—a servants' entrance, he'd thought.

Descending from the bus, Doc's unfeeling feet tripped him, clipped hands useless to break the fall. He landed facedown in the open-air holding pen, pulling Stirling with him, furious at the hu-miliation though the guards took no notice, not even bothering to haul them to their feet. The handcuffs and leg irons were linked by a chain running between them, this chain in turn clipped to a belly chain, the knotted loops forcing him into a bent, shuffling gait, unable even to mimic a defiant stance or carriage as he as-cended the broad fan of steps leading to the barred entrance of the sally port.

Inside, they'd waited in the holding cell for the Receiving Unit, a featureless room with a raised gunwalk where three guards paced with sawed-off shotguns at the ready, low enough and close enough that they could rap the newly shaved head of a con with a blued muzzle. Most of the arrivals had done time: you could tell by the way they held themselves—self-contained, not making much small talk, many with inked forearms. It took time to earn your way into Tyburn. The joke went,

Q: How does a con graduate to Bone Hill?
A: He fucks up everywhere else.

Two shakedowns—pant cuffs and shoes, a pat beneath the arms and up the legs; strip...check under scrotum, between ass cheeks, in mouth, between toes. Grippe, Doc remembers, had searched him: Grippe had been merely stocky then, a young guard with fashionable sideburns and an afro tamed by a tight hat, his nose not yet swollen from too much drink, job new enough that he still enjoyed swaggering among the inmates. He'd run his hands up the insides of Doc's legs in a cursory, clinical manner, yet eyed Doc's body with greater scrutiny than that of any lover, the search an unsettling juxtaposition of intimacy and impersonal examination to which Doc has never become accustomed.

Naked, he was sprayed with anti-louse disinfectant and issued prison denims stenciled with the number that would name him for the rest of his sentence—125630. A number now low enough that it commands respect from the veteran cons and new fish alike, respect for time served as an old-school convict.

Doc stretches, clasps his hands behind his head. One of the kid's slender arms hangs from the upper bunk.

The shackles they used when you rode the chain felt like a branding, cinched tight enough to burn. Doc had complained of the pain to Stirling after the anti-lousing, neither noticing as Grippe approached. Stirling muttered, "Ever tried to run with your feet asleep? Hacks don't have to waste no bullets on someone trying to run when they know he gonna sprain a ankle in three steps." They stood massaging raw wrists and listening to Sergeant Biddle, long since retired, lay out the prison rules in a low monotone.

Grippe stepped up and leaned in too close, his dark face impassive. "Y'all feeling lonely? Need a little help, someone to talk to?"

Doc still isn't quite sure what it was about Grippe that set him off—the swagger, being the first at the prison to check his nuts, feeling that a house nigger was trying to fuck with him. But whatever it was between them, it appeared that day and in the sixteen years since, their enmity has festered.

"Why? Does being a house nigger mean your ass is for sale, too?"

Biddle paused his monologue.

"What's your name?" Grippe said, face flushing red beneath his dark skin.

"Kane, William Ro—"

Grippe slapped him in the face, then poked the stenciled number on Doc's denims. Around them it quieted. Doc tightened his jaw, aware that they were the center of attention, cautioned by Grippe's masked expression.

"What's your name?"

"125630."

Grippe slapped him again. Doc tasted blood.

"125630, sir."

Grippe nodded once, perhaps disappointed by such a quick study. "That's right—*sir*. I ain't no house nigger and no brother to you, neither. Call me sir, mister, even righteous motherfucker. You ain't got no brothers here but the rest of this trash." He'd motioned at the other arrivals. "The kind you deserve."

It was the beginning of a ritual, tonight performed for the kid. It is Grippe's reminder that Doc's name has been deeded by the Federal Bureau of Prisons, a reminder that it is the goal of the prison—or Grippe—to match an institutional personality to his institutional name.

The cellblock is still. Doc listens to silence settle following evening lockup, a lull that marks the close of each day. He wonders if there is a collective memory of the first day; if the other cons, too, feel the same buried thoughts stir at the echo of the closing gate; if they pause for a moment of reflection.

2

Frank opens the metal locker set into the wall beside his tiny desk, his back to Doc, who perches on Frank's bunk. Frank's stringy hair is brushed to cover a shiny, pink bald spot on the top of his head. *Ain't no white boy looks good bald, 'cept maybe Telly Savalas,* Doc thinks, embarrassed for Frank. Embarrassed, too, to be here. He doesn't want the razors, doesn't need the trouble they'll bring.

Frank works loosely with the D.C. Blacks, the largest power base in the prison. Persuasive and white, Frank has a few prison guards muling drugs and virtually anything else short of guns. In return for filling their orders, the D.C. Blacks handle what Frank calls his collection service. Doc helped him in the past, though this now falls to the younger D.C. Blacks, the ones with more time, less hope, more rage.

The cell has the dusty smell of mold and a section of the cement wall glistens with a damp stain edged in gray. The plumbing of the building is old, perforated with small leaks. Water seeps through the mortared seams of rooms, soaks through porous brick, wends its way down, leaving crystalline traces of its passage. In the oldest, deepest parts of the sprawling prison complex, disused rooms resemble subterranean seeps, encrusted with mineral growths like those that fill the pockets in the layered limestone beneath the foundation.

The cellblock's white noise subtly shifts. Both Doc and Frank look to the entrance. Frank smiles, relaxes. "Well, well. How's the stomach, Suspence?"

Suspence, shirtless, looks pained by this. He steps in, his large frame stooped as if from the burden of his muscles. "I don't wanna interrupt or nothing," he says in a quiet voice.

"Sure you do," Frank grins.

The hair on Doc's arms prickles. Suspence keeps his body turned toward Doc and sticks close to the opposing wall, avoiding eye and physical contact. This is hard to do: the cell is only five-and-a-half feet wide, nine feet deep—any time there is more than one person in a cell it becomes a game of Twister to preserve personal space.

Suspence's bare chest is a record of prison time: tattoos run the lengths of his thick arms and cover his chest—spiderwebs over the elbows, a barbed tail curling around his left nipple and disappearing over a shoulder puckered by a gunshot wound. A red weal jags across his stomach, still fresh enough to have the centipede look of stitchmarks. Doc scans for swastikas, for an Aryan Brotherhood teardrop, but sees none.

Frank hoists himself onto his desk, his thin shanks pale below the pant cuffs. His toenails are yellowed and curled. Doc wonders if they hurt where they press into the tips of his toes.

"You want Marlboros," Frank says.

Suspence nods, his face long-boned like that of a hound.

"And I want to fuck your mom. Life ain't perfect," Frank says. "Lucky for your mom," he adds. Frank enjoys his own humor and his face is expressive. At times Doc has seen him converse with himself and the shifts in his face have been exhausting just to watch.

"I gotta have some cigs." Suspence's sharp body odor mingles with air thickened by smoke, bad breath, and sweat.

"And I gotta have your mom," Frank says, running a hand

through thinning hair. "Now, I know your mom would charge me for it, but I give her a little dough, she gives me head, and everybody's happy."

"Not me." Suspence's expression hasn't changed, the immobility of his face suggestive of some deeper paralysis.

Frank smiles, surprised. "No, not you," he agrees. "But you could be. Just have to master the barter system." He glances outside. It is early evening and most of the population is roaming or in the TV rooms, relaxing after dinner, enjoying a free period before Five Count and the nightly lockdown.

Frank's cell, like all in Tyburn, provides only enough room for one person to move comfortably, though it is fitted for two. The double bunk occupies the left wall of the room, running along the length of it and ending a foot in front of the barred cell door. Frank has hung a blanket over the bunk end closest to the door, blocking the view of tonight's selection of goods. They lie beside Doc: soft drinks, cigarettes, magazines, candy bars, freeze-dried coffee.

"C'mon, Frank," Suspence says. Doc notes his flattened nose and the pale slivers of scars around his eye sockets. He wonders if Suspence boxed. *That, or the boy got a lack of personality*, he thinks.

Frank taps a cigarette from a pack of American Spirits and lights up with a stainless Zippo. It glints cleanly, catching Suspence's eye. Frank takes a few short puffs, further clouding the air.

"I go to a lot of trouble to provide what people need. The administration gives you a place to shit, but you need a tittie mag to read and I'm the man. Even get a fuck doll in here on occasion. Takes money and time. You reading me, Suspence?"

"I'm good for it," Suspence says.

Frank grimaces. "Hah." He places two packs of cigarettes on his desk. Suspence reaches for them with even deliberation, almost as if they are his due. As he turns, his watery blue eyes fix Doc with a flat stare.

"What the fuck kind of name is Suspence?" Doc asks a moment later.

"His name's Spence, for Spencer."

"White-boy humor," Doc says.

"Fucker ain't rational," Frank says. "And he doesn't—It's like he's too still. You start to find yourself waiting to see what he'll do, because anything, *anything*, is better than that loom of his."

"Ain't no one rational looks like a chalkboard someone forgot to erase."

"That's his cellie, Max. Practices on Suspence 'fore he scratches those that can pay."

"Don't sound like no deal to me," Doc says.

Frank stubs his cigarette. "Heard about when he got cut?"

Doc shakes his head. "What for?"

"Likes to bet on NASCAR, but don't like to pay. About three weeks ago he gets stuck in the stomach. Gets stitched up in the butcher shop and pretends to be unconscious—like there's something wrong. Goes on for one, maybe two days. Acts like a zombie anyway, so I guess he's convincing. Thinks that if he don't open his eyes or talk the doc's gonna send him somewhere else for treatment and maybe then he makes a break for it."

Frank shakes his head. "The doc holds his hand above his head and drops it to see if he's faking. His arm hits the side of the bed—it'll land on your face if you're really in la-la land—and he knows what Suspence is up to. So he announces he's gonna have to reopen the wound and dig around to see what's wrong. Dig around. Hah. Shithead's up and running, forgets that he's handcuffed to the bed and dislocates his arm. Got so much adrenaline in him he's howling and won't let no one near him. Too big for anyone to want to, anyway. Stupidity like that is an art. Makes life unpredictable. Gives an element of—"

"Yeah, okay." But Doc is grinning, appreciating the spectacle. For both of them too many years have passed unmarked, blended by an unchanging routine. Variations from the order are links to the past, handholds for the memory so that the years can't be compacted into the description of a single day. The cons who act in these events are like celebrities, accorded an odd respect for having established themselves, even temporarily, in the prison lore.

"All those tattoos...He ain't a member of the—"

"Nah," Frank says. "He ain't got the one that matters. Not that I seen, anyway."

" 'Cause I don't have to tell you that we don't sell to no Aryan Brotherhood."

Frank pulls a roll of Saran Wrap from the locker to the right of the desk. Like everything but the bunks, the locker is set into the concrete of the walls. He removes ten toothbrushes, a pack of razors, each sliver wedged into a paper sheath, and several rolls of surgical tape. Doc notices that Frank's cheeks have begun to sag. In the harsh light of the cell he looks tired. He wonders if Frank sees the same age weighting his own face.

"It ain't my business," Frank says.

"Nope," Doc says, sliding the toothbrushes and Saran Wrap into his loose sleeve, pocketing the razors.

"We got a parole hearing coming, Doc. Two weeks."

"I know it." He is annoyed with Frank for reminding him of the obvious, for fixing him with a stare that seems so reproachful. "It's bad enough having to act like a fool, without you remind me 'bout it," Doc snaps.

Frank sighs. "I know how it is. I'm just saying that—"

"You can't just quit."

Frank nods unhappily.

"Anyway, Grippe's already making noises. Wants to fuck me again. And you know the hearing officers already made up their minds. Just want to sit with Grippe and join in the game of cat and mouse."

"Fuck Grippe," Frank says.

"We all been praying and it ain't happened yet," Doc says.

"Keep the faith."

Doc smiles enigmatically. "Faith got nothing to do with it. Got to take initiative when the deck's stacked against you." He pauses at the cell door. "I got a new fish in my cell. Byron Cripps. Don't sell him nothing. He gonna have enough problems without having to pay you hundred percent interest."

"Okay, Doc, okay."

It is nearing Five Count. Doc walks beneath the rotunda. At the center of the vaulted space a guard sits in a box of shatterproof glass. The glass is thick and yellowed. The guard looks like an insect trapped in amber. Doc hears the soft bounce of a ball. A guard emerges from where Cellblock D spokes from the hub of the rotunda, a tennis ball in his hand. He winds his arm back and crouches slightly, then straightens and lobs the ball at the underside of the dome. Doc watches the green ball rise and pause, still twenty or thirty feet beneath the dome's arch. The paint of the dome's underside is fissured, flaking leaves of paint having split from the stone, seemingly held in place by the cobwebs that festoon the ceiling's arc. The ball drops and Doc follows it to the palm of the guard. The guard smiles when their eyes meet. The on-duty guards toss the ball nightly, a time-killing ritual. As far as Doc knows, no one has yet hit the ceiling. On sleepless nights he'll sometimes listen for the quiet bounce.

In Cellblock B a repetitive banging announces that Hammer's been released from seg. Hammer, rotund, perhaps thirty, habitually knocks together whatever's around: tray to table, bunk to wall, shoe to bars, et cetera. He's been doing this for six months, and most of his time has been spent in a padded cell in seg. During his first stay in solitary he'd used his head against the wall. Now he spends his stays in isolation drooling from Thorazine. There is betting over how soon he will be transferred. Odds laid on the mental institution.

The kid lies in his bunk reading a *Batman* comic Doc has left out next to a stack of *Scientific American*s. "Yo, can't no one shut him up?"

Doc shrugs.

"Twenty minutes," the kid says. "Been doing that twenty minutes."

"Give it another five. He don't wear himself out and someone'll get into it."

Doc sits on his bunk and pulls the Saran Wrap and toothbrushes from his sleeve. He rolls them into a towel along with the razors and surgical tape, then lies back in his bunk, flipping through a comic.

Outside, the banging continues. Several people have begun to shout. "Hammer, you motherfucker!" yells one. "I gonna hammer my dick in your ass you don't—" More yelling. Guards clatter up the stairwell and the cons fall silent, listening. The banging stops. A few loud grunts followed by silence.

"Like I said, five minutes," Doc says. He puts a hand on the lumpy towel. By morning Cornelius will have affixed the razors to the sides of the toothbrushes with the melted Saran Wrap, making shanks that are good for slashing, but not, thinks Doc, for fatal puncture wounds. It is a small consolation for a man with four years left to his sentence and an upcoming parole hearing. He palms the sweat from his forehead, wipes his hand on the mattress.

He wonders if Old Man Ellis has rid his jacket of the gambling records, as promised. With no gambling record, Doc is clean enough that any objections from Grippe will simply appear vindictive, and it is possible that Doc will be released. He smiles, anticipating the sight of Grippe's face when he realizes what Doc has done. Ellis is thorough, smart enough to cover his tracks, and Grippe protests at enough of the parole hearings that his objections and memory of the gambling incident will be easy for the Parole Commission hearing officers to write off as either wishful thinking or a simple mistake. It will be a sweet moment.

He wishes Cornelius would hurry. A thirty-second cell search will erase his good time, his prospective parole date, land him in solitary. And he doesn't want the kid to find out who Cornelius is. It won't do the boy a bit of good to know that this is the brother of someone he'd had killed—it will just leave Doc with less control over the situation.

The kid crinkles a comic-book page.

"Don't fuck up the covers, you want to keep reading," Doc snaps.

"Okay, man, be cool. One of them scorpions crawl up your ass?"

"Y'all need to learn a little respect. Got to preserve respect 'fore everything else. Part of the code," Doc says.

"Don't need to know nothing 'bout your code," the kid responds.

"Don't know what you need to know 'cause you a fish. Goddamn Pepsi Generation. Your momma was around, you'd still be sucking her titties."

"Yo, that's more than you ever had."

"Young fool, I sucked your momma's titties and your grandmomma's, too." Doc hears another crinkle. "Don't be reading when I'm talking."

"You gonna talk no matter what." The kid's voice is calm.

Presence, thinks Doc. "One more thing. You listen, then go back to reading 'bout Batman apprehending sorry-ass criminals like yourself."

The kid grunts.

"Only one kind of con in here: Them that lives by the convict code. The rest is inmates, fuckups, lops, fish, psychos. Convict got honor; ain't no prison gonna beat him."

The kid turns a page, noisily.

Doc sighs, gets up and goes to the sink to cool his face. He looks into the polished metal mirror above the basin, the kid's face reflected from where he sits on the top bunk. Fine blue veins web his eggshell skull, visible beneath his light-brown skin. He seems too delicate to endure the unrelenting pressure of Tyburn and the nature of its confinement. This thought makes him seem both beautiful and alien to Doc in a way that he's loath to think on.

"When you gonna quit acting like you the only one that's been around?" the kid says, setting aside the comic. "I ain't no punk. I run more product than you *ever* seen. I ain't no sorry crackhead, no fuckup thief. And I *definitely* ain't no fish. So you can quit with the granpa convict shit. Only thing I need I got," he says, tapping his head with a forefinger.

Doc turns to respond but the kid is no longer watching him.

Grippe's wide, sagging body blocks the open door of their cell, every inch an obstacle. He smiles.

"You comfortable in here?" he asks Doc. "The mattress give you enough? Got to stay well rested."

Doc keeps his face blank and his eyes away from the folded towel on his bunk.

Grippe looks about solicitously. He runs a finger along the top of Doc's locker, drawing a line through the thick dust. "Clean cell. I'll put in a word about that." He looks at the kid for a long moment. "Don't be making noise for Kane. Old man needs his sleep for his parole hearing—something you ain't never going to experience."

"I got a lawyer gonna schedule one ASAP," the kid says. "See what he has to say 'bout guard brutality, too."

Grippe turns to Doc. "This the smartest punk-ass bitch you could find for a cellie? Too stupid to suck dick, I bet."

"So you saying you smart enough to suck dick?" the kid says.

"You want to gum your food for the rest of your stay, keep talking."

"Didn't choose nothing," Doc says.

"Ain't the story I got. Heard you was getting *lonely.*"

In the silence of Grippe's departure and Doc's relief, the kid asks, "You get to choose your own cellmate?"

"You think I'd choose your trash-talking ass?"

"I got *personality.*"

"You ain't got shit." *Less than shit*, he thinks. *Think you know the score. Damn.*

"That motherfucker better watch it," the kid says.

"You the one better watch it. Watch that mouth, too."

"Don't be pulling that granpa shit on me."

"Yeah, that's right. Forgot that you know it all." *Like the fact that you gonna be scheduled for a hit by my crew 'cause you been set up just like you set up those witnesses.* He wonders how long he can stave off the inevitable.

A few moments later the cellblock intercoms blare, "Five Count lockup," in a distorted crackle. Cons start to walk the tiers, heading for their cells. Cornelius, a long-standing D.C. Black like Doc, glides in. "Sorry I missed the party," he says. Doc steps forward with the towel, getting between Cornelius and his view of the kid even as Cornelius's eyes slit and his face tightens. His obsidian-black skin and hard features give the impression that he's been chiseled from some unforgiving stone; it is impossible for Doc to imagine that Cornelius was ever a child, ever anything but the unyielding man before him.

Doc would like to yell at Cornelius for being late, to say that his timing almost cost Doc four years of time, but instead he presses the rolled towel to Cornelius's chest and turns him back toward the tier. "You just be patient," he whispers in Cornelius's ear. He is almost surprised to find Cornelius's shoulder warm where his hand rests.

"Fuck patient," Cornelius mutters.

3

The cafeteria smells of food and sweat, tinged with something rotten. Voices rise and fall, amplified by the high ceilings, a sonorous roar, the voice of the pen.

Across the room Doc sees the kid perched in the fuckups' section and nods to himself. Whites cluster against the east wall around a pocket of the Aryan Brotherhood; blacks line the west wall, grouped by area—New York, D.C., California—as well as by gang and religion. Mexican, Puerto Rican, and Cuban *carnales* sit to the south; a buffer of outcasts—Asians, Indians, gays, crazies, the kid among them—are grouped in the hall's center. The guards, armed with truncheons, loiter near the serving line, a spot of beige against the faded-blue field of prison denim.

Doc knows the kid isn't happy being with the fuckups, feeling it an affront to his touchy street pride, but he's safe for now. Many of the new fish now free of the Receiving Unit have already run into trouble, marked as soon as they approached the wrong table.

Why you worrying about that boy? he thinks. *Had any sense and he'd be no concern of yours. Ain't a damn thing you can do for him 'cept keep him company when he sinks. Ain't a thing nobody can do.* But this isn't quite true. Like it or not, any trouble the kid gets into could fuck up his parole. *Got to get with it*, he thinks. *Don't go and let him start no fire on the first floor of the house when you stuck upstairs.* His eyes seek Ellis, find him with the other D.C. Blacks, and he feels a momentary comfort at the sight of the old man.

Elston, a spindly black Doc first met in a long-ago stay in NYC's jail, the Tombs, joins Doc in line.

"Yo, Houdini, whassup," Doc says.

Elston grins. He recently escaped from Atlanta by impersonating a building inspector, using just a clipboard and some technical jargon. The guards let him walk right out the front gate. The theory is that here, even if he succeeds again, he'll find himself standing in the middle of a desert. His Atlanta escape has made him popular with the convicts and he is rarely alone, as if proximity will allow the other hopefuls to beat the odds. Even as he and Doc move through the line convicts pat Elston on the shoulder as if touching a lucky penny.

Doc picks up several plastic forks and knives. In the past there were metal ones, but too many were used as shanks, patiently sharpened against the cement floors, the hilts thickened with tape stolen from the infirmary.

They fall to chatting about the Tombs, then to the differences between Atlanta and Tyburn as they get their food. It's still strange for Doc to speak with Elston: The last they'd seen each other they'd been scared kids, really, awaiting sentencing and trying to bluff their way through their stay at the Tombs; more than once Doc had kept Elston from being raped. Out of touch since then, it is difficult to reconcile the aging man before him, hair peppered gray and receding from a high forehead, with the scared youth he'd once known.

"Difference is," Doc says, "that here even the motherfucking bugs is tough. Cockroaches can't cut it here. Just scorpions and centipedes. A whole new level of mean."

"It ain't so bad," Elston says. "Try to work outside in a Georgia summer and hell looks good."

"We got hot here. Hundred-ten, hundred-fifteen for days on end."

"Yeah, but it's a dry heat."

They near the end of the line. "You settling in okay?"

Elston nods. "Got some homeboys from the City."

Beneath the smell of the cooking something putrid passes beneath Doc's nose.

Stirling Bison's shoulders shake as his laugh booms across the table. The whole crew is present, including Old Man Ellis, who is engrossed with an issue of *GQ* he's propped against his water glass. Proximity to Stirling's bulk makes the wizened man look even more diminutive.

At an adjoining table sit other D.C. Blacks. Several Doc doesn't recognize, though he knows they've just been transferred from Leavenworth.

Stirling smiles wider still when Doc sits down. "Hey, we was just talking 'bout your new puppy dog." Part of his left ear is missing, giving it a pointed tip.

"Yeah. It bother you the way he walk around sniffing your ass?" Bunt asks. His wide forehead is wrapped with a black bandanna. He is short and round and with the bandanna on he reminds Doc of a bowling ball. He's one of the oldest D.C. Blacks, has been inside almost as long as Doc.

Their smiles belie a certain tension. Doc glances at Cornelius, dourly silent, his coal-black face inscrutable. Ellis has stopped reading; he, too, is watching Cornelius.

"Just wish you could get someone close enough to smell yours, you skanky crusty fuckup. Stink worse than the food," Doc says.

"Got to get us some new crew requirements: No crusty motherfuckers," Stirling says. There is a chorus of "uh-huh" and "amen." "You heard of soap, Bunt?"

"Why you think he wear that rag?" Doc says. "Hide his unwashed, nappy head. Gimme your peaches," he adds.

"No fucking *way*," Bunt says.

"Who runs this place?" Doc asks.

"Not you, motherfucker," Bunt says. He reaches up and adjusts his bandanna.

"Yeah, you right. But Stirling here want you to give 'em to me, too," Doc responds.

"I'm the fucking peachmaster here, hey, and I want my peaches," Stirling shouts. He is smiling, his angled eyebrows raised. He strikes the table for emphasis, and others at surrounding tables look over, evaluating intent, the potential for violence. Stirling is a presence not to be ignored—six feet seven inches of edged mass and a forceful personality that dwarfs even his physique.

"Peachmaster?" Bunt asks.

"Yeah, on account of I gotta watch over all you fruits. Now give me my due, fool."

Bunt isn't quick enough, and soon his tray rests between Stirling and Doc, who divide the peaches. When Bunt retrieves his tray there is little left but coagulated grease. He looks up. "Whyn't you take nobody else's meal? Why you got to disrespect me?"

Stirling lingers over a mouthful of peaches, smacking his lips before responding. "Well, you was to shut up once a while and maybe bad shit wouldn't happen to you." He pushes his fork into another soft wedge of peach and two tines break on the tray. "Fuck. Ain't never gonna get the hang of this plastic shit." Doc hands him a spare fork.

"You better," Bunt pipes, fingering a knot in his bandanna. "First it fake forks, and now we just a step away from plastic food. Cornelius was saying they got this new grease back there that's like that Teflon shit. Sit in your stomach 'till you die, know what I'm saying?"

"I never said that," Cornelius says. He sits with his head close to his tray, shoveling his food down.

Bunt glares. "Did so. Too much sun on that bald head of yours just made you forget."

"I don't even work in the kitchen," Cornelius says.

"You got a problem with bald?" Stirling says.

"That ain't what I meant—" starts Bunt, but Doc interrupts: "He just got a problem when somebody's bald *and* ugly," he says to Stirling. " 'Course, that still apply to you."

Stirling holds up a fist, the skin whitening over the scarred knuckles. "Gonna have to take y'all outside and instill a little respect."

"That metal plate in your head been picking up too many *Superman* movies, you think you gonna do that," Doc says.

"After I work you over and we both in the Hole you gonna wish you got my reception," Stirling says, tapping at his skull where a metal plate—the result of a boiler-room explosion a decade earlier—sheaths part of the bone. "I'm gonna sit there enjoying the Playboy Channel and your sorry ass be talking to the scorpions."

"Velvet jackets," Ellis says disgustedly, shaking his head. He looks at the others and holds up the magazine for all to see. The ad features men in green and red velvet ensembles. "Young fellas ain't got no idea what to wear no more. Look like lawyers tryin' to dress like pimps."

"Why you always complaining 'bout that shit like it matters?" Bunt says, still worked up over the slight to his authority. " 'Round here all you got to worry is whether you want to roll up the cuffs of your denims, know what I'm saying? And you, you don't even need clothes nohow—need a good coat of varnish or woodstain or some shit. Weatherproofing. All that fashion shit, it's *moot*."

" 'Moot'?" Stirling says.

"Yeah," Bunt says.

"That ain't no word."

"Get a dictionary, motherfucker. M-O-O-T."

"Two bucks," Stirling says.

"You on," Bunt says.

Doc rises to get a cup of coffee. As he'd hoped, Ellis trails him to the coffee urns.

"I don't want to assume nothing, Ellis, but I got that hearing real soon . . ."

Ellis cuts in front of Doc and watches the dark stream of coffee fill his cup. He wears a slight smile. "You ain't never been in trouble with no gambling slips, hear? That's all you need to remember this time around." He puts a hand to Doc's wrist, gripping it tightly in his dry fingers, fixing Doc with eyes watery and bright.

Doc suppresses the urge to grin. "Right. No gambling."

"*Never*. Like you forgot what the word means."

Doc follows Ellis back to the table, realizing he's forgotten to get himself coffee. The smell of rotting meat settles again. The others pause with their eating.

"Three weeks and they still can't fix that smell," Cornelius says.

"Getting bad again, all right," Doc says. "Was getting better up 'till yesterday."

Bunt points to Ellis, who's now flipping through another series of ads. "You know what that stink is, don't you? You like that motherfucking *2001 Space Odyssey* HAL computer and this prison's like your spaceship. Run the scene and *know* the score, right? Wouldn't let no stink like that in your house unless you got a damn good reason."

Ellis shrugs without looking up from his magazine.

"You ain't got no idea?" Bunt looks disappointed. "I been smelling it in my cell, too," he adds.

"That ain't no surprise," Stirling says. He points to a vent on the wall above them. "See them streaks all around the edges? Bet they got the sewage lines rerouted. New legislation to give our fine federal retreat what you call punitive ambiance."

"You the one with the fucked up vocabulary," Cornelius says.

"Got a problem with air circulation," Bunt declares. "Gonna get all the little brothers like me and send us in to scrub the vents like Team Aunt Jemima, know what I'm saying?"

"Didn't wear that rag on your head and maybe you wouldn't look like no Aunt Jemima," Doc says.

"Ain't no comparison 'tween Ugly Motherfucker here and sweet Aunt Jemima. She too good for you motherfuckers to even talk about," Stirling says.

"I used to dig her," Bunt says. "Maybe she why I always have this thing for older women." He shrugs.

"Stirling's momma was the one made me think the same thing," Doc says.

"We going outside right now," Stirling says.

"Now don't go getting all upset. I wasn't the only one. And anyway, least I can say you had a fine momma. Bunt look like he came out of some fucked-up test tube."

"They got a bandanna gene?" Cornelius asks, his rocky face betraying a rare smile.

"Got a crusty motherfucker gene," Doc says.

After dinner Doc gets Stirling alone for a moment as the group heads from the cafeteria. "Need to talk."

"I know it," Stirling says. "Cornelius won't shut up about that kid."

"So when you going to have time?"

"Soon. Boy ain't going nowhere. At least as long as Cornelius listens to me. For now we got bigger issues."

4

Two days later dark clouds mass. The air is hazed with dust and the afternoon sky glows in brilliant shades of purple and green. It is otherworldly. Doc and his coworkers, returning from the textile shop before Four Count and dinner, pause to study the sky. To the northeast loom depthless black clouds freighted with threat.

One of the cons whistles. "Gonna have a hell of a storm."

Others nod. "Could use the water."

The wind kicks up, strumming the high-tension wires strung between the towering walls of the Yard.

"It ain't water," Doc says.

"Well it ain't snow." The others laugh.

"Dirt," Doc says. He leaves the group, aimed at the main prison building.

"What?"

"Dust storm," he says over his shoulder. He walks quickly, shoulders hunched. There will be no dinner tonight, he knows, and he wants to scam a little food before the storm hits.

The prison is locked down completely by Four Count with news that there will be no release until the storm has passed. The inmates of Cellblock B stare from their barred doors, trying to glean some clue from the view from the outer cellblock windows. Doc notes the silence. Such quiet seems to accompany the significant moments in his prison existence, affording him a chance to concentrate on the moment's import.

The voice of the storm arrives with the mindless howl of wind that has accelerated over the desert flat. The seethe of windblown sand against the windows and walls fills the cellblock. The lights dim and the wail of rushing wind climbs as it scrapes over stone cornices and rams into the unyielding bulk of the walls. Fine dust sifts from hidden crevices. Doc feels grit in his teeth, senses the force of the wind through small, seismic shifts in the floor.

The kid stands beside him, hands grasping the bars. "Never seen nothing like this in D.C.," he says. There is a twitch to his smile.

Doc swallows. "This ain't D.C."

"I know."

"Ain't like no place." Doc runs his finger between his mouth and gums to clear the grit. "Somewhere you ain't never supposed to be," he says, inspecting his finger and wiping it on a pantleg. He closes his eyes and listens to the storm, tasting the sweat on his lips. It feels as if the prison is somehow afloat, the crash of the wind like the weight of waves breaking on the stone, the entire structure seeming to rock from each blow. It is as if the prison has been cut loose to drift into seas where the known referents of the natural world are askew, convicts and guards alike lost in these new and menacing waters.

Doc has been through dust storms before, but this is no comfort. It is unnatural to see sand falling from the sky, to witness in this storm the epochal fury of a judgment out of all proportion with the crimes committed by those within.

A window bursts, and Doc opens his eyes to a cascade of glass. Dust billows through the opening of the shattered outer window. He and the kid retreat to the back of their cell. Doc rips up a T-shirt and they wet these and keep these pressed to their mouths.

Throughout the night the storm pulses. They sleep fitfully, rising every two hours to place their hands on the cell-door crossbars during the cell counts performed by teams of nervous guards.

With morning the storm abates, the air still blurred by dust. Prisoners wear torn sheets about their heads like kaffiyehs and hold wet cloths over their noses and mouths. When the cellblocks open—two hours after breakfast and after three separate counts— the prisoners walk over floors thick with drifted dust. The cafeteria food is gritty. In spite of the windstorm the room still smells powerfully of rot.

Following breakfast the cons are divided into work gangs. Doc is paired with Bunt, Cornelius, and four others. Two tired, surly guards lead them to the Yard, where they are to clear a drift that has blocked the basement windows on the back side of the administration building. Around them the dust has settled over the twenty-two-acre enclosure in rippled, Saharan dunes.

Doc walks ahead of his group. To his left, he sees a set of barefoot tracks in the face-powderlike dust. At one point there is a stutter in the spacing and the imprint of a body, the outline curiously crisp. Handprints to either side of the form are marked by four fingers, each missing the thumb. The guards have passed it blind. He stares at the imprint, mouth dry and sticky with grit, and the image blurs under the breeze and shifting dust until it fades invisible. He does not mention the sight to Bunt or Cornelius as they come up beside him, imagining it to be an anomaly, a result of too little sleep.

They set to digging. Around the Yard other crews do the same; indoors others sweep and scrub floors and walls. Dust roils in the air, settles, and roils again with every attempt to collect it. The guards have several crews running wheelbarrows out to the prison cemetery, where it can be dumped and somewhat contained by the desiccated shrubs ringing the backside of the hill.

Doc digs and tries to shake the image of the imprint in the dust, shying from thinking on it directly. *Going to make parole just when you too crazy to appreciate it,* he thinks. There are other signs of something amiss: It seems to him that the sun is somehow closer, larger, the hard edges of the prison blunting beneath the weight of the heat. The air trembles and Doc feels as if he is trying to shovel water as the dust eddies about him and sifts back to fill every hole left by his shovel.

The guards are irritable from lack of sleep and too much overtime, their steady complaining acquiring a monotonous drone, their figures obscured by the haze of dust. Doc digs steadily, trying to lose himself in the rhythm of the work. Cornelius shovels in sync, the deep black of his neck and chest oiled with sweat. "How long you expect me to wait?" he says, his voice just audible above the shovel's rasp.

"You let me handle it," Doc mutters through the cloth covering his mouth.

"Wasn't your brother that got capped."

"Couple weeks don't make no difference," Doc says.

"Every minute he's around is a disrespect," Cornelius says. "He disrespecting the crew, disrespecting me. Disrespecting you."

"Heard what I said. Don't fuck with me the week before my parole hearing. Ain't got no patience for that."

"You seen who he's spending his time with?"

"So he got friends. You jealous?"

"Don't you be disrespecting me." Cornelius pivots and lofts a shovelful of dirt into the air, the arc of it taking it far over the nearby wheelbarrow.

"You got it backward, you think that."

"It can look like an accident," Cornelius says.

"Bullshit, motherfucker. There ain't no accidents happening to my cellmate this week, hear?"

Cornelius jabs his shovel into the dirt, eyes slitted and just visible between the strips of bedsheet encircling his head.

"No accidents," Doc repeats. "Motherfucker is accident-proof long as I say he is."

"You ain't the whole D.C. Blacks." Cornelius's torso flexes with another stab of the shovel, his body black and as combustible as coal.

"I'm enough."

Later, pausing to wipe the dirt from his eyes, Doc notices that the guards have quieted. Standing with them is Lieutenant Raven. Tall and gaunt, he has the build of a mantis, an impression heightened by a bald head and bleached eyebrows that arch above large gray eyes that are now staring at Doc. He wonders how long Raven has been watching him. Raven blinks, turns away.

Doc hides in the shade of the prison wall with a few others to escape the sun. A chalky layer of dust encases his arms and chest. Bunt, his customary bandanna now tied over his mouth, stands before Doc and studiously scrawls FUCK YOU on his own chest with a finger, the dark of his skin shining where the dust has been scraped away.

"You got the *C* backwards."

Bunt sits and unties his bandanna. "How you feeling?"

Doc shrugs. His head aches, filled with the furnace roar of the sun.

Bunt looks at him closely. "You looking pale."

"Gimme a minute. I'll be fine."

Doc and the kid leave for the showers as soon as Four Count ends. A long line of tired workers extends from the tiled chamber, their hair dusted brown, crusted dirt around their eyes and mouths. The concrete floor is muddied and wet. Doc's eyes rove over those in front of him: Bunt about to enter the showers, a subdued Hammer a few heads up. He is thankful for the crowd, thankful that Cornelius isn't around.

As the line shuffles forward the kid says, "Whew. How you supposed to get clean in a place that smells like this?"

The smell of mildew is powerful, complemented by bleach, soap, and the sweat of those in line. Doc inhales, for a moment surprised that he hasn't noted it. But of course he has, it's just that for him it is such an integral part of his surroundings that by now only its absence would draw his attention. "Best get used to it," he says. "Prison is nasty just like it is gray. The way things is."

"Ain't no excuse for that smell. Bad enough having to sleep in a cell with a open toilet and me laying on some mattress all stank up by fifty other dudes used it before me. This the one place you go where you supposed to get *clean.*"

The line inches forward and the standing water on the floor deepens.

"Gonna get athlete's foot on top of it all," the kid says, lifting a foot out of the water. "Feel that bacteria already. Making me itchy and shit." A few other cons have gone so far as to wrap bags around their feet to protect them from the murky shower water.

"That's the way of it." Doc is tired, still light-headed, and leans against the wall for support. "Whole place stinks. All that sweat and bad breath and sewage just soaks in." He closes his eyes, feels the water lap at his feet as someone exits. "All that fear and hate and pain soaking in." He opens his eyes to the kid staring at him skeptically.

"All that craziness soaking in."

"Shut the fuck up," Doc says, unable to muster a smile. "You got more to worry about than hygiene."

The kid waits. Doc says nothing.

5

ushing up from his fingertips, the burn of tiring muscles running from his forearms through his shoulders and into his chest, Doc breathes to the rhythm of the push-ups and counts off, "One, two, one, two, one." The kid slips into the cell, breaking his concentration. No longer able to force his arms to carry his weight, Doc stands, flicking the sweat from his eyes.

The kid settles atop the bunk, legs dangling. He's pulled off his shirt and trousers and lolls on the mattress in his briefs. "Yo, why'n't you count how many you done?"

Sunlight glances into the cell, highlighting the smooth shape of the kid's shaven head, chiseling features both sharp and delicate from the darkness of his skin. Doc imagines running a hand along the clean angle of the kid's jawline, imagines circling his hand behind the kid's long neck to cup the heavy, rounded weight of his head in a wide palm. His pulse sounds in his ears.

"Don't matter so long as I do 'em."

The kid pulls a soft pack of Camels and a book of matches from his crumpled shirt.

Doc nods. "That's nice. Already got you a friend."

The kid shrugs. He has a soft, undeveloped musculature.

"Dumb motherfucker. Didn't I tell you not to act like a mark?" Doc says.

"Yo. Ain't no one messing with me 'cept you."

"That ain't cigarettes you just took, you dumb nigger. That a favor. I know you don't got no money to pay for no cigarettes. Prison commissary's closed after dinner. I see you with a pack in your pocket I can read it just like someone put a real-estate sign on you say *Sold*. Same sign say you weak; say that hunting season begun."

The kid holds up the pack. "This don't say nothing but one-hundred percent tobacco. And what the fuck do you know 'bout my finances? I deal with motherfucking *millions*! I move weight you can't even imagine. I know all I need to know 'bout finances."

"Past tense."

"What?"

"Use past tense, fish. Maybe you *dealed* with millions, but not no more." Doc shakes his head. "Need a new attitude, you gonna survive a life jolt." He finishes wiping the sweat from his body with a soiled T-shirt. The air is still grimed with dust and the shirt comes away streaked brown. He puts on a fresh shirt.

Out on the tiers men are circulating, some wandering the cement walkways, others visiting, holed up in dim cells. The afternoon heat is still thick. Late-summer light laps at the windows.

Doc finds Stirling sitting in his cell fiddling with small, brightly colored bits of plastic. He has them arranged on a mapped board. He refers to a piece of paper and makes a few adjustments. "'Bout time. Don't you know world domination waits for no man?"

Doc sits and examines the plastic army figures spread over the topography of the Risk map.

"Look to me like you misremembered my domination of Kamchatka."

"I'm gonna kick your ass all over the Urals, just like I did last time in Kamchatka. You the one busy misremembering."

"Huh." Doc leans back against the low bunk. Muted conversations drift from above and below, a subdued tone running beneath the echoing cacophony of louder yells and exclamations.

Doc palms dust from beneath Stirling's bunk and sifts it over the territory marked *Middle East.* "For realism," he says. Stirling smiles, shakes the dice. They fall to playing, occasionally muttering threats.

"See that six? You gonna hurt after this," Doc says.

"Temporary. Italians ain't kicked ass since B.C."

Doc rolls again and laughs. "They just busted a cap in your ass."

Outside, an argument builds, cut short of its crescendo by a reedy voice that Doc recognizes as belonging to Bayler, a guard. "You got a complaint? You put it in writing—"

A flurry of responses slap over one another.

"Fuck you, hack!"

"Yo, chill out, man—"

A knot of cons mill at the tier's end. Bayler stands between two men, his pressed uniform somehow slovenly on his pear-shaped body.

"You backing him?"

"You best shut—"

"That's it, you two fuckers come with me," Bayler says.

"Aww, man, fuck you. I ain't done nothing—"

"Backed him, motherfucker."

But the two cons follow him, perhaps glad for the interruption—a chance to save face without violence. The others disperse, openly disappointed. Doc and Stirling return to their game. Doc mutters something about loaded dice. Stirling shuffles a deck of cards, the size of his hands making the gesture mildly comical.

"Wouldn't make no Vegas dealer, that's sure," Doc says as he watches.

Sterling tallies up the results of the latest stage of their ongoing war. He looks up triumphantly. "Hey, hey! That's right. I am the *man!*"

Doc rolls his eyes. "Ain't no reason for me to have been assigned to a new cell. And 'specially not no cell with that kid," he says. "Grippe don't have the energy to work that on me just for kicks."

"Don't have no more patience than when you got here," chuckles Stirling.

"Too old for patience. Been patient sixteen years."

"So," Stirling says, "we going to discuss Byron Cripps, lately of LeDroit Park, Washington, D.C.?"

"I know all that shit. Ellis talked to me. I want to know what you plan to *do*."

"Hey," Stirling says, holding up a hand. "Patience. You sound like Cornelius." He slides the game beneath the bunk. "When he went up on RICO charges he got a list of witnesses and killed eight of 'em. He got proactive on one of ours: Cornelius's little brother, Sartorius."

"Family got some fucked-up names."

"You want to hear this or not?"

"I want to say straight out that I got parole coming up. I *don't* want no disappeared cellie. Can't afford it. Cornelius just going to have to wait. He the one needs to learn patience."

"Wait 'till you know it all. You hear how big this boy's operation was? Boy was *large*. He was gonna move on a few crews in the area when he got stung. Had big plans to expand."

"So?"

"One of the operations he wanted was ours. Run by D.C. Blacks just out of Leavenworth. Chester Nutt and a few others I don't know. Don't need to tell you that we need boys like that or we don't get no product in here."

"So what," Doc says, not wanting to make the connection. "The kid's finished with that shit now. He can't do nothing."

"His operation's still going. Feds put a big dent in it but the motor's running." Stirling stares intently at Doc. "They put him in here with you because they want to make him an example: Kill witnesses and get killed directly. Hope that maybe that's a deterrent to the partners they didn't catch."

"We don't have to do nothing," Doc says, feeling tired, already anticipating Stirling's response.

Stirling holds up a hand again. "The hacks think we gonna run the gears on him on account of Cornelius's bro. They put him in a cell with one of our heavies and wait to see the blood. Even better that the one that does him is close to getting out when he blows it. Like scorpions in a jar. Grippe probably volunteered your ass." He runs a hand over the damaged side of his skull, absently fingering the point of his ear.

Doc shakes his head. "Don't feel right."

Stirling stretches his arms in mock surrender. "So what's your call? That we got humanitarian guards that think this kid had all the bad breaks, and arriving here is the worst of all? Maybe they thinking, *Damn, we gotta help this little black brother. Give him a big brother to look out for him.*"

"Where you hear about this takeover stuff? You talk to Chester?"

"I got sources," Stirling says.

"We're getting used," Doc says.

"Yeah," Stirling says. "So what? Got to take care of business for *ourselves*. I can't help if it makes the Feds happy. Kid can't come in here and not get no payback for Sartorius. It's too much disrespect. And Cornelius ain't going to let up. Wants that boy but *bad*."

Doc's voice climbs. "I got a parole hearing tomorrow. And no matter what happens, come four years I will have done my time. I don't want this shit. I don't care who you planning to give the job to—I'm still the one that's gonna suffer if he disappears. You know Grippe will see to that."

"You so worried 'bout the straight and narrow, what about collecting for the gambling debts? You didn't have no complaints about being involved in that."

"Just cause I don't complain don't mean I don't got complaints. I told you I'd take care of the shanks, which I done. We got an understanding that it don't go no further. Not with me on short time."

Stirling nods. "You clean, all right." He rubs his hand over the game box and looks up. "But the rest of the population don't know, and if they did they wouldn't respect it. When those boys that owe us money get cut, everyone gonna know our crew done it, even if there ain't specific names. You one of us. So you can be clean, but what you gonna say? And rumor turns to fact real quick in here."

"Said you should wait. Why you got to hit everyone at once? Makes life hard. Especially for me now I got Grippe nosing around. You move on that kid on top of that and you might as well sign me up for another ten years." Doc pinches the bridge of his nose. "I ain't staying in here on account of no vendetta with that kid, hear? I don't care what Cornelius wants."

"Goddammit, Doc, don't be giving me that. Just 'cause you short time don't mean you can start thinking like a Square John. You been yelling at that kid about respect so much you forget to listen to what you was saying? You got duties and you got associates and that's *all* there is." He gets up and goes to the sink, where he drinks some water from the spigot. "You get parole and I'll try to hold Cornelius off 'till you gone. You don't get it and all bets is off."

Doc nods, knowing he's going to have to see Cornelius himself to gain more assurance, and wondering, too, what he can say that will give Cornelius pause. He leaves Stirling, returning to his cell. The kid is still slouched on his bunk, feet hanging before him, comics and magazines scattered over his sheets. He is smoking.

Doc splashes water over his face, behind his neck. He regards the kid. "Ain't you got nothing better to do?"

The kid exhales a stream of smoke, refusing to break with Doc's stare.

"And where you getting money for those smokes? Someone

already moving on you and you too stupid to know it. Who you spending time with?"

The kid says nothing, his lax posture and almost feminine beauty an invitation for violence, desire.

Doc begins to pace. "They testing you. Show them you hungry for attention and they'll use you."

The kid inhales, the tip of his cigarette waxing bright. "You paying lots of attention to me," he says, smoke curling out with the words. "What do you want?"

"Fuck you, fish," Doc says. He leaves, making his way to the fifth tier of the cellblock. The heat here is intense. Though the light is fading, most of the inmates have left their lightbulbs partially unscrewed, convinced that even such a slight addition to the ambient heat would be overbearing. The tier is almost empty, those unlucky enough to be assigned here enjoying the cooler climes of ground level. Doc moves to the end of the tier where, pressed against the railing, the setting sun glares from the narrow windows gouged into the outer cellblock wall. It is the only place he can go for such a view.

The evening light flares, illuminating the surrounding plain in tints of gold and scarlet. Noise from beneath erupts in bursts and ricochets from the concrete, steel, and stone.

Doc closes his eyes, trying to clear his thoughts. Sweat beads on his forehead, trickles behind an ear. After a long moment he stares outside. In the distance a herd of wild animals moves on the darkening plain, silhouettes wavering in light that is shifting down the spectrum, yellow to red to purple in the moments before twilight.

The animals resemble camels. Doc's dream of his return to D.C., of following Dead Earl to the ruin of his earlier life, surfaces with a sickening vividness. The heat has dizzied and disoriented him, the bars of the tier railing slippery beneath his hands. Something startles the camels and they bolt as a herd. In their absence he sees the lone silhouette of a human figure just visible in the twilight. Just before it fades from view completely it raises a hand and Doc knows that, could he see better, that hand would lack a thumb. He shivers. *There ain't no camels and there ain't no Earl. Both dead and gone. Long gone. And D.C.? Same as it ever was, far as you know.*

6

Doc cracks his knuckles. He hears the rasp of Grippe's voice in the office beyond. "Who they got in there?" he asks.

Frank shrugs. "Unlucky punk. Mezzo-soprano Grippe's singing his favorite aria."

Seven convicts sit in the cramped waiting room outside of the parole-board office. The space reeks of sweat. Doc has pressed his uniform, the creases still sharp, and doesn't want the board to mistake the smell of the others for him; he wants nothing do with these others, resents that they will be heard along with him.

"Hey, Gordo! Don't go and have a heart attack on us. Board already made up its mind," Frank says to a fat man with a stringy mustache sitting opposite. The man's denims are limp with sweat.

"You don't know nothing about it, *cabrón*," the fat man says.

"Sure I do. Been here what," he looks to Doc, "ten times?" Frank asks.

Doc nods.

"They just got you here so you sweat while they sit around with their thumbs up their butts." Frank grins. "Anyway, they ain't going to approve no parole for you."

The fat man looks at Doc. "Tell your friend he better shut up he want to make it in that room."

"I ain't no message boy," Doc says.

"Don't take it personal-like, beaner. They just don't like spics. Niggers, white trash, slant-eyes, neither. It's egalitarian hate," Frank says.

The man leans forward. "We get away from this door, *chingado gringo*—"

Frank laughs. "You ain't doing nothing, beaner. 'Behavior in the penitentiary will be the primary criteria with regards to evaluating your eligibility to receive parole.'" He gazes at the man, eyes flat. "You want out so bad you're wet like you just crossed the Rio Grande. Don't you threaten me, you fucking wetback."

A moment later the man looks away. Frank's shoulders loosen and he turns to Doc. "What you gonna do when I get myself paroled, Doc? Won't have nobody to spend these hearing days with."

"Can't help but think that if they parole your irritable ass, mine's already gonna be back on the street."

"Got the better chance, that's sure."

"Yeah?"

"Yeah. *Corrections Today* magazine. Says that burglars," he points to himself, "got the highest recidivism rate. They know they'll see me again if I get out. Murderers got the lowest. They know if they let you out they can give your bunk away for good. It's just a matter of time until the odds kick in. Or 'till they need the extra bunk space."

An inmate opens the door and walks woodenly between the others, not bothering to shut the door behind him.

"Denied," Frank says.

In the hearing room Doc sits in a folding chair before two Hearing Officers from the Parole Commission. He feels Grippe staring at him from where he leans against the wall to Doc's right. Beside him stands Lieutenant Raven.

"William Robert Kane. Aged fifty-five." Doc nods. The bald officer addressing him has a high pink forehead and widely spaced blue eyes his glasses magnify. He looks like an exotic fish. His nameplate reads *J. Herrig*. Behind him a wide, barred window reveals the prison parking lot. Heavy thunderheads color the sky metallic gray.

"Sentenced 1977 to twenty years for first-degree murder. Subsequent loss of good-behavior time and an additional four-year sentence for dealing narcotics on prison grounds."

Doc fixes his eyes on his thick fingers clasped over his knees. He is conscious of his arm and chest muscles pressing against the rough cotton of his uniform. Herrig continues to cover familiar ground: his salient-factor score, the history of his institutional behavior, a recap of his past crimes, past parole recission hearings. A cool, charged breeze issues through the window.

"We are, of course, concerned that if released you will resume the habits and behavior that landed you here in the first place," Herrig's partner announces in a loud, sharp voice that jabs at Doc. His nameplate reads *A. Davidson*. Beneath the folding table that serves as their desk, Davidson taps his foot rapidly against the cement floor.

Doc remembers Ellis squinting at him at the coffee urn. *You ain't never been in trouble with no gambling slips, hear? That's all you need remember this time around.*

"There hasn't been no trouble with me the last eleven years," Doc lies.

It begins to rain, water pattering on the hardpacked ground. Doc stumbles on. "Ain't been involved in nothing violent since that trouble with my son-in-law landed me here. Got involved in drugs and I paid for that, too. Haven't had a dirty piss—urine test since I did the prison's Narcotics Anonymous, and that was ten years ago."

"Tell us about Moises Tailor, your deceased son-in-law."

Doc has expected this question but slows his response, not wanting it to sound as well rehearsed as it is: He's practiced what he will say until it no longer provokes the actual memory of the incident. "He beat my daughter," he says. "But killing him was the wrong thing. Made me worse than him." But he doesn't believe this, not at all, and such oversimplification feels as dishonest as any lie he's told.

"You think that your actions—that is," Davidson consults the record for show, "the use of the *shotgun* wasn't called for?"

Doc shakes his head. "Wasn't none of it called for." But fuck, what did this fool know about the logic of violence? Different rules for different worlds. *You ain't no different from me,* he thinks, even as he keeps his gaze lowered to his interrogators' nameplates, *not neither of you. Just too ignorant to know it.* They seem to be waiting for more, but Doc finds himself without the patience to dance more. "That's all," he says.

"That ain't all," Grippe says.

Herrig clamps his thin lips together and closes his eyes for a moment.

"Check his jacket. He was in the Hole for gambling," Grippe says. "You didn't read that part. He's a suspected—hell, a definite member of the D.C. Blacks."

Herrig shuffles through Doc's records. He looks up, "It's not in the file from the regional offices, and I don't see it in this institutional file, either. Any other proof?"

"He hangs out with them," Grippe says. He turns to Lieutenant Raven. "Ain't that right, Lieutenant?"

"I don't know, Officer Grippe, I'm not making the accusation." Raven's voice is relaxed, well modulated.

Grippe's mouth opens, closes, opens again. "What?"

"What I said."

"Then what the hell are you here for?"

Raven blinks, a slow lidding of the eyes the only break in his reptilian stillness. "That's enough, Grippe."

"Tattoos? Documents?" Davidson asks impatiently.

Grippe turns his attention to the man. "Nossir, but I don't need 'em to know."

"That's hearsay, Officer Grippe. The gambling?"

"It's in his jacket. Check again. A couple, three years ago, I threw him in seg. I got a letter in there 'bout that. 'Bout the gambling and the sentence. Hell, why do you think he's still waiting for parole?"

"What I have is a letter from you asserting gambling," Herrig says. "And a letter denying any incident ever occurred, from William Kane, Inmate 125630, and absolutely no proof to back your claim—no record of a stay in segregation, nor any record of a hearing from the ICC. All of which implies that this charge is based on a nonevent and that we *should* have had this hearing some time ago. This inmate security file is a complete mess." He raises and drops the folder in emphasis.

Grippe lumbers forward, the bulldog snuffling at an empty dish. "I gotta look." He snatches the folder from Herrig and thumbs through it. "You got an incomplete report. He ain't rehabilitated. You know it and I know it."

"What I know, Officer Grippe, is that without the proper documentation your opinion is, ah, distracting," Herrig says. "We appreciate that you've seen fit to elaborate on virtually every inmate we've reviewed today. Perhaps you'd like a break?"

Grippe's face clenches. "What about his new cellmate?" he says. "This kid Byron Cripps was one of the biggest dealers D.C. ever had. You think the two of them ain't been talking? Maybe considering how to kick start things again if Kane goes back to D.C.?"

Motherfucker, thinks Doc, somehow surprised that Grippe would try something so desperate. *Should have seen it coming.* A bead of sweat trickles down the side of his rib cage.

Davidson's mouth pinches. "You have evidence for this one, too? A written agreement perhaps? A recorded conversation?"

Grippe glares at Davidson, wheels to Doc. "No," he says, finally. "I don't got proof."

Doc keeps his eyes fixed on the scarred hands tumbled in his lap. He forces his shoulders to relax. *So you ain't got the balls to do it. Don't even know how to lie, Uncle Tom.* The relief he feels at this, though, mixes with something else.

Herrig asks, "Do you have anyone to go to if you're released? Family still in D.C.?"

Doc stares at his hands, unwilling to reveal his face. The skin about his knuckles is wrinkled and ashy. Blisters mark his palms from all of the recent shoveling. "I'm an old man now. Got kids that grown up I wouldn't recognize." The blurred face of his young son, Willie, surfaces. *Boy, what you doing now? Where you at?* Aged eight when Doc went in, now twenty-four. *Prison? College? Married? Dead?* "Got a boy and a girl and ain't neither of them would recognize me in a lineup."

The murmuring of waiting cons slips beneath the door.

"Don't matter where I go. It's all me."

"Is there something that will give you the strength to cope outside of prison, a touchstone of sorts? Religion, perhaps?" Herrig asks. "We're concerned, of course, that the pressures of the outside could prove too much, that you might turn again to violence or other illegal activities . . . to the familiar"—he gives a quick laugh— "in the face of the demands of readjustment."

Doc meets the eyes swimming behind the thick lenses, sees the hands steepled below Herrig's chin—soft, manicured, pink.

What the fuck you know about coping? Doc pictures the Valley of the Undead, the junkies' haunt where he began dealing. He imagines Herrig walking these streets, Oxford shoes crunching over spilled glass, stepping around a junkie splayed on the sidewalk and fouled in his own shit. He knows Herrig's thoughts: *God, get me out of here.* Doc's desire been no different in his youth. But there are locations where you looked not to God, but to the self for delivery: The Valley of the Undead was such a place, and so, too, was Bone Hill. And so now, "Just me."

"Just you?"

"This ain't no place for an old man."

Herrig waits, but Doc remains silent. Thunder cracks, rumbling through the walls.

Davidson looks to Herrig, then clears his throat. "It appears to the board that continued incarceration will serve no further useful purpose. It is further apparent that there is a reasonable probability the prisoner—William Robert Kane—will live and remain at liberty without violating the law, and that his immediate release is not incompatible with the welfare of society...."

Doc's blood sounds in his ears as Davidson reads. In the wake of the judgment he is too stunned to respond. He rubs his face slowly, then stands, avoiding Grippe's eyes.

"Jesus Christ," Frank says as Doc passes him in the hall, "they give you an extra sentence?"

Grippe catches him in the rotunda, spinning him by the shoulder and leaning into his face. "You don't get out this way." His voice is low.

"Then maybe you should have followed up on those *allegations* you was making." Doc resists the urge to push Grippe back.

Grippe's jaw works. "You ought to know why I didn't. If you'd learned anything in here you'd know why."

Doc turns away, leaving Grippe to stare after him.

7

The bar is a dusky silver, worn by the passing grips of thousands. It flexes under the weight of the forty-five-kilo plates—black and rust-speckled—that jangle on either end, rising five, six, seven times, then wavers, the hands gripping it white-knuckled, corded forearms trembling. The arms powering it up extend fully in a final push before the bar falls back into the grip of the stanchions. Doc breathes deeply, waiting for the spots swarming behind his eyes to disperse.

He moves smoothly into a second set, pausing with his arms extended, aware of someone standing near. He groans silently but continues with his set, eyes flicking to the truncheon looped in Grippe's belt just behind the holster for handcuffs.

"You ain't as slick as you think."

Doc shrugs. His pulse jumps. Has Grippe found Ellis out?

"Talked to Warden Duchamp." Grippe looks at the ground and then up. He seems genuinely hurt, and there is an inflection to his voice bleeding through that is disturbingly childlike, disappointed. "Got him fooled like all the rest, like Raven. But not me, Kane. I know you. Knowed you since day one in here and you're still the same as you was."

The tension eases. Grippe's complaint is practically an admission that the warden has no interest in investigating a sloppy inmate file. "I read that the cells in your body change every seven years," Doc says. "Every hair, every bit of you. Maybe it's eight years, I don't know. Point is, I been in long enough for two reconstitutions. I ain't close to who I was when I come in here." He stares hard at Grippe. "I'm different, just not the different you want me to be. *You* the one that ain't changed since day one."

"I know you, motherfucker," Grippe says. "This ain't about cells. It's about character. People like you," he gestures around the Yard, "got none and ain't anybody in society that wants you back."

"You just out here to threaten me? Whyn't you just throw me in the Hole? Go on my record whether I should be there or not, and then you get what you want."

"What the fuck you think I'm talking about? I got standards, Kane. Integrity!"

"Like that shit you pulled with my cellie? I didn't ask for no transfer. 'Specially not that violent motherfucker." But he sees that Grippe has no idea what he's talking about. "Or what about that shit you tried to pull at the hearing? Ain't nothing to no drug deal. You know it."

Grippe looks embarrassed. "What matters is what you did, not what I almost did. I know you changed those records. You ain't learned a thing."

"Then I guess this conversation's over, ain't it?" Doc leans back and starts another set. But Grippe pulls on the end of the weight bar and Doc has to jerk his head to the side, the bar striking the weight bench and several of the plates sliding free to clatter on the ground.

"Don't you dismiss me, you inmate fuck!" Grippe shouts. "You ain't out yet!" The angry red flushes up into his dark skin like metal heating. His breath smells of whiskey.

Doc is up and squaring off, light-headed with anger, aware of the stares from other cons in the Yard. "You pushing too hard, you drunk mother—"

"Enough."

Grippe's head snaps around. Lieutenant Raven. Doc relaxes slightly; outnumbered, there is less of a demand to make a stand. Raven raises a hand to the mirrored window of the nearest guard tower and then lets it fall. "We have a meeting in my office, Sergeant Grippe," he says in his dry voice.

Grippe opens his mouth but Raven raises his hand again, forestalling a response. He looks to Doc, face expressionless, "Sergeant Grippe is no longer available to help you. If you need anything, come to my office."

Doc nods. Grippe, deflated, follows Raven.

He watches as they disappear into the prison, unsettled. Guards don't fight in front of inmates, just as inmates don't rat on other inmates.

There is something amiss, but he is still thankful for Raven's intervention. He resets the bar, sets the plates, and counts off a quick series of military shoulder presses, the deltoids bunching along his bare back. As he finishes, the high-tension wires strung above the Yard begin to vibrate and sing, thrummed by a hot, dry rush of wind that flows over the perimeter wall. Dust roils above the packed earth.

An early-morning crowd plays handball against the perimeter wall, regulars as eager as Doc to be out early on a Saturday morning, free from work, with hours to fill before lunch. They bat balls against the south wall, their shoes squeaking on the concrete squares that extend back from the base of the towering wall.

Doc makes a note to visit Ellis for advice on dealing with Raven and Grippe, as well as to thank the old man for fixing his files. He wonders how one alters regional files and smiles. *Ain't a damn thing the old man can't do.*

The nearby handball players bring to mind when Ellis hired an incarcerated baseball player for a drug scam. He'd have the guy play on one of the prison teams. Once a game the man would knock the ball over the prison wall, usually near the close of the game. Outside of the prison he'd have arranged to have a guard walking rounds who would get the ball and pull a switch, tossing back a replacement hollowed and stuffed with drugs.

Doc grins as he pushes through another set of military presses, the burn of muscle fatigue constricting around his back. He is the only one driving iron so early, but soon the weight pile will be crowded. Already blocs of cons are beginning to roam the Yard, circling like enemy tribes.

He jogs slowly around the Yard. The largest cellblocks extend north and south, three hundred yards of granite joined at either end to the perimeter wall, capped where they meet by the silver-domed hub of the rotunda. Two newer cellblocks spoke from the rotunda into the prison yard. The twenty-two acres of the prison grounds are encircled by brick and coiled razor wire and marked by six guntowers. On the far side of the Yard rise the other prison buildings: the hospital, power plant, disciplinary housing unit, and the sprawl of the industries building, where Doc works sewing mail-bags. As he runs, little puffs of dust hover in the wake of each foot strike.

He's glad Stirling hasn't told him when to expect the knifings—it would just make the waiting worse. Being out of the loop makes him feel more secure, though he knows such security is illusory. When the knifings occur, Grippe will come for him, and even as he deals with this, Cornelius, armed with one of the shanks Doc gathered, will come for the kid. *Fixed yourself good. Better than Grippe ever could.* No matter that paying fealty to Stirling by involving himself, even in a token role, was an obligation.

He lengthens his stride and alternates his pace, sprinting, slow-ing, sprinting again, until his breath rasps. By his warm-down lap, he's decided to talk with Cornelius. But what to say to the kid? Inevitably he will learn that Doc is a D.C. Black and will take steps to protect himself. He may already know. *He decides to move first and you got no one to blame but yourself, old man.*

Something shifts beneath Doc. He stumbles as the ground shiv-ers. Around him others look warily about. A low rumble, more felt than heard, is followed by silence. For moments longer no one moves, people intent for signs of the tremor. But there are none. Movement resumes, announced by the slap of a handball. Doc completes his loop. Beneath, in the limestone pockets that riddle the bedrock and are themselves fissured with fine cracks, pooled water ripples from tremors too slight to be felt.

8

Y o, I need me *The X-Men. Iron Man*, too," the kid says, a rolled-up comic in one hand. He flushes the toilet, which doesn't respond.

In the wake of the tremor an aged sewage pipe beneath Cellblock C has ruptured, flooding undetected for several hours. Now the prison is filled with the reek of an opened bowel.

Doc looks up from *The Amazing Spiderman*. He's spent ten minutes on the first page, his thoughts revolving around what to tell the kid and when. "Ain't getting nothing after unleashing that stench. Bet the last dump you took's responsible for that sewage explosion."

The kid tries again to flush. "Obviously you ain't smelled your own breath."

"Ought to have waited. They said they was gonna cut the water off."

"When you got to go, you got to go. Now, what else? Yeah, need me *The Punisher*. Sucker is bad-ass."

Doc waves a hand in front of his face and wrinkles his nose. "That it?"

"Naw. Got to get me some of the classic shit: *Superman*, my own *Batman*s, and, lessee—yeah, *The Terminator*."

"Movie rip-off ain't no classic."

"Ain't got to be old to be a classic."

Doc rises and hawks and spits into the sink. "You just remember who all it is getting you this shit. Show some respect."

The kid cracks a smile. "Yeah, yeah. You know I ain't serious."

"Huh." Doc looks down at the order forms piled on his small, folding desk. "I ain't got more than four forms." He feels a thrill, knowing that there are no more subscriptions for him to renew, not for himself, not here.

The subscriptions are free, three-month samples that the magazine publishers deliver before unpaid bills cut the subscription. Ellis sends the mail from outside so the publishers don't see a subscription request stamped by the prison. After every cancellation, Doc changes a letter in his name and sends it in again, a fresh account for the computerized subscriber lists. He's had *Scientific American* for so long that Stirling and Bunt have both used their names and most variants thereof to keep it going.

"I got Book-of-the-Month Club, too, you want it."

"They got any action books?"

"Shit, I ain't going to read you the damn catalogue."

The kid pages through the catalogue, lips moving as he reads. "I don't got to pay for nothing?"

"What did I say?"

The kid shrugs.

"I said you didn't have to pay nothing, so why you doubting me?"

"This going to ruin my credit rating?"

Doc chuckles. "You know it. Going to throw your ass in jail. Now what you want, *Batman* or *Superman, The Man of Steel*?"

"I am the Man of Steel!" shouts Hammer. He stands before their open cell, his arms stretched above him as if attempting to fly. His head twitches, jerking to the left repeatedly. Tardive dyskinesia, brought on by toxic antipyschotics.

"Shit," Doc says. "Get the fuck out of here, Hammer."

"Yo," joins the kid, "whyn't you fly off the tier, you so indestructible?"

Hammer slaps his palms against his barrel chest. "Kreegah! Tarzan bundulu!"

"Get your nappy ass back to your cell," Doc says. "Keep this up and I ain't going to win no bet. I got money says you make it to the end of the month."

" 'Bundulu'?" the kid says.

Hammer howls and runs down the tier. They hear him attempt another Tarzan cry as he climbs the stairwell.

Doc shakes his head.

"You ever get *Tarzan*?"

"That's another comic I got editorial issues with. Any hero ought to be a nigger, it's Tarzan. Ain't no white boy got business being no African hero—ain't credible. Not even in motherfucking South Africa."

"Don't go racializing 'bout comics. Ain't no sense to it. Just enjoy what they got."

"You like to read so much, why don't you enroll in one of the courses they got here? Those Pell grants ain't gonna be around forever."

"I ain't in for that school shit."

"That's what I'm talking about! Ain't gonna get nowhere, you don't better yourself. Just gonna slide around at the bottom of this big shitpile."

The kid shrugs. He has a studied, laconic indifference that never fails to annoy Doc.

"Ain't you bored yet?" Doc says. "You got no job. What the fuck you doing with your time?" He passes a hand through his wiry hair. " 'Least get a job."

"Don't matter," the kid says.

"Don't matter."

"Life jolt, right? Do whatever the fuck I feel like. Fuck your classes. Fuck your work." He walks out on the tier. "And fuck you," he says quietly.

Doc mulls this over. Soon, though, he's standing with Stirling at the edge of the second tier. Stirling lights a cigarette, the length of it tiny and delicate in his hand.

"He gonna find out about me," Doc says. "If he don't already know."

"You give the word and he's gone," Stirling says. "I already had two fights with Cornelius 'bout this. He don't want to wait no more."

"Just do what you said: Keep Cornelius and the rest quiet. When I'm gone . . ." *Kid made his own bed. You didn't have nothing to do with it.* He feels guilty thinking this, but more disconcerting is the idea of leaving Stirling, whose presence and bulk have always been a comfort. A mass that's kept his orbit and patterns centered. He wonders how it will be without such friends, if he'll ever make new ones he'll understand half as well, men he can read from the slope of a shoulder, the lift of an eyebrow, the shift of an eye.

"So you going to sleep in the same cell with a kid who got a beef with the D.C. Blacks? When he knows you one of them—maybe the one with the contract on him?—what if he decides to get proactive on you like he did with those witnesses?"

Doc sighs. "He ain't done nothing yet. And no one but a fool takes on a crew alone. Not with no place to hide."

"He ain't stupid just 'cause he young or don't know the rules here. Boy like him got to be sharp. Watch him close. And the day you out, he's gone. He probably already stirring up trouble."

"He got no weight in here."

Stirling's cigarette butt arcs over the tier's edge. "Stubborn motherfucker. You want to go see Ellis, play some cards?"

"We got a fourth?"

"Maybe Bunt."

They descend the stairwell. Near the cellblock gate the kid stands with a group, Elston among them. Doc recognizes Ivory, as well as two others—part of a small crew from New York. Doc knows Ivory for a loner, a shark, and doesn't care for the sight of this mix. *He the best you could do?* Doc thinks. But it's likely Ivory is the only kind of ally Byron can hope for.

The group quiets as the pair nears, men edging back from the narrow exit with a studied lassitude and indifference. Elston removes his glasses to clean them with a shirttail, while the kid tracks Doc with a flat stare.

Stirling, slightly ahead of Doc, heads straight at Ivory, who blocks the exit. Ivory raps a soft pack of Camels against the flat of his palm, packing the tobacco. He is tall, maybe six foot six, and sinewy. His hands seem elongated and disproportionate even for his height.

For a moment there's no sound but the steady smack of the cigarette pack against Ivory's palm.

A smile appears on the front of Ivory's sharp face. "Cigarette?"

Stirling bulls ahead, brushing hard against Ivory, plucking the cigarettes from him in the same motion. "Part of what you owe," he says, and continues on, not looking back, Doc moving with him into the rotunda.

"What the fuck was that?" Doc asks in a low voice.

"You tell me. Motherfucker think he gonna start something? With me?"

But Doc wants to know what the kid is willing to trade—or has traded—for protection.

"Dead man," Stirling says. "Ivory ain't just getting cut for what he owe."

"Relax. He got no weight, like you just illustrated. Ain't got to kill him."

Stirling looks down at the balled cigarette pack in his fist. He lets it fall. "All right. But he ain't gonna be smiling when we done with him. Not even if he pays what he owes. Send Cornelius after that nigger. And that kid." Stirling kicks the pack to the side. "I want that kid gone. Punk ain't making no trouble. Not here. Not in my house."

"You let me handle it," Doc says. As long as it's his job he's got a chance to delay the inevitable until he's safely away.

"You *ain't* handling it. Not that I see."

9

ust outside the doorway Ellis is silhouetted against the brightness of the Yard. Doc steps into the sun, leaving the hum of the sewing machines behind.

"I knew you was involved in this."

Ellis cracks a smile, the lines around his lips deepening into crevices. "Figured you could use a break."

"Had me a break."

"Yeah, I remember something 'bout a successful parole hearing," Ellis says. His frayed denims are monochromatic gray and ill-fitting, as if of a previous generation of uniform reminiscent of stripes and chain gangs.

"How you get the Parole Commission to miss my gambling?"

"Files get lost. Not all fellas got complete jackets. Be a whole different story when they computerize this place."

"But regional files? Grippe giving you any heat? He been after me."

This elicits a shrug from Ellis. The sun's glare and heat is like a physical assault, hammering in tandem at the stone of the penitentiary walls and buildings.

"I stuck to what you told me," Doc says.

"I knew you would, Doc. This place ain't beat you."

Ellis has never made mention of his own parole hearings, but Doc has wondered for a long time why none seem to come up, especially if the old man can grease the wheels as he's done for Doc. He claps Ellis on the shoulder, feeling the knobby collarbone under his hand, happy for Ellis's company. "Need to get us some hootch."

"You ain't still hungover from that pruno Bunt cooked up?"

Doc laughs. "Be too old to enjoy life when I stop repeating my mistakes." It had been a good time; a moment with Ellis that had briefly allowed him to forget about prison and enjoy a drink with friends as he would were he free.

Doc, Ellis, and Bunt had gathered in Bunt's cell three weeks earlier, during TV hour when the rest of the prison—guards and cons both—was clustered around the TVs watching a heavyweight boxing match. Black on black was a safe kind of match, so the guards didn't mind slacking a little on their rounds to watch the fight.

Bunt's tier was empty, the cellblock silent and uncharacteristically empty, almost private. His cell smelled so strongly of Right Guard it made Doc's eyes water. Bunt had fermented pruno from oranges, sugar, wheat germ, and moldy bread placed in a sock—mold for the yeast—so he wouldn't have to strain it from the booze. The bucket had been sealed a week, the pruno potent and raw.

"Why you got to use so much deodorant?" asked Doc, wrinkling his nose.

"I ain't aiming to get caught, nigger." Bunt's voice climbed an octave. "Hacks smell my single-malt spirits and they throw me in seg so's they can drink it themselves, know what I'm saying?"

" 'Single-malt'? Single-sock, you mean. And this deodorant is like a big sign."

"You ain't being no respectful guest."

Ellis took a cup and eased down against the wall. Doc sat on the bunk with Bunt and watched Ellis, struck by how withered he looked. Some cons joked that Ellis, here before anyone else, will be here long after, the only man to serve a life sentence and then get another tacked on when he lived through it.

To Doc it is a sad joke, though, because it is the truth. Ellis will remain long after the others leave, lying in a grave on Bone Hill, the prison graveyard that is the prison's namesake. For Doc and others it is a place best ignored and avoided, embodying as it does the deepest fear of all the cons: that they will never escape, not even in death.

They drank in silence, inhaling deeply from cigarettes to kill the taste. Doc felt warm and secure, watching Ellis pull a second cigarette from a pack and light up, his delicate fingers working his lighter. Then Ellis, as Doc knew he would, began to speak.

"Momma said my fingers was my future. Surgeon or a pianist, she said these fine hands was gonna make me all the money I need." He held up a long-fingered hand and turned it slowly. "But we was poor, didn't have no money for piano lessons or doctor's school."

Bunt cut in, his broad forehead bare of the usual bandanna, shining from the shadows of the bunk, wide face already animated by the pruno. "And you had to walk through a lot of snow and work every day—"

"Show the man some respect," Doc said. He'd been in long enough to have heard most of Ellis's stories. Their rhythm and familiarity were comforting.

Ellis nodded to Doc. "Like I was saying, Momma saw these hands and saw my future, or part of it, leastways. I did make money with these fingers, but the Feds catch me three times, and I ain't engraving no more plates. Be happy you ain't in as counterfeiters. Be happy you got sentences gonna end 'fore you do."

He drank again. "What's important ain't what happen to me, it's what my momma clue me in to; can tell a lot 'bout the future of the man from the way he looks, the way he acts. My momma was right 'bout me, except she my momma, and didn't see I wasn't in for no hard work. Just saw my good points, like they all do when they looking at their young fellas."

Doc poured more pruno for everyone, thinking of dimly-remembered childhood nights spent struggling to stay awake as his grandfather's voice rumbled in the dark beside his bed.

"There's them that say you can see the whole history of a man, what's been and what's gonna be, just by looking at him. I think they's some truth to that," Ellis continued. "Take Doc, here. Got him a sad mouth, them muscles, them thick fingers. Built for a life of struggle. Bunt, you a small and slick and round fella, like some rock that water wash over. Life pass you by 'cause you never involved."

"That's what I told the judge. He didn't listen, though," Bunt said.

Doc smiled, but Ellis didn't seem to hear. "Long time ago when I was etching plates, pulling in enough money to wear clothes so natty they wasn't no woman gonna say nothing 'bout my plain face, I spent most nights at a place called Mo D's. Ran a joint in Chicago. Had it set up like a flower shop: 'Roses.' Was the front for a speakeasy during Prohibition, and made some money on its own so Mo D kept it up. Go behind the counter, step through a big metal cooler—one like where they keep flowers cool in buckets of water—open a rear door and you walk down into the real joint. Slick, keeping that around. Make you feel like you was up to something illicit, slipping behind that counter, like you was in on some big secret. Used to say we was going to pick roses 'cause there was so many fine women there. If you was a nigger with any standing you was going to be seen there at night."

Bunt burped and Doc elbowed him. "Damn," Bunt said.

"So me and the fellas I was working with started making good money. Sold a pair of plates to the Chicago mob and was happy enough to be alive with the money that we felt like celebrating. Hadn't never gambled, but when I went down there I knew I'd be back. Had a fine woman on my arm, Selena. She got these shimmery black sequins running down her body like she dressed in night water, high cheekbones, soft New Orleans accent. Like a wild bird come to roost on my arm. She work for Mo D, but it was easy to think that there wasn't nothing to that. Plenty of other fellas around and she take me, and I'm thinking to myself that she can see a little deeper than most, see a man of character." Ellis paused to drink and take a drag from his cigarette.

"Went to the blackjack table and we watch. Could probably tell I ain't played much, but she know men, know 'bout touchy pride. We watch and it ain't hard to figure it out. I'm trying to be smooth, hand her a bill and let her bet it. She win, I wait a little more, and I'm thinking, *This ain't a skill game. Just count the tens.* I bet, double my stake. Three more like that and I know I got it, and she there purring into my ear, all sleek lines that hurt to look at and I'm feeling like I got me a whole new life. All those hours with a jeweler's lens pressed in my eye, all those headaches from staring at them little blank plates 'till they got the kiss of money on them, all of it feeling like a bridge, like I finally crossed and there ain't no going back to barefoot Mississippi, split-pea soup and looking at the ground every time a white man around. Feeling light on my feet, the whole world of opportunity out there and I know I'm smart like Jesse Owens is fast." He stared at the two on the bunk through the cigarette smoke. "Y'all probably felt just the same way when you was dealing."

Bunt blew smoke rings, the blurry hoops hanging in the still air.

"Next week I'm back and the same feeling rush over me. See Selena coming across the floor and it's a lock—everything working like it ought to. I win at blackjack, at roulette. Feeling big even when I drop a thousand in one poker hand. Don't mean nothing. Can win next time." He chuckled quietly.

"Over the year I won a lot. But in the end I lost more. All that money dry up. Couldn't beat a system set against me 'cept by leaving." Here Doc caught Ellis's eyes flash as he paused in his story. "And Selena, she cover that angle. I'm thinking she love me almost as much as she love gliding around that room with all that talk and shine and money. My cash is gone in twelve months, and one night I'm working on a set of plates for Mo D and I'm thinking, *What have I done that I got to work for a high-profile nigger?* My partners I ain't seen in three months 'cause they want nothing to do with a man like Mo D, a fella who got enemies. Three months later and I'm doing my first day of hard time and I'm wondering how the ball got rolling this way. See that roulette table and that ball bouncing and rattling around to a pattern all its own and I see me watching it, thinking I can predict that pattern and others— like Selena's—besides. And that's when I know you can't ever know all the angles."

The trio sat silently. Doc shifted uncomfortably, surprised by the sudden mood shift.

Ellis drained his cup. His eyes were dark and brooding. "Said you can tell a lot 'bout people from the way they look. Fellas here turning gray and hard inside. Everyone the same color as the prison." He set down his cup and shuffled out.

"Don't be looking at me like that, nigger," Bunt said defensively. "I don't even gamble."

"Give me another hit."

Doc is happy now, out in the Yard with Ellis, that the same emotions are not evident in the old man's eyes. "So how you get me out of work in the middle of such a fine afternoon?" he asks. It's a rare opportunity to walk in the sun with the Yard empty, never mind the heat. He has to concentrate to keep a dumb grin off his face. The two squat against the perimeter wall, tucked in the narrow band of shade it affords, while around them the ground bakes in the heat, the air warping and twisting.

"Was thinking about all that complaining you been doing in the cafeteria. 'Bout that smell. Thought you could use some fresh air."

"Hard to eat in there. They ain't cleaning the pots or something."

Ellis gives a hint of a smile. "Stimple, he's the fella that heads prison maintenance. Warden started smelling something bad in the admin offices and told Stimple to fix it. He been trying, but with all that sand everywhere he been busy. Ain't nothing changed 'bout that smell 'cept it's got stronger and the warden's 'bout ready to fire his ass."

"And you real concerned about Stimple's sorry-ass maintenance-man career."

Ellis nods. "Stimple is a reasonable man. Always good to have a fella like that around."

"Huh."

"He's nervous. I ain't saying desperate, exactly, but he's ready to listen to suggestions 'bout the cause of this odor. Blueprints don't seem to much match the actual buildings, see. Shapes is right, I guess, but a lot of details is missing. Stimple need someone who knows the prison enough to look where he wouldn't know to."

"Stimple gonna be awful grateful when you discover the problem." Doc is smiling. He wipes the sweat from his face and neck.

Ellis nods again. "I ain't saying I can find it, but if I do, he just might be."

They stand and walk toward the cellblocks. Doc doesn't look forward to fishing rotten meat out of some forgotten air duct, but Ellis has supplied him with more good fortune than he believed possible.

Inside Center Hall the faint smell of rot sours the air. Ellis shuffles ahead and turns into the lieutenants' office, motioning for Doc to wait. Doc shifts from foot to foot, staring at the sign posted next to the scarred oak door. It reads, *If you ain't a lieutenant at Tyburn, you ain't shit.* He chuckles. Lieutenant Raven's dry voice edges beneath the door. Old Man Ellis reemerges, a ring of keys dangling from his left hand. Raven is with him. He smiles thinly at Doc.

Doc remembers being part of a crowd watching a baseball game that Raven wanted ended after the cons had ignored the cell-count announcement from the intercom. One con had contested— the game was a close one, and not easy to give up—telling Raven to fuck off for a few minutes, then swaggering up to the plate. Raven, then a new guard working as a Yard Officer, turned on his radio and murmured into it.

"What, you gotta call backup?" said the con.

Raven shook his head. "Just reserving an empty bed in the infirmary."

It was too late for the con to back down in front of the others. "Won't need no bed when I'm done with you," the con said.

Yard Officer was a position to be avoided because it left you exposed and alone among the cons. If someone wanted you, you could only hope that the Wall Post guards were awake and watching from a gun tower.

Raven had to understand the con's position, that he would back down if Raven waited for reinforcements. And so the con was as surprised as the rest when Raven stepped up—a lone guard approaching an inmate armed with a baseball bat in the middle of the prison population—his long arm looping out, the truncheon catching the con squarely on the temple.

It was not the violence so much as the audacity that was startling. It was tacitly recognized that the cons had to be given a certain amount of leniency if the prison were to run at all. That Raven was willing to risk so much to enforce a literal reading of the prison rules made little sense. Guarding inmates was a job, not a calling. Anyone so seemingly rigid was to be watched and avoided, much as a man touched is to be shown a distant respect and, perhaps, fear.

He'd stood there, calm, with the same thin smile Doc now faces.

Raven hands Doc a pass. "One hour," he says. Satisfied by their silence, he reenters the office.

"Got to keep a close eye on that man," Ellis says. "He taking a liking to you."

"Was at the parole hearing. Shut down Grippe midsentence."

"That boy bad luck for you, Doc."

"Both of them."

Outside, Ellis shakes the key ring like a trophy. Long skeleton keys jut from the assortment of smaller silver and gold keys. The jingling skitters up the wall behind them and Ellis pauses. He listens and shakes them once more, looking like some wizened shaman. Far ahead, the squat cube of the disciplinary housing unit—the Hole—wavers, sunken into the ground as if capping a yawning pit that will soon engulf it. As they walk he says, "Prison like an old body you got to be familiar with. Got a personality and a language," he smiles. "Got halitosis, too."

Doc grins back. Ellis seems to turn any conversation into a game, weaving inflection and expression and seemingly pointless stories together to form a pattern of meaning for any listener acute enough to trace it.

Ellis moves slowly, skirting the edge of the Yard for the shade of the walls. Coils of razor wire hang high overhead, spooled on overhanging supports. "Built this place in 1872," he says. Doc knows that Ellis hasn't invited him out merely for a break from routine or to help with his odd jobs. "First federal penitentiary. Took them close to ten years to make the old part. Had convict laborers they'd march in from an army stockade. Worked them digging and laying brick and stone twelve hours at a stretch, feeding them garbage, driving them hard. Cons who gave too much lip worked with a twenty-pound ball chained to their leg. Carrying the baby, they called it, 'cause you had to cradle it every time you needed to march."

These stories fascinate Doc, make him feel a part of something larger, of a tribe with its own legends and heroes, part of something permanent that doesn't end when a sentence is served or a transfer effected.

"Guards quit even if they couldn't afford to. But for the cons there wasn't no out. Just a condition of their sentence. Funny, ain't it? Lincoln sets Nevada up fast so he got another antislavery state and then they pack us out here to build this place." He spits. "That's history for you."

A small dust devil coalesces and twirls across the empty ground before dissipating when it strikes the unforgiving bulk of the perimeter wall.

"Read up on the official prison history and you see the first fella to die here was Jackson Harding in 1877. Tuberculosis. Got the first space up on Bone Hill. It true he dead, but he wasn't no first. Had a number of fellas that died building this wall." He slaps a hand—hard—against the stone of the perimeter wall. The large blocks are chiseled smooth and fit tightly in a series of interlocking joints. The wall rises thirty-five feet, changing from stone to a course of brickwork.

"Dug a trench thirty-five feet deep and filled it with stone to support this," Ellis says. "Those that died working ain't recorded 'cause there wasn't no prison yet to die in, and no cemetery to put them in. Back in the forties used to hear these stories from the old cons, fellas who knew fellas been here from the start. Said they's a lot of bones under these walls." Ellis's eyes focus on Doc. "Real convenient, see, to have a deep trench around waiting to be filled. Just roll you in and brick you over."

Ellis speaks briefly with the guard stationed at the entrance to the Hole, who checks their passes and waves them through, ignoring the blare of the metal detector reacting to the keys in Ellis's hand. It is hot and gray inside. The floors of the center hall gleam with a thick layer of wax. To either side the cell doors are sealed. As their shoes squeak on the concrete, hands extend from the food slots, angling watch crystals to see who's entered. The air smells of bleach, sweat, and vomit.

Two guards round a corner, a prisoner slung between them. He wears a padded helmet, and as the guards drag him he tries to catch up but his legs move sluggishly, lifting slightly only to stall, as if he's forgotten midmotion that he means to walk. Doc catches the roll of white eyes in the shadows of the helmet, hears a gurgling, unintelligible utterance.

"—fuck out the way," says one panting guard, and then they are past.

"How much you got riding on Hammer?" Ellis asks.

"Fifty if he goes in a month," Doc says, attempting a smile. "You?"

Ellis manages a sly silence.

"You going to fix the bet and I want to know," Doc says.

At the rear of the hall Ellis unlocks the stairwell and they drop two levels. Doc sticks close to Ellis's bent form.

During Doc's sentence he's been sent down to the Hole three times, and each time Grippe has placed him in the remote side-pocket cells, where isolation is so complete that even noise is barred from entering. Each time he'd entered the windowless nine- by five-and-a-half-foot cubicle defiant, resolved that he'd beat the time, measuring days with the contraction of muscle during endless sets of pushups, sit-ups, and isometric exercises, pushing into the pain of exhaustion to free his mind of thought, keep it too tired to dream. Each time he'd failed. Steel, cement, matte-brown walls, movement limited to pacing a strip of floor between the toilet, bunk, and sink—it was too constricted, and soon the hallucinations started.

He's seen others emerge from the Hole broken, dragged out with their mouths agape, drooling and incontinent from too much Thorazine or Prolixin—the Prolixin shuffle, they called it—sanity having long since escaped the confines of segregation. And, too, he's heard stories: distant cells without light or forever bathed in it, cold and dank and lost in a labyrinth of old stone and subterranean seeps, the cons living through years of isolation, emerging with their thoughts as deeply sunken as their eyes, left to shuffle the prison halls in contemplative silence.

During Doc's last stay in seg, Grippe had visited. After three weeks of total isolation, Doc was even glad to see the man who'd sent him there. He'd watched Grippe's face pinch—showers were such a rarity that even Doc was not inured to his own reek. It was a strange visit. He still wonders if it occurred, or if his mind invented it.

Grippe had set down a lunch packed in a Styrofoam cup and leaned against the far wall, looking Doc over and shaking his head, the gesture strangely genuine.

"You just got to bend," he'd said. "Talk to me about the gambling. Your next parole hearing comes up and I'll put in a good word."

Doc didn't trust his voice to work and looked instead at the lunch.

"Accept what the rules is about, Kane. They ain't arbitrary." And in his eyes there was a naked need, a look that said he meant it, that it was important to him that Doc get out.

Doc tried to speak, cleared his throat and tried again, his voice louder than he'd expected. "I accept rules," he said. "But we ain't got the same ones. Not in here, and not outside, neither."

"Goddamn you," Grippe said, leaving Doc with his thoughts for two more weeks.

Getting out of the Hole had been another kind of punishment. "The Bonus Round," as Bunt called it. He remembers the end of that stay: the overwhelming wash of movement and noise issuing from the crowded cellblocks; his eyes watering from the seemingly vibrant blue of a faded uniform; the touch of a breeze exquisitely intense. His keyed-up, starved senses had left him unable to focus, helpless in the face of so many stimuli, unable to process or filter or cope.

And now you got Cornelius running around with a shank you supplied, and the kid and Ivory together. He curses.

"What you making noise about?" Ellis asks.

"You ever been in seg?" Doc asks.

Ellis raises his eyebrows. "What do you think?"

"How long?"

"Long enough to learn I wasn't going in again. Like they say: First time's an accident, second is stupidity, and the third time you deserve what you get."

"I never heard that."

"How many times you been in?"

"Three."

"Like I said."

A third locked door reveals the boiler room. Sewage and water pipes cross and recross overhead, a latticework tangled with old and unused pipes, some of which have gaping rust holes. It is dank and musty here. Ellis pulls a small Mag-Lite from his pocket and hits the beam when the wall switch fails to spark more than one anemic bulb. A line of industrial-size water tanks loom out from the back wall, their bulk somehow menacing. A scratching runs through the metal near Doc's head.

"Rats ate all the bugs," Ellis says with a grin. At the back of the low-ceilinged room, beyond the boilers, is another door covered with a greasy layer of dust. The knob gleams when the beam of the flashlight strikes it.

The door opens noiselessly into a room with several rusted file cabinets and a warped floor where some of the planks have come free of the joists, revealing further depths to the prison. Ellis kicks the rightmost cabinet with his foot. "Gotta warn the rats." He pulls a key from it and opens the middle drawer with a piercing squeak. Inside, yellowing papers wilt in dark-green folders. In the space behind these he pulls a worn blueprint, smoothing it on his knee. "Amazing how much paperwork gets lost."

Ellis traces the light over the blueprint. "Remember this: Left twice, right twice, down, left, right, down, left three, right. My memory ain't worth a damn. Lucky for you."

"Whyn't you just write it down?" Doc asks.

"You ever get thrown in the Hole for gambling slips? I seem to remember something 'bout that. Remember something, too, 'bout how hard it is to get rid of written records."

"Yeah, all right." Doc leans in for a closer look. The blueprint is soft with age. The blurred lines seem to waver. It is divided into five rectangles, each an overhead of a level in the central administrative prison wing. "Didn't know there was five floors."

"Got five floors here, too. Got a floor beneath this. Long time ago they used to keep the violent dings there. Had Lawrence

Bonny 'till the papers heard about it and made 'em brick up the whole level," Ellis says.

Doc shivers. "Don't care what he did. Should have just killed the sick mother. This ain't no place for the living."

"They's worse places than downstairs. Got rooms been forgotten about before they built this part of the prison. I got lost a few years ago and found the storage room where they kept a old electric chair. Look like a big insect waiting to jump."

Doc gets up. "I got the instructions, so unless you got something else to show me."

Ellis pauses for a long moment. "Parole board say okay."

"Uh-huh."

"Heard that the D.C. Blacks need to collect on some gambling debts."

Doc shrugs.

"You the only short-timer in your crew, ain't you?" Ellis says.

"Me and Bunt. So what?"

"Well, you a short-timer and I know you a man of principle. Seem to me that sometimes a man of principle can be a little too rigid. Not bend when the wind comes."

"Don't you never come out and say what you mean?" Doc asks.

"Not once," Ellis says in a flat voice.

"Why the fuck you bring me down here, Ellis?"

Ellis sighs. "I'm sorry, Doc. I don't need to lecture no grown man. No disrespect meant."

"All right, then," Doc says. "We got your *directions*. Let's get the fuck out of here."

But Ellis shakes his head. "There's something you got to see. Something I found, that I been thinking about." He shuffles to the far corner of the room and opens a door with a clouded-glass pane.

"I ain't up for this," Doc says.

"Just come with me. This ain't something I can show anybody else."

"You sure we safe down here?" Doc asks, as he steps through

the doorway and into a narrow hallway of corroded brick that appears warped by the weight of the building above, the floor sinking unevenly where the ground has softened and settled. A web of cracks spreads across the ceiling. Doc walks softly, afraid that even brushing the wall will bury them, remembering the tremor he'd felt while weight-lifting.

"This place ain't no worse than the rest. Got sinkholes everywhere." Ellis's voice comes out tight and fast. "Architects was so damn busy designing this place to look like the Capitol building—you know you living in the Senate Chambers, Cellblock B?—and caught up in all these ideas 'bout enlightenment through surroundings—sunlight, big architecture—that they didn't bother to look beyond the building. Had most of the wall up and laid most of the foundations when it finally rained and they found the first sinkhole. Too late to move by then. Been some cave-ins in the past—a big one 'bout thirty years back. It was to rain out here more and they'd have a problem, though." Ellis's patter is unusually fast, stripped of its Southern languor, his voice tight.

Doc's mouth is dry. He's never heard Ellis sound so tense.

At the end of the hallway Ellis pauses at a wood door banded with metal. He pushes a long skeleton key into the lock and twists. There is a soft click and then he steps back. The beam of the flashlight rests on a damp patch of floor.

"You first," Doc says.

Ellis shakes his head. "Together. We go together."

The flashlight's beam exposes a pair of corroded chains that angle from the far wall to support a metal cot. Light glints from long, yellow teeth set in a fleshless grin.

That night Doc lies in his bunk trying to erase the memory of the desiccated corpse's smile. It is long after Five Count. The cellblock is filled with the somnolent, almost inaudible sound of so many dreaming prisoners, their whistling exhalations a soothing, nocturnal cadence. From the echoing space of the rotunda he hears the soft bounce of a tennis ball and the slow steps of a guard on his rounds.

"Now you know," Ellis had said when they had surfaced from the Hole and were again traversing the length of the Yard.

"Next time you feel like sharing, find some other lucky partner," Doc had said, but Ellis wasn't listening.

"Found it six months ago and I knew it meant something," Ellis said.

"Don't mean nothing but that some poor motherfucker messed with the hacks and got a permanent bit—the kind of sentence nobody wants."

"Been in my head every day." Ellis spoke quietly, effortfully. "Found it and felt like it meant something, you know?

"If Bone Hill got a face, that's it," Doc agreed.

"Don't tell no one about this," Ellis said.

"Whoever that boy was, he deserves a proper burial. Ain't no way to be left."

"No," Ellis said emphatically. "That ain't no one person. Not no longer."

"It's a body," Doc said. "A corpse. Or it was a corpse. A skeleton, now."

"That ain't no one person," Ellis repeated, the lines in his face so deep and numerous that his skin looked to have a grain to it. "History is what it is. And you tell someone and pretty soon word gets around and then a crew gets sent to clean it up and then what's left?"

"What does that matter?" asked Doc.

"It matters!" Ellis stopped and got in his face. "It matters! That ain't there and then people can pretend it didn't happen! Can say there never was no message because there never was no event. No skeleton, nobody to make no skeleton." He'd glared at Doc. "You just shut up about it. I shown you and that's that."

"All right, Ellis," Doc said softly. "I'm sorry."

"You just remember what you seen."

But Doc's not sure he understands. Facts don't work here as they do on the outside. What has happened, what is rumored to have happened, what is rumored will happen—they all vie for eminence. The result is a bizarre, hybrid reality thick with incertitude, doubt, suspicion, inconstancy. A world that is the very antithesis of the ordered social contract, the legalistic equations of time served as it relates to crimes committed. It is a world that refutes the validity of such equations. And when facts rooted here—riots, dead bodies, shankings—twist their way outside they are easily discarded, as if what constitutes them is suspect.

Doc wonders if there's anything from his sentence—any lesson or habit—that will serve him when he's released. Above him, the kid shifts. Doc's eyes open, but there is no light in the cellblock, the inky black of night coiling in the air.

The kid shifts again, the springs of his bed squeaking. There is a rhythm to the movement. The kid is masturbating. Doc listens to the quiet rustling and feels himself flush, grow hard. *Who you thinking of?* he wonders, envious that the kid has fresh memories of past girlfriends to hold up to his mind's eye.

The creaking increases in volume and speed. He hears a muffled moan, a final shift. Doc moves his hand to his cock, hating himself even as he begins to fantasize.

10

Doc stands before an industrial-size sewing machine making U.S. Postal Service bags. His job for the past sixteen years, today the familiar drone of the needle lancing through the canvas fails to soothe him. With his pending release, the protective sheath of prison routine has slipped away, leaving him raw and irritable, feeling the rasp of each passing moment.

Others stand with heads bowed, shoulders and arms shifting as they adjust the position of the canvas or toss finished bags into the baskets at their feet. They lean close to their humming machines, nodding like disciples to a murmured prayer. Sewing pays relatively well. Like most of the skilled work that requires training, it is reserved for prisoners with long sentences. Doc thinks the kid could get a job here, maybe stay out of debt, get away from Ivory. *And what? Get him a bank account? Money ain't no good to a dead man. You going to help, you got to do something.*

A cool breeze wafts through the room. Outside, the sky is blanketed with dark rainclouds and it is raining steadily—the first real downpour in two years, especially surprising so soon after the shower a few days earlier.

He finishes one bag and begins another, the motion so ingrained by repetition that he manipulates the canvas by feel as his eyes wander to his warped features mirrored in the reflective metal surface of the sewing machine. Sixteen years of standing and sewing, shoulders sloping, hair graying, wrinkles bunching on his forehead. How will the kid look after so many years? What will his eyes show as they look back on a stretch of twenty years, and forward to another twenty, and twenty more after that? *He ain't lasting no twenty years, and you neither, 'less you stay careful.*

He's not hungry at lunchtime, has no desire to feel the rain. He hears its steady rush and the sudden yells of cons running to the cafeteria. That such an event caused the work crew to crowd the door at the lunch bell strikes him as pathetic, filling him with frustration because it reveals the stultifying and unchanging routine of his life. Doc walks to the office of his work-detail officer, Flippy Santana. Flippy smiles at Doc, covering the phone's receiver with his hand. "You staying to beat quota?" A big order of mailbags is due. During a production rush the cons get a bonus for every bag produced over their daily quota; a rare chance to make extra cash. And yet rain is even rarer—the mud and humidity a reminder, for many of these men, of the wet climes of home.

Doc continues sewing mailbags, the basket at his feet half-filled. Three cons remain inside. Two belong to the D.C. Blacks, new members just transferred from Leavenworth. He vaguely remembers hearing about them. Luster and Kordell. Beyond Lorton Penitentiary there is no place for D.C. to warehouse its criminals but Federal prisons like Leavenworth and Atlanta. So many have been funneled into Tyburn that they make up ten percent of the population. The third con is also familiar—white, muscular, with long blond hair and watery blue eyes. Doc can't place when they would have met, or why. All are new to the jobs.

Flippy opens his door and leaves. The jobs are so prized that he doesn't have to worry about leaving the machines briefly unattended, and often spends the lunch hour circulating among the other on-duty guards.

Doc thinks of the kid's surreptitious masturbation the previous night. There was a time when the sight of any woman in the prison—a rarity, though sometimes they came through on government tours or he glimpsed one from the BOP admin offices—would leave Doc fantasizing for weeks. But the comics and issues of *Gent* and *Hustler* are the only escape he now allows himself. Years ago he didn't need them, but then the faces in his dreams, those of his ex-wife and old lovers, began to smear, resolving into the contours of a familiar hack or con.

Last night's fantasy has left him depressed. It is disheartening that his fantasies involve familiar prison faces, involve violence. Sad and electrifying both, the fantasy of fucking the kid, exulting in the control and pain inflicted, even more so when the kid's face shifted to that of Grippe, their cries indistinguishable.

He can't shake the image of the kid, the creamy glow of his skin and the perfectly balanced features. There are few in his position that wouldn't press their advantage. But Doc denies himself sex in the same spirit that he performs his daily workout: Both are about holding true to an image of himself as he was before prison, married and fit. An image he is afraid to examine, afraid he might see that he is not what he once was, afraid he's become something women should fear.

The concrete floor shivers from a tremor, and he grabs the sewing machine to steady himself. Looking around he's surprised to see the room empty. A muffled scream reaches him and he curses for not seeing it earlier, now placing the blond: Suspence, the man from Frank's cell. He moves down the row, unbalanced by another tremor, thinking of Ellis's description of the sinkholes. The trio fights behind the wall of canvas rolls they've been stacking. Suspence is on the floor, but it isn't easy to keep him there. Kordell—rangy, with hard muscles—struggles to hold Suspence's arms locked behind his back, using his knee for extra leverage. Luster straddles Suspence, one hand pressing the side of his prey's head to the floor, the other gripping a toothbrush, the razor metallic red. A thin wail and now Doc is close enough to see the blood, an entire cheek sliced open in a wound that arcs toward

Suspence's ear, revealing the skull's wide grin. Doc sees the room from yesterday, sees the smile of Bone Hill.

Blood seeps into Suspence's hair, pools beneath his head. His shirt has been ripped halfway off, and on the pale, tattoo-embellished skin, Doc sees a deep-blue tattoo on the underarm, still red around the edges. He jerks into motion when he recognizes the shape. It is a half-teardrop, a tattoo worn by the Aryan Brotherhood.

"Dumb motherfuckers!" hisses Doc. The one with the peeler, Luster, looks up in surprise.

Doc points to the tattoo, watches the realization sink in. "Get out," he says.

"This Sean Spencer! Owe us big and that say he a wannabe AB! Let's do him!" Luster lifts the razor, his dull face tight with excitement. Doc cuffs him, Luster falling to his side, slipping in Suspence's blood when he scrambles up. Kordell scrabbles away. The three face each other over Suspence, who backs against the wall, a hand pressed to his parted face, blood weeping from between his fingers. He has blood in his eyes and blinks furiously.

Doc lowers his voice. "I tell you it ain't for you and you listen."

"Getting soft, Doc," Luster says.

"Look at me, motherfucker. I five-foot-seven and weigh two thirty-five. You don't want my kind of trouble." He moves in, hands at his side, aware of the shank dangling from Luster's hand. "And you say my name again, fuckup, and two people leaving in boxes."

"Maybe you and him," Luster says, eyes flicking to Suspence.

Another shift from the floor, this tremor more violent than the first. A canvas roll falls from the stack, crashing into a sewing machine.

Luster and Kordell look to one another and Kordell backs away, turns to run. "You dead!" spits Luster before jogging after Kordell. Doc doesn't know who he's threatened. He's tempted to follow, feeling the unsteady mass of the room around him as he had the weight of the Hole when helping Ellis.

Suspence tries to bolt past Doc, but Doc grabs his hair, pulling him up short. Caught, Suspence wheels and clips Doc with a strong right hook to the temple. He still can't see well, and the following flurry of punches are no more than glancing blows. Doc ducks, jabs Suspence's damaged cheek. Suspence howls, the sound slurred by blood, and falls to the floor.

"Got gambling debts you ain't paid, that's why you cut. This ain't nothing to do with the Aryan Brotherhood. When they ask about it, you gonna profess ignorance. Ain't got *nothing* to do with the AB. Lie about it to 'em to start a feud and I'll gut you."

Suspence grunts. He's got an eye cleared of blood and it's fixed on Doc, memorizing the face.

"You want to live, remember what I tell you." Doc sprints for the door.

Outside, convicts and guards mill about the Yard. As Doc slogs through the mud he looks over his shoulder and sees the yaw of the furniture mill and textile plant. Chunks of mortared stone are falling from the upper reaches of the walls, embedding themselves in the muddy ground. Doc casts an anxious eye to the distant bulk of the cellblocks, praying they stay intact. A collapse will destroy his hopes of parole. He has a fleeting image of the thousands of cons pouring over rent walls to the staccato of gunfire. It would take years to set things right. He'd have to serve out his sentence and then some.

Cons spilling from the nearby buildings mirror Doc's fright, but those already out howl in delight at the sight of so much destruction, of a dream realized. Rain beats into the thick mud, weights the uniforms of the guards and inmates. The Yard PA rips through the air: "Lie face down! Spread your arms and legs! Remain motionless!"

Even as Doc wonders if he can sprint to the cellblocks and his cell before it gets any crazier, he prays that there won't be a riot. The prison can turn to ash for all he cares, but not until after he's free of it. A contingent of guards in full riot equipment enters the Yard like a swarm of dangerous insects: black helmets with Plexiglas face-shields, gas masks, flak jackets, and three-foot truncheons. Behind, several guards labor with a forty-millimeter grenade launcher and canisters of tear gas. Prisoners begin dropping to the ground before the guards reach them.

"Facedown now! Facedown or we fire!" crackles the Yard PA system. Doc drops to the ground at a loud pop, thinking a gun has been fired. The mud conforms to his body and oozes into his clothes, hiding the blood. The windows of the southwest guntower split and fall, shatterproof glass shearing in jagged plates as the metal frame of the observation deck twists. A wide crack appears at the base of the tower, wending through the stone and brick, pausing halfway up the forty-foot climb.

From this, traversing the Yard, a line of collapse burrows toward the prison industries buildings, which list far enough to the side that they look as if a strong breeze will complete the leveling. A cinderblock wall separates raggedly from the building front, exposing the dark recesses. The wall tilts off axis by three, four feet, pausing in the wet heat.

Guards move among the prone convicts, spectral in the rain, shades descending in the aftermath of battle. Doc buries his hands deep in the mud, covering the blood.

Back in the cell that evening he finishes washing his hands for the fourth time.

"A week?" the kid says.

Doc grunts. The air in the cell seems too viscous to circulate. Lockdown is going to be hell, made worse by the kid's incessant questions and the fact that the upcoming week in the cell is time when he could be out on parole.

"Look at them engineers down there," Doc says. "You think they gonna let us run around when they worried the walls is going to fall in?"

Below, the second of two teams of architects and engineers—

suited, sweating in their starched shirts—walk the cellblock. Damage assessment will continue throughout the night; no one expects to get much sleep.

"They so concerned 'bout my health, they could install air-conditioning," the kid says.

Doc lights a rolled-up newspaper with a lighter.

"Yo, what the fuck you doing! It's already hot enough."

Doc crouches where the wall meets the seam of the cell floor in a groove a quarter-inch wide. "Get down here with a shoe."

The kid rouses himself, curious. He leans over Doc's shoulder as Doc presses the makeshift torch to the seam and works his way around the cell. One scorpion and two centipedes, as well as other, less familiar insects scurry from the flame and are unceremoniously flattened.

"That's a lot of bug," the kid says, looking at the waffle sole of his shoe.

"This don't mean you can quit checking the sheets and shoes."

The kid climbs his bunk. "What about cigarettes? They gonna let us out to go to the commissary? They got to."

"No shopping specials when you in lockdown."

"You got cigarettes?" the kid asks.

"Not for your sorry ass," Doc says.

"Man, you enjoying this. Got you a captive audience to preach to."

Doc walks to the sink and splashes water on his face. He's only wearing briefs, his muddied clothes having been washed in the sink and hung to dry from the bars of the cell door. "Wasn't me started no conversation."

"Need me some smokes."

"Need me some quiet."

"Damn. Just get me one. It ain't me that started lockdown," the kid says accusingly.

Doc shrugs.

"Heard Ivory almost got it. You set that up, too?" the kid asks.

"I didn't set up nothing. And you'd do good to avoid that nigger," Doc says. "He ain't got nothing but what you don't need."

"Like you some Mother Theresa."

"You don't know shit. Start running your mouth and you ain't gonna be in a position to learn shit, either."

Hammer is making noise again, a steady, metallic boom coming from farther up the tier, a sound like a bunk being violently rocked against a wall.

"Got to sit and sweat for a week and you flexing on me for nothing," the kid complains.

"Flexing? What would your skinny ass know about flexing?"

"A week. Can't handle no week of confinement. Not with no smokes."

Doc laughs. "Can't handle no week? You got life confinement! A week ain't even a blink!"

"No," the kid says.

" 'No'? You got some special deal with the warden? Selling your ass for quick release? A suck job for a year's good time?"

"That ain't what I meant."

"But you got it all figured out. How to beat a life sentence in three easy steps. Never mind all the others that's tried and failed," Doc says.

"I ain't like them," the kid says.

"You ain't."

"Ain't like you, neither," the kid says.

"You right about that. *I'm* getting out."

"No, I mean I *ain't* like you. I'm a player! Got sent up in what you call highly politicized circumstances. Things is gonna settle. I know shit about my situation you don't."

"Like what," Doc says.

"Like I said," the kid shouts, "I ain't got no life sentence! Be out soon. Just like you."

"You still ain't said how."

The kid throws out his arms. "What the fuck? I ain't got to tell *you*. It ain't easy to explain, much less make sure that you get it."

"Go ahead and try me," Doc says, with an effort to keep his voice flat.

"It's hard to say, you know? But people like me don't get no life sentence. Feds and all the rest is gonna forget what I done in a couple of months. Then I be out."

"They gonna forget *you* in a couple of months. Then you never be out," Doc says.

"I ain't having this conversation no more," the kid says.

Doc shakes his head and controls his voice, careful not to shout. "Got to accept your time here. You don't and you ain't gonna treat it as real, ain't gonna take it serious. And that's what a life jolt is."

He holds the kid's eye for a moment before turning to pull a few *Amazing Spiderman* comics from his locker. "You want to read?"

"Gimme that *Batman* one with the shit 'bout Arkham Asylum," the kid says grudgingly.

Doc takes the comic. A letter is affixed to the mailer cover. "Looks like you got mail."

"Yeah?" The kid leans forward, hand out.

"A bill," Doc says. He chuckles. "Bet it says they going to turn you over to a collection agency any day." He hands the comic and letter to the kid, his hand brushing the kid's leg as the kid reaches for it from where he sits on the top bunk. Doc's hand lingers a moment and the kid pulls away, looking at Doc silently.

Doc goes hot in the face and jerks his hand back guiltily, dropping into his bunk without meeting the kid's eyes.

11

In the TV room the cons have settled down for the evening's movie: *The Good, the Bad, and the Ugly*, which is due to start after an installment of a detective show they like to watch, which combines live footage with the reenactments of cases. Inner Circle sings, "*Bad boys, bad boys, whatcha gonna do, whatcha gonna do when they come for you...*" as cop cars race down a highway.

Bunt, as usual, is dissatisfied with the TV fare. "Yo, ain't there any ball on?"

"I got all the ball you need to see right here, motherfucker!" yells Cornelius.

"Ball—?"

"You want ball—"

"All right, all right. Fuck y'all," Bunt says, crossing his arms and glaring at the TV.

Onscreen two policemen and a German shepherd chase a barefoot, muscle-bound man through a yard. The man pulls himself over a fence, but too slowly. The dog gets his foot.

There is a chorus of jeering. Everyone is excited to be free of their cells; there have been several scuffles since dinner.

"Damn, gets caught and gets rabies all in the same night," Stirling says.

"Dog's mouths is cleaner than ours," Doc says. He sits near the back, his feet up on another chair, Stirling bunched beside him. Stirling is an active watcher of TV—with every shift of his body he rocks the metal frame that holds the whole row of chairs bolted to the floor.

"Shut up with that *Scientific American* shit," Stirling says.

"That's what happens if you got too much muscle," Bunt says, standing and flexing a bicep. "He was to be in slim, fighting shape like me and he would have been over that fence like Speedy Gonzales!"

"You slim like a bowling ball, you nappy motherfucker," Doc says.

"You better make like Speedy and get the fuck out the way of the TV!" yells Cornelius.

"Show sucks my ass," Bunt says.

When it's time for the Eastwood movie Doc grins contentedly. He likes watching the westerns more than most, dreaming about wandering through the vast landscapes, wondering what it would be like to be alive in a time where you could ride far enough west that you could escape the law, people, even your own past, in the immensity of the land. He slouches low, relaxing as the opening credits roll.

He glances over at Stirling, who looks pleased and happy. Lockdown ended midmorning, and within the recirculating population the eleven men just out of the prison infirmary bearing stitched and bandaged faces haven't created the stir they normally would. Damage from the cave-ins has slowed the administration's investigation. Guards and cons alike are more concerned with the prison repairwork: the damaged furniture mill and textile plant provide most of the prison's revenue, the loss of profit eclipsing the knifings.

Luster is the only D.C. Black to have been sent to the Hole, having bragged about his handiwork within hearing of a guard. Doc guesses that Suspence will keep quiet, given that he and Kordell are still in the general population. The real question is whether there will be any retaliation.

After the show people disperse, enjoying a chance to stroll before evening lockdown. Doc and Stirling pause on the third tier, looking down toward the cellblock floor and the cons milling about. "Should have killed him, Doc."

"And then what? Like giving a corpse twenty more years of my life."

Stirling smoothes his pantlegs with his wide hands, his brow knit, the fleeting pleasure of the movie dissipating in the light of these demands. "Got two people that saw it. Think you soft. Word gonna get out."

Doc snorts, though he knows Stirling is right. Everyone prowls for weakness and they'll scent him like sharks drawn to bloodied meat. "And what? Think they's them that's gonna try and turn me out? Ain't nobody gonna touch me."

"Spencer gonna try. Every time he look in the mirror and see that face he want payback."

Doc hears the truth in this. "He try to use the AB and he cut his own throat. They don't have no truck with personal vendettas. Ain't gonna provoke the whole of the D.C. Blacks over his personal debts."

"So he come on his own. What then? He try to take you in the showers and you do what you got to do, and either he's dead or you are. No matter what, you gonna face the same kind of situation you had. Just won't be nobody to do the work for you this time. This time you gonna be responsible. Or you gonna be dead."

Doc pushes back from the railing. "Him I can handle." But he's not sure and for a moment resents the trap of circumstance. Better that he had kept out of it altogether, though with parole looming that had been impossible. By saving Suspence he's as good as asked for a contract to be taken out himself.

Stirling stares straight ahead. "You got so much to lose you can't even afford to step into the ring. And you still ain't handled what you said you would."

"The kid ain't done nothing since he got here. We could just leave him be. Got enough sources of heat."

"He ain't done nothing? Then how did Ivory know we was gonna move on him? Huh? Someone warned that motherfucker, and we missed him. Clayton ain't never going to be what he was." Stirling shakes his head. Clayton was the D.C. Black sent to cut Ivory. He ended up with a broken elbow, popped knee ligaments, and had his razor applied to his own eye. Ivory had known exactly where and how to strike to permanently cripple the man. "I ain't saying you said anything to him directly, but that boy saw something and put two and two together."

"So I'm responsible for the fuckup with Ivory?"

"You ain't and you is." Stirling puts a hand to Doc's shoulder. "I don't like this no more than you, my friend. Taking somebody out brings a lot of heat."

Doc sighs. "A week. Give it a week and then let Cornelius loose. Ellis says the warden and ICC be done reviewing my file by then." It's almost two weeks since his parole hearing, but the collapse has delayed the paperwork. Doc is no stranger to the stunning inertia of bureaucracy, but at this point in his sentence it seems targeted and cruel, worse than being worked over by the guards.

"Shit," Stirling says. Heading along the tier toward them is Grippe.

"Nice work, shitheads."

"Why thank you, Sergeant," Stirling responds. "I've always prided myself on my shoveling technique."

"I ain't talking about cleanup, Inmate Bison. Talking about your boys' handiwork. Leave it to you motherfuckers to make the prison population even uglier."

"I don't get the reference," Stirling says.

"You just remember that I'm investigating. I get one of those swiss-cheese motherfuckers to sing and you two are going to permanent lockdown in Marion."

The pair is silent at this. Marion is a level-six penitentiary under twenty-four-hour lockdown. While there is some measure of glory in doing time at Bone Hill, Marion is different—most of those who go in enter with a sentence that precludes release until they've become old men who've spent decades under lock and key, acclimated to the silence of a frighteningly solitary existence. You leave without the strength or inclination to brag about your time.

"This white boy, he don't know shit about the inside 'cause he's never been," Doc says as he and the kid walk to Frank's commissary in the minutes before Five Count. "Judge decides to fuck him over and sends him to Bone Hill even though he ought to be in a level one somewhere. First couple of days he's okay, but then he comes back to his cell and someone lifted all his books."

"What kind of books?"

"I don't know. Law books or some shit. Point is, someone's testing him. Seeing if he gonna make any noise, see if he's connected. But he ain't. Next day this brother sits by him in the chow hall, offers him a cup of coffee. They get to talking and this white boy, he's so excited he practically tells his life story then and there. People ain't good at being self-sufficient, see. Got needs. And a need," Doc points a finger at the kid, "is a weakness."

"You going to go and ruin a good story on me?"

"All right, all right. Couple nights later, this boy is up in his cell and two guys come up, knock him around and got his pants down around his ankles when his brother from the cafeteria shows up and scares 'em off. Pretty soon they got an arrangement."

"He pays the dude for protection."

"Think that's all, Brainiac?"

"Sex?"

"Ain't there nothing curious about the timing?"

"Setup?"

Doc smiles. "Now you getting it. The brother steals the books to case his prey. Then he finds out what kind of money the boy can provide. Gets his crew to fake the rape. That's a real scam 'cause the victim, he's *happy* to be paying the money and he ain't never gonna know that the guy he's giving it to is the one that made his life hard in the first place."

"I could've thought of that."

"Your friend Ivory *did*. That's what I'm talking about."

The kid grins. "He's the man."

"What makes you think a man that can pull that kind of shit won't do it to you?"

"Pull what kind of shit?" Grippe says, coming up from behind them in the rotunda and interrupting their trip. Doc curses under his breath; Grippe is without letup. During lockdown he'd come to his cell twice a day or more to taunt him. There is something perverse to such attention, as if he is so desperate to keep Doc in Tyburn that he's willing to goad him into attacking.

"You talking about Operation Ginsu Knife, Kane? 'Cause I got questions, too."

"Yo," the kid says, "whyn't you go back to reading your Johnny Walker labels instea—" But before the kid can finish, the cold, smooth end of Grippe's truncheon is softly touching the underside of his chin—there is an unsettling blend of menace and something sexual to the way the two pause there. Doc wonders if Grippe has his own designs on the kid, if the unrelenting abuse and attention is a cover he's loath to lose with Doc's absence.

"You'd do good to train your punk a little better, Kane."

Doc says nothing.

Grippe smiles. "Let's all of us go and take a piss test."

"Go ahead," the kid says. "What you gonna do, extend my sentence?"

Grippe raps him lightly on the lip. "You got a poor imagination if you think that's all I can do." He turns to Doc. "And I don't want to hear shit from you about shy kidneys. You ain't clean and it's over."

"It ain't going to be that easy," Doc says.

They both come up clean, but not before Grippe has them march to the infirmary and sit an hour, waiting to take their turn before his watchful eyes.

12

I n the shadow of the perimeter wall two men jump and dive, their shoes squeaking in the summer quiet, the irregular slap of the handball against the face of the brick wall snapping out.

The kid is playing well, but can't compete with his lanky opponent's reach. Doc stands nearby, breathing heavily from a run around the Yard. He spits.

Ivory Ferrel holds the red handball up in the kid's face. Ivory has the height of a professional basketball player, though it's a sport he hates. "Five dollars says I can take you on this shot."

The kid smiles. "Don't matter. I got five points on you."

Ivory leans into his face, lips splitting to reveal tightly bunched teeth. "Yeah, well if you gonna win the game, give me a chance to lose a little less money."

The kid is still smiling when he says okay, smiling even when he loses the point. Ivory catches Doc watching them, and in five quick serves the game is over. He moves with the boneless flexibility of a snake.

"Damn, Ivory. Gotta show me them moves. You old, but you got the moves."

"Luck. You the better player." Ivory palms the kid's head and smiles with the front of his face before walking away, his eyes sliding off Doc. Just as he passes, he mutters, "It's all about *anticipating*."

Doc thinks of Clayton. Sooner or later the Blacks will drop him now that he's an invalid. He has a long sentence, and the friends that are here to protect him will ultimately make their way out of Bone Hill. Clayton's in for a multiple homicide—forty to life. It wouldn't surprise Doc to learn that Ivory maimed Clayton instead of killing him because he might have some use for him down the line—it's easy to pressure someone who's weak and unprotected. Doc watches Ivory's receding figure and shivers.

The kid bounces the handball as Doc approaches.

"Want to transfer cells," the kid says.

"That so."

"Ivory say he can make it so I get a single."

"What, like you can entertain your women there? You gonna play the part of a bitch spreading your ass for Ivory's johns, you ain't careful."

"This ain't a conversation I want to have."

"How much you owe Ivory?" Doc asks.

"Nothing."

"How much is nothing?"

The kid looks at his feet.

"Nothing? Well, nothing ain't easy to pay, 'less you got a job or got family sending money." As Doc walks away he looks over his shoulder. "Maybe he let it go for a *favor*."

The kid lingers for a long while, bouncing the ball until others move in for a game.

What you waiting to pull, Ivory? Doc thinks dejectedly. He watches the fading light from the top tier of Cellblock B, wondering what it will be like to see it glowing from the smooth ribbon of the Potomac, colors softened by the humid air of his hometown. He sees footage of D.C. on the national news at times, on those rare occasions when a politician delivers a speech from somewhere other than on the steps of the Capitol Building or the Supreme

Court. Glimpses of home that seem less and less to mesh with the contours of the town he preserves in his memories. He knows that it will be different when he gets there, that his nostalgia for his past will seem indulgent foolishness in the face of this new life, but that doesn't prevent the daydreams, doesn't prevent him from wishing he could pick up as if he'd never left. As if he still had his wife and children waiting for him. As if his old friends would remain, expectant. As if somebody would be there to take note of his arrival, to remark on his victory over Bone Hill. It's been hours since he's learned that the paperwork for his parole has been processed, that he's to be released in two days, but this hasn't brought with it the anticipated euphoria. More, what he feels is a deep unease.

"You ain't got the face of no free man," Ellis says in approach.

Doc is glad for the interruption. He tries to shrug off his discomfort, forcing a grin for the old man.

"It's like I got too much to feel," Doc says.

Ellis nods. "Well, we ain't got no time for that at the moment. Got work to do before dinner."

"All right," Doc says, "just as long as you ain't got no more life lessons for me."

The kitchen is quiet, the convict cooks immersed in the meal's preparation or wheeling full trays of food toward the cafeteria serving-counter. Several men cluster near the meat locker, smoking and enjoying the cold issuing from the half-open door. They ignore Ellis and Doc.

The two enter a storage room stacked high with crates of generic food. In one corner a black shape darts between two boxes. One of the forty-pound flour sacks leaks from the corner. A crust of old food covers the exposed floor. Ellis asks Doc to shift a box of canned tomatoes, revealing a trap door.

"Who'd you get to move this the other times?" Doc asks, grunting as he pushes it to the side.

"Other times?" echoes Ellis. "Wasn't no other times. We just following a hunch. Got it in my mind that maybe some rats get themselves caught in a old air duct from time to time. I figure it must be one that's out of the way. Else Stimple would have found it."

Doc grins. Ellis won't reveal anything about this unless Doc pries it out of him. But he knows Ellis must have had someone around to do the grunt work like lifting this box and if Ellis has really planted dead rats in an air duct, Doc is sure that Ellis was not the one to directly handle them.

A wooden ladder leads down, the floor here dusty and dry. Ellis twists on his Mag-Lite. Over his shoulder Doc sees footprints in the dust—different-sized feet, both coming and going. They stop in a low-ceilinged room, the stone floor and walls fuzzed with gray fungus. A vent set into the wall has the grating removed. On the floor rests an empty sack, a pair of canvas gloves, and ten feet of coiled rope. Doc eyes the vent dubiously.

"You'll fit. Get those gloves on and take that sack in one hand." Ellis hands Doc a bandanna to cover his mouth. "Probably gonna find some pungent rats."

Doc looks at his wispy companion. "Pungent."

"What I said."

"And how do I get out of there?"

"Just inch out backwards."

"Damn," Doc says. "No wonder you need me. I bet the fella you had putting those rats up there got stuck. Now *he* the one making the stink." He takes the coiled rope and loops it around his neck and shoulder before tying the bandanna over his nose and mouth.

The air duct is a tight fit and the smell causes his eyes to tear. To squeeze through the narrow passage Doc must stretch his arms straight ahead, inching slowly with the friction of his whole body.

Within a few feet he is sweating, breathing hard. The warm metal of the vent seems to press on him above and below, from the right and the left, inexorably closing in. He feels as if he is being crushed by the prison, the overwhelming sense of confinement causing his heart to flutter in his chest like a trapped and panicked bird.

He coughs as his breathing quickens, inhaling rust flakes that leave a metallic taste on his tongue that mixes with the rot in the air.

He pushes faster into the thick smell, a buzzing in his ears, relieved when the light illuminates a small pile of rotting rats where three vent-shafts angle off. Something moves and he jerks back, his head striking the metal paneling above with a hollow boom. He retrains the light on the pile of carcasses. The fur is dull brown and black and seems to twist. He realizes that the buzzing is coming from bluebottle flies. A plump maggot wriggles free of a rat's eye socket.

Doc places the open mouth of the sack beside the pile and grits his teeth as he reaches with a gloved hand and grasps the first carcass. Flies bump against his face. Moving the rats to the sack is a slow, awkward process without room to properly bend his elbows. The rats on the bottom of the pile seem older and are little but fur and deliquescing meat. By the time he finishes sliding them into the bag he feels sure the stink permanently impregnated the skin of his hands and face. He ties the sack shut with the rope and backs away as quickly as he can, the rope's end gripped in one hand.

Doc falls from the vent to the floor, banging his shoulder on the floor. He stands and strips off the gloves before patting the caked rust from his knees and chest and forearms. "Didn't tell me 'bout no goddamn insects, Ellis."

"Death an ugly thing."

Doc spits. He turns and reaches for the rope end hanging from the vent's mouth, pulling hand over hand until the full sack falls from the vent and lands wetly before them.

"Sure you got them all?" Ellis asks, his face pinching with the smell of rot.

"Saved one for a snack," Doc says. "And why didn't you just leave them in a sack in the first place? Tie it up with a rope and pull it out if you got to add some."

"Seems to me that would imply that somebody was directly responsible for them rats, which we know ain't the case."

Doc hawks and spits again.

"Pile of dead rats. Makes you think."

"Ain't no metaphor in this," Doc says, prodding the bag with a foot, "so don't go getting poetic." But he's impressed: Only Ellis could take a pile of rats and turn them into enough leverage to get Doc's parole files changed, to say nothing of the many other favors he's probably managed to get out of the administration.

"Let's get out of here," Doc says, moving to leave.

"Best pick up that sack before you start walking," Ellis says. "We got a deal to close."

"You ain't gonna leave them here?"

"Got to close the deal. Even the warden's got curious 'bout so much stink."

Doc laughs. If any con were to present a sack of rotting rats to a guard, much less the warden, they'd end up in seg for years. But Ellis, he'll probably get a commendation. So much time in the prison has left him far better prepared to use the system than those who nominally wield the power.

"Now pick up that sack," Ellis says. "I'm too damn old to be doing no labor."

Doc spits yet again. The taste of rot stubbornly adheres to his mouth.

At dinner he drinks only water. His crew is clustered around Stirling, whose physical presence dominates the table. He is the center of gravity here, the force that holds them in their synchronized orbits and provides the order within the chaos of conflicting needs and desires.

Bunt is reading from a letter. For several months he's penned notes to a man in New York who'd responded to an ad he'd posted in the *Sun*'s personals pages: "5' 10", DWF, ash-blond hair, big boned/voluptuous, alluring/appealing. Enjoys fun in the sun, soaking up the rays, quiet romantic times. Seeks correspondence with older, mature gentleman. Looking to start loving again."

Bunt has gradually escalated the pitch of the letters ("I think of you each night before I fall asleep in the hopes I'll dream of you," to "Only a year until I'll be released into your arms!") as well as the accompanying demands for money to buy "law books so I can get out sooner." The latest letter seems to be the big break-through: his unsuspecting boyfriend has sent a mail-order set of black lingerie.

As Bunt reads, Doc interrupts. "Don't he know there ain't women here?"

In a falsetto, Bunt says, "He's in love! It's no time to be rational!"

They all laugh. "You'd make one fucked-up bitch," Stirling booms, shaking his head; and at this the others laugh hard enough that Bunt looks slightly hurt, the cheer that inflates his face leaking a bit.

"He going to be disappointed, all right," Doc says with a smile. Everything about Bunt is round, even the moles that dot his full face. His body is like that of a chubby schoolboy who has yet to hit his growth.

"Yo, let's see that underwear!" Cornelius says. There is an edge to his voice that Doc hears clearly, sees in the tightness of the muscles of his face.

Bunt glances around, then half pulls them from his pant pocket.

"Who you got muling the letters for you?" Doc asks.

"Ain't saying," Bunt says. "You find your own work force."

Cornelius jerks the panties from Bunt's hand. He sniffs appreciatively, then pulls them on his head.

"It's Pantyman!" he says in a deep voice. Every mood of Cornelius's has about it a violent intensity that is barely controlled. As if humor could impel him to violence as easily as hate, goodwill as easily as jealousy.

Bunt rips them off his head. "Keep your damn hands off, 'less you want to buy 'em."

"Could wear those instead of them nappy bandannas," Cornelius says.

"You get anything else?" Stirling asks.

Bunt waves the credit-card receipt that came with the underwear.

"You go shopping and I want a cut," Stirling says.

"You know it. Figure I can order a few TVs 'fore he complains. Send 'em to my brother, he pawns them, and then it's *direct deposit*, know what I'm saying?"

Stirling laughs—it is a sound they all enjoy. "You the man, Bunt. You the man."

The kid sits several tables away in the midst of Elston and his New York crew, talking animatedly to Ivory. Doc watches them. *Forget that boy.* There's a tightness in his chest as he admits that he will do whatever's necessary to crawl from beneath the crushing mass of so much stone.

After dinner he goes to Bunt's cell and passes the hours before Five Count drinking pruno with his friend until he is too drunk to think.

"We going to be friends on the outside?" Bunt asks. He is due for a parole hearing in a few months, with only two years left to his full sentence, and the question is more than idle.

Doc nods. "Have a few *real* drinks together."

"Even though we ain't supposed to have nothing to do with each other?" A condition of parole is, in the language of BOP-ese, that the parolee avoid former inmates of penal institutions. A means of discouraging the bonds forged in prison.

"Shit," says Doc. "I aim to be different on the outside, but not *that* different."

"Doc," Bunt says, leaning in close and looking into Doc's face to let him know he's serious. "I ain't never want to come back here. Never."

Doc holds his gaze.

Bunt shakes his head. "Maybe you ain't going to be too different. Me?" He looks away. "I ain't like you. I can't come back here." He clears his throat and drinks quickly.

"You all right, brother," Doc says quietly. They drink silently for the next half hour, Doc returning to his cell just before the nightly lockdown.

The kid sits cross-legged in his bunk, smoking while fiddling with something. To his left is a stack of Doc's issues of *Gent*. Beneath this a crescent of surgical tape shows. He covers the magazines and tape with the corner of his blanket when Doc stumbles in.

"Yo, man, you get beat? You okay?" He slides down and steadies Doc.

Doc pushes him away and collapses on his bunk. He can't close his eyes because the slow spin of the cell accelerates when he does. "Don't be embarrassed 'bout reading my tittie 'zines. Just remember you got to ask."

"Kind of hard to ask, is all," the kid says, oddly flustered.

"Got to hang on to the pleasures you got. Ain't gonna start trouble beating your meat," Doc mumbles.

The kid smells the brew and starts to laugh.

"Yo, where you get that stuff? You got any more?"

Doc smiles, mumbles, "Just beating the Man, thas'all...."

"You got any more?"

"You too young."

"Twenty-one! Legal."

"Not for the shit I drink, you ain't. Get in your bed. Ain't got the energy to be talking." Doc plants a foot on the floor to slow the whirling cell and breathes deeply.

"Doc?"

"Whassup?"

The kid is in his bunk again, legs dangling from the side, kicking at the air.

"How you get here?"

"Same as most, got caught." He chuckles. "Killed my son-in-law for beating my girl. Got a few more years tacked on for dealing dope inside."

"So why you always on me? I ain't done nothing worse'n you."

"It's how stupid you is in here. Don't listen. They's a code to prison. Code to everything." He starts to drift, but the kid's voice cuts in.

"You still got family?"

"Yeah."

"And they visit? Bring you Christmas presents and stuff?"

"Used to. Been in here so long . . . I had family," he says sharply, struggling to sit up. "Had memories."

Willie, Rose. But he can't even recall the faces of his son and daughter, just the curve of a smile, the angle of a chin. At the start of his sentence, he sometimes heard the cries of children playing outside, their shouts arcing over the penitentiary walls. Back then, there had been an anemic town sheltered beneath the prison: gas station, a few sag-roofed, low-income guards' houses, a market, all of it looking hurriedly nailed down, like a temporary mining camp. Over the years the children's cries faded, as did the images of his own kids, their faces as blurred in his mind as the finger-smeared writing on the ragged, cloth-soft letters he keeps.

It is quiet, Doc's labored breathing audible. The kid quits kicking his legs. "I ain't never getting out, huh?"

Doc is silent. The kid does not know if Doc has heard or not. He runs his thumb over the grain of the surgical tape long after the prison lights are extinguished.

13

n the hour after Three Count, Doc skips breakfast. He walks the
perimeter of the Yard enjoying the relative cool of the morning,
the sun just edging over the horizon and visible only as a paling
in the sky above the high penitentiary walls. His head aches
fiercely. He vomits, stomach twisting tight, forcing up the last of
the pruno. He's begun to sweat and feels better for it, pushing
himself to twice run the length of the Yard to work out the im-
purities. The ground is ridged with footprints, the treads of tractors,
the grooves from wheelbarrows, all of it hardened into the desert
clay, which even now is covered with a fine layer of sand. It reminds Doc of the pictures he's seen of petrified dinosaur tracks
leading across stone flats, a record of past journeys lightly pressed
into the rock.

Today his work crew is shoveling dirt into the collapsed por-
tion of the Yard by prison industries, and he is glad for the physical
labor, enjoying the feel of the shovel as it sinks into the dirt and
the smooth motion of his body twisting as he lifts the weighted
shovel and sends the dirt sifting into the sinkhole. There is too
much to think on; it is easy to give himself up to the motion, to
give up another day—his final—to prison routine.

Bunt passes with a full wheelbarrow of dirt he's collected from the cemetery where the fallout from the dust storm was piled. "You having a good time?" he says, his sweat-streaked face tight-lipped. " 'Cause I am. Ain't nothing more uplifting than moving dirt from one motherfucking place to another."

"You can put it down on your résumé," one of the guards says, watching them. "Crack-head, convict and landscaper. Fuckin' Renaissance man."

"What do I need a résumé for? I already got a job fucking your momma."

The guard laughs. "And you're welcome to it."

During the lunch break, Doc naps in his cell and then, roused by the noise of inmates returning from the meal, pays Frank a visit before afternoon work call.

Doc wishes he could remember more of the previous night's conversation with the kid. He's seen less and less of him since Ivory began hovering about like a late-afternoon shadow, his sharp face watchful, measuring.

Frank sleeps on his bunk, a copy of *Vanity Fair* over his face. His chest is lightly furred, skin taut over his small, hard belly.

Doc clears his throat. "Sit at the desk," Frank says from beneath the magazine. "Only so much you can learn about Sly Stallone before the injustice of his success shuts down your brain.... You getting nervous?"

"A bit. Yeah."

"A bit. Hah. I would've gone crazy by now. They held it up what, two weeks?"

Doc shrugs. "Warden, ICC. Everyone got to feel important, use their stamp."

"I wouldn't be so philosophical."

"You ain't me," Doc says. "Just 'cause I ain't sweating don't mean I ain't sweating." He prods Frank's supine form with his foot. "You sold anything to Ivory recently?"

Frank makes no move to lift the magazine. "Nope."

"Nothing?"

"Don't sell to him no more. He been broke for months now and still owes me. Stirling says he's gonna take care of it."

"He will," Doc says.

Frank sits up. "Got a lot of shanks floating around. Keep an eye on who's ending up with them."

"You mean Suspence?"

Frank sits up and shakes his head. "I wanna be clear about this: I ain't sold him nothing like that, and he wasn't part of no AB when I let him in here with you last month. I don't have no beef with you or that boy. Not neither of you."

"All right," Doc says.

Frank's eyes protrude a bit more than usual, and his breathing has quickened.

Doc purses his lips. "You'd want to make it known, though, he was to come around looking for something along the lines of a shank."

"I'd want to make it known, yes," Frank says.

"Thanks."

"Hah."

The kid and Ivory are at the wall again, shirtless and gleaming, framed by the white square painted on the surface of the stone. The kid is falling over himself to get to the ball after each hit. Ivory twists, arches around him, speeding and slowing the tempo of the game, dropping a few points every time the kid slows from discouragement. Doc watches from the edge of the concrete bleachers, facing away from the baseball game under way. After a few minutes he sees Ivory stop and holds out a hand. He says something and the kid shakes his head, looking at his feet. Ivory slaps him, grabs him by the jaw and continues talking.

"Look like you already carrying that weight, Doc."

He turns to see Ellis on the bleachers, all but lost in the folds of his baggy uniform.

Doc climbs to sit beside the old man, pleased to have been

noticed. "Just the weight of a hangover. Always afraid I'm gonna go blind after Bunt's pruno."

Ellis stares distractedly at the kid and Ivory talking down below. "What's so important 'bout that kid that you get that look?"

A sharp crack of a ball against a bat, cheers and shouts as a man runs the bases, slowing to a strut over home plate, waving his hands celebratorily.

"It's getting out. Feel like I'm balancing, getting close if I can just concentrate, but then this fool child appear, waving his arms and needing my attention."

Ellis continues watching the game. "Most times I say a man's got to stand up for what he believes in. But now," he rubs the back of his neck, "you best do what it takes to leave. That kid ain't your business. Only got room in your life for parole."

Ivory walks off toward the baseball game. Doc rises.

"They's a lot of us who ain't gonna make it out, Doc. Death walk the prison grounds with a big smile for a reason. But you," Ellis looks into Doc's eyes, "You get out and it one victory for us." He turns back to studying the Yard, humming softly.

Doc leaves Ellis and approaches the kid, feeling the old man's eyes on his back.

"Let's you and me take a walk," he says. He can see the swelling starting around the kid's right eye. The kid falls in step, head hanging.

"Thinking maybe you could use a good-paying job."

When the kid doesn't respond he continues. "Going to be a job in prison industries sewing mail bags and army T-shirts. Pay good and ain't too hard. I can fix it so you start in my place, you want."

They're near the prison industries buildings. The collapsed section of the Yard has largely been tamped level with fill, but the ground closest to the split guard tower is cordoned off with rope. A deep pit has opened here that will need to be capped. The sharp, yellowed edges of limestone blocks glow like old bones where the pit narrows to a split between the stone that is pitch-black.

"Yo, I heard someone working there sewed a guy's face with one of them machines. Don't sound like no place I want to be," the kid says, looking at Doc to gauge his reaction, but Doc isn't really listening, his mind elsewhere.

They've reached the Hole. The bricks are covered with so many layers of paint they look to have been melted by a century of hot desert wind.

Doc nods toward the building. "Used to throw you in there for walking on the wrong-colored tile in Center Hall. Do something the hacks didn't like and you got a sweatbox with just a hole in the center. Smell like a sewer, and nothing but dirty cement to lie on. Just you and the bugs."

Doc guides him to the back wall, grabs his hand and presses it against the smooth paint. "Feel that heat? Come out at night and it still be there. All that anger running through here for so many years. . . ."

The kid jerks back. "Ain't no heat but the sun, and the way you talking, I bet the same damn sun's fried your brain. Now what you gonna show me? The cave-in open a tunnel out of here?"

"No wonder you doing time. Got a mouth so damn big, probably got witnesses for things you ain't even done." At the outermost curve of the perimeter wall Doc motions around him in a sweeping motion. "Convicts built this after the Civil War. Ain't no getting over, and no getting under. Four feet thick, so forget about going through."

He points to where the course of masonry ends and the brick begins, some ten feet above the ground, layered like the strata of a road-cut hill. "Had a bunch of stonemasons at work on the wall. Heard they can't make walls like this no more. Stonemasons fit it together so that it ain't nothing but stone and gravity. This part gonna be here long after the brick and cement get old and crumbly."

Doc turns to the kid, who meets his stare with a bored look. "You and me and every convict in here builds his own wall. Can keep things out, and if you ain't careful, can trap yourself in. I got my wall. Got respect, got my crew, got my muscle. Ain't no Ivory coming my way. But you," Doc pats the wall, looks the kid up and down, "you building a wall keep you in even tighter than this one. Ivory probably just had a little talk with you 'bout your finances. Says you got to do a little favor to work it off."

The kid stands very still.

Doc grabs the kid's forearm and pulls him to the wall, almost jerking him from his feet. He places the kid's hand on a crevice in the stone wall where something angles out: the side of a jawbone with a few jutting teeth.

"Ain't real," the kid says.

"Real enough," Doc says. "I like to think some con wedged in there. Give us all something to think about."

The kid pulls his hand away, rubbing at his wrist.

"If Ivory beats on you, maybe you go to the hacks, complain 'bout the treatment you getting. 'Course, they ain't gonna pay you no mind, 'cause they've already tried to do you one worse than Ivory." Doc leans against the wall and stares at the kid. "You should never have been in no cell with me. You and the hacks both know you ain't got no friend in the D.C. Blacks. Cornelius and a few others like you even less than Ivory. But the hacks, they read your record, decide life in Tyburn maybe ain't enough for what you done. Die in here and it ain't nothing to them. Think maybe I'm the one to do the favor."

"You."

"You know I'm with the D.C. Blacks. Ain't you wondered why nothing's happened to your ass yet? Ain't you wondered what's gonna happen when I'm gone?"

The kid stares at him, eyes flat. "You know less than you think, old man."

14

D amn." Stirling puts a hand to Doc's shoulder. "Twenty years and now you gonna be gone."

Doc clears his throat.

"Still, we got a lot of brothers coming in. Another year and there ain't gonna be none left on the streets. 'Cept you. You dumb, but not dumb enough to break parole."

"My last day in here and you finally right about something."

They walk through the rotunda to Center Hall as they have countless times together, their footsteps magnified by the cavernous space. Doc hadn't known what to expect on his final day, but wasn't surprised when Stirling dropped by his cell after the morning head-count.

A large leaf of plaster twirls from the ceiling to the floor, landing before them. Stirling snorts. "Dust storm. Cave-ins. This place ain't going to outlast my sentence."

"I don't know," Doc says, "seems more like a settling, you know? Like this place is just getting comfortable."

"Shit. Least when you go I ain't losing no one with a sense of humor."

Doc laughs. "You right. I'm just talking shit."

They'd eaten breakfast in the cafeteria where Doc joked with the other D.C. Blacks at his table, taking the hazing, promising to get laid enough for everyone, feeling the anticipation build, an added feeling of satisfaction when he bumped against Suspence on the way out, insulated from the cold glare by the warmth and respect of his crew, by a release just a day away. *Leave it behind like I'm leaving you,* he'd thought, meeting the stare from the scarred face. After that he and Stirling had lingered a few hours in Stirling's cell, playing dominoes and trying to finish their Risk game, uncharacteristically quiet, both lost in thought, touching the memories of the past, shared decades.

It is now midafternoon. Bunt is in the kitchen, taking advantage of the lull after the general prison lunch to cook a Cajun sauce for Doc's final supper. Ellis sets plates on a stainless serving-counter covered with a white tablecloth. There are two bottles of wine. Doc smiles at the sight of the serious old man so carefully placing the dishes. Ellis nods to him, picks up a cloth and begins polishing the glasses. Stirling laughs. "Hey, you the man, Ellis! There ain't nothing you can't get."

"Almost nothing." Ellis points at the plastic utensils. "Plastic," he mutters.

Bunt lifts an open rum bottle in invitation and Doc and Stirling join him at the stove, passing the bottle, the burn clean and smooth, leaving a cool numbness in its wake.

They drink without saying much, watching Ellis finish his meticulous polishing. Bunt sets the pasta and salad on the table and they pull up their stools. When the wine is poured Ellis lifts his glass. "Doc, you a good man. Hope you find a good place."

Stirling lifts his. "And may that good place be between the legs of a fine woman."

"I just want to thank everybody who made it possible to be here—Officer Rosen; Warden Duchamp; my former friend Tyrel Scopes, who snitched on me; the D.C. Superior Court—"

"Shut up, Bunt," Ellis says mildly.

By the end of the meal the wine is gone and another bottle of rum is making the rounds. The conversation has waned. From the outer halls the dim sounds of the other cons returning from work filter in.

"Time to wrap it up," Stirling says, rising.

The others reluctantly follow suit. The door squeaks open as the first of the inmate cooks walks in to prep for the dinner shift.

"Ellis, what do I got to do to get the Doc discount on a bottle of rum?" Bunt asks as they head for their cellblocks.

"Ain't nothing for free," Ellis says. "Doc worked for it. Charge you fifty for a fifth."

They fall to haggling over prices, voices slurred with alcohol. Stirling wants to get in a last round of Risk before cell count. He and Doc leave Bunt and Ellis for their tier, passing Doc's cell en route. The kid sits backed against a wall, his head in his hands. Doc slows. "Let me catch up with you," he says.

Stirling's eyes dart to the cell. "Waste of time," he mutters.

"Just a few minutes," Doc says. In the cell, he prods the kid with his foot. "Hey."

"What up." The kid looks dejected, his gaze fixed to the floor.

"You getting all depressed now that you going to have to go and find a new cellie?"

The kid bites his lip. "I been wanting to talk," he says, voice almost inaudible.

Doc waits.

"Not here. Outside, maybe."

Doc shrugs. "All right, Double-oh-seven. You lead the way."

The kid says nothing as they make their way to the Yard, his eyes downcast. As they step into the late-afternoon sun, he pauses to squint into the glare, then turns to Doc. "This the last time you gonna be out here, huh?"

"Moving on to bigger playgrounds," Doc says.

They walk toward prison industries, where a final work crew is just breaking up.

"You scared?"

"Nah," lies Doc.

The men from the crew pass by. Cornelius is among them, a shovel over his shoulder. He slows, watching the pair, the black of his face somehow so dark as to be unreflective.

"Yo, Big C," Doc says.

Cornelius nods to Doc, then leans and spits, an eye on the kid. "See you around," he says, continuing on his way.

In front of them runs the collapse line, most of it filled with packed earth, though the deep pit remains near the base of the split guntower. Parked at the pit's edge is a small bulldozer.

The kid walks to the edge, stepping over the staked ropes that mark it off and peering down. "Where you think it goes?"

Doc joins him. "Ain't no tunnel outside, that's what you thinking."

The kid shakes his head, a wan smile on his face.

"What you smiling for? Bet you just happy 'cause after tomorrow you don't have to listen to me no more."

"Some of that," the kid says. "And 'cause now I get that single I been wanting." He turns and smiles widely, clapping Doc on the shoulder. "You enjoy your last day?"

"Yeah," Doc says. "I did." He smiles. He notes that the kid has bruise marks on his throat, like dirty fingerprints on his skin and is about to ask a question when the knife enters his stomach.

He looks down at the bloom of blood on his shirt. The kid jumps back, as if shocked by his action. "Ivory and Suspence is paying for you to taste the knife." He says it like an excuse. Waves the knife for emphasis.

"Wha—"

The shank darts at Doc again, withdrawing too fast for pain, like a light punch.

Doc stares dumbly at the kid, hands pressed to his stomach; it is not the act that immobilizes him, but the kid's stare, his eyes like a snake's: black and flat, dead. He is so transfixed that he is as surprised as the kid when the flat of a shovel blade impacts on the side of the kid's skull. The kid crumples soundlessly. Blood streams from his nose. Cornelius shifts his grip on the shovel's stock. He hefts it like an ax, swinging, the edge of blade splitting the kid's parietal bone and lodging deep in his skull.

Doc watches from his knees, his hands pressed to his stomach.

Cornelius works the shovel loose of the kid's temple, then levers the body into the pit. It slides down the incline and over a lip of limestone, disappearing. Cornelius jams the shovel in the dirt, scraping the blood from it. "You going to die?"

Doc shakes his head. Blood seeps over his fingers.

Crouching in front of Doc, Cornelius pulls open his shirt and wipes some blood away. He looks steadily at Doc, then takes off his own T-shirt and wraps it about Doc's waist, cinching it tight. He buttons Doc's shirt over this and smears dirt over the bloodstains. "Get up," he says.

Doc shakes his head.

"You want to get out? Then get the fuck up. Your guts ain't going nowhere."

Doc struggles up with Cornelius's help. It feels as if he is watching himself from afar, the attack, the pain, the circumstances so remote as to lose their import.

"Hurry," Cornelius says. " 'Fore you bleed enough that it gets noticed."

In his cell Stirling and Bunt lean over him. "This gonna hurt, but you best keep quiet," Stirling says. He has a bottle of fluid which he shakes vigorously. Bunt pulls up Doc's shirt, removes the blood-caked T-shirt, then wipes at Doc's stomach until two dark puncture wounds show, already bruising around the edges.

Doc steels himself as Stirling pours the mixture in the bottle into each wound, feeling a burn, and beneath this a deep soreness. "You listen: Got Betadyne and water to keep you clean. When you out tomorrow watch for fever. You start running one and you know you got hit in the wrong place, find you a doctor. But it don't look like you got hit in the gut," Stirling says.

Bunt smiles. "All them sit-ups did you some good. Got enough muscle to deflect the shank." He wipes the excess fluid from Doc's wounds and tapes gauze over each. There is surprisingly little blood.

Stirling places a hand on Doc's shoulder. "Bunt gonna help you pack."

Doc follows Stirling with his eyes until he disappears from view.

Bunt loads a duffel bag with Doc's meager possessions he hasn't yet put away. "Hacks see you cut and parole ain't happening. You can't move stiff. Otherwise they nail you for sure."

"The kid," Doc whispers.

"What the fuck was he thinking? That we wasn't gonna catch him?"

"The kid," Doc repeats.

Bunt stands over him. "Gonna be okay, man, okay. When Grippe come for Four Count, you ain't seen the kid. They ain't gonna find him, hear? Never. Stick to your story."

Doc nods. He tries to remember the fight, but it is a blur.

At Four Count the gates to the cells rumble shut, and soon Doc hears Grippe's heavy footfall. Doc sits up, wincing, stands and approaches the front of the cell, gathering himself. *A day like any other,* he thinks, repeating it in his head like a mantra.

"Count off," Grippe says, barely glancing in. He seems curiously subdued.

"That it? No final object lesson?"

Grippe clicks his counter. "I don't feel like celebrating, that's what you mean."

"125630."

"This ain't no victory, Kane. You'll be back."

"The hell."

"You just prove it, you hear. You never changed. You going to get out, fuck up again, and make it that much harder for good blacks everywhere."

"I changed. Like I told you before."

Grippe shakes his head. His voice is low, and Doc can see his shoulders sag. "Count off," he says again, looking past Doc to the upper bunk. When no response is forthcoming it registers that the kid is not in the cell. His face hardens. There is no smile of victory, but rather a raw and unmasked anger. "Motherfucker. Where's your bitch?"

Doc shrugs, trying to look unconcerned, though his heart races. "Ain't seen him."

"You fuck. Day before your release and you got a missing cell-mate." He radios in the news to the on-duty lieutenant and then looks again at Doc. "You motherfucker."

But an hour later, Doc's cell a mess from a thorough search, he is back in bed feeling the throb of his wounds, sleepily drifting, thankful Raven was the on-duty lieutenant and kept Grippe from banishing him to seg on a mere suspicion of involvement. Instead, Raven has red-tagged his cell, keeping him confined to his bunk until his release.

At first he sleeps, dreaming of walls made translucent by the sun, suffused with a rose light. Behind them he sees blurred movement, indistinct shapes approaching and receding, gradually sharpening as the walls thin. He rises and pushes against his cell wall, the cement now gauzy and soft enough to stretch, wrapping around him like a glass sheath as he moves forward. But as far as he moves and as thin and transparent as the wall becomes, he cannot seem to press through, the sheath hampering his breathing, choking him as he pushes on.

He wakes to a jolt of pain from his abdomen, and groans. The dim light reveals the imprint of his face on the wall, eyes closed, mouth partly open. As he stares the shaded pockets of his face-cast merge with the level surface of the wall, disappear.

The following morning Doc's cell is searched again and the convicts suffer through a long, hot day of lockdown while the guards comb the prison for signs of the kid. Those in adjoining cells call to Doc to see what he knows, and while he says nothing, soon there are rumors that the kid has found a network of caves and is out, maybe miles away, emerging from some hidden pile of rocks, already on the run, his imagined freedom a vicarious thrill.

After getting lunch in his cell—a Styrofoam box with a sandwich and piece of fruit—Raven appears. He unlocks the cell door, nodding to Doc as his eyes sweep the cell, settling on Doc's uneaten lunch where it lies on the chair.

"Didn't expect to see this day."

Heat boils in the cellblock. Doc's sweat-soaked bandages burn his wounds. "What day is that?"

Raven's lips flatten into a faint smile. "A day when a cafeteria sandwich goes uneaten."

Doc watches Raven.

"We haven't found your cellmate," Raven says. His eyes move about the cell.

"I told you all I know, Lieutenant. Ain't no way I would do nothing to get in the way of today."

"That isn't what Sergeant Grippe thinks."

"He thinks a lot of things 'bout me, ain't none of them good."

Raven's eyes pass over Doc, a cursory look, catch at his waist for a moment before gliding off. His thin smile returns. "An inmate disappears and a lot goes with him: the cost of housing, of food," he pauses, "we don't even pay for a box. And recidivism's never a problem."

Doc keeps his face blank.

"Had the man here who did it," Raven continues, "and I might even thank him."

When Raven leaves Doc looks down at his waist. A dark spot of blood the size of a quarter stains the denim.

15

oc moves stiffly, his head up. It hurts to carry his bags, but he doesn't betray this as he passes down his tier for the final time, Grippe a few steps behind. Doc pauses before Stirling's cell. Stirling reaches his arms through the bars and grasps Doc's shoulders in his huge hands. "Guess I win that game of Risk."

Doc tries to smile. "Yeah." He swallows a breath.

"Don't go and get all juicy, Doc."

"Think you can handle all them boys on your own?"

"You know it."

"You tell Ellis and the others—" He feels his knees weaken and is glad that Stirling's hands are there to steady him. He does not want his friend to release his grip. There is so much he wants to say, though he doesn't think he could find the words to convey all he feels. Not now or ever.

"They know, Doc. Just get out of here. You leaving Disneyland. Time to breathe some air, to get some pussy."

"Let's go, Kane," Grippe says.

Doc turns with his eyes to the floor, the gray cement blurring.

In the rotunda he stands for a last look at the red- and white-checked floor of Center Hall. His shoes squeak on the tile. Near the front gate, a faint breeze cools the sweat at the base of his neck. He pauses, smelling the thick, sour rot of sweat, urine, and fear that issues from the prison like its very breath.

"You ain't won nothing," Grippe says. His face holds the same flush it has for days, his eyes a jaundiced yellow. He looks sick with anger.

Out in the drive a taxi waits.

"Damn straight," Doc says. "I earned it."

Grippe studies him. "I don't think so, Kane. Ain't no one would call you rehabilitated."

"I *paid* my dues. You got sixteen years and parts of me I ain't never gonna see again. You got your pound of flesh."

"It was never about that, Kane."

"The hell. Take a good look at this place. Ain't about no re-habilitation. Your man, Raven, he's what it's about. That's why he's lieutenant and you ain't never gonna get promoted. He's the future, man, not you, you damn house nigger."

He walks to the prison steps, gazing at the horizon's wide sweep. The wind sighs over the flat, the circling of a lone crow the only movement.

He is not surprised to see that the town that used to surround the prison has wasted away, leaving in its ruins a greater sense of emptiness than if nothing had been built. All that remains are boarded-up cinderblock houses, and roads that emerge in places from drifted dirt, surrounding the walled prison in a faint grid.

The taxi's horn sounds, jolting him into motion.

The crow settles heavily on the fence beside the gravel drive. It caws once. The fetid air of Bone Hill disperses as Doc descends the steps into the hard Nevada light.

PART TWO
Dead Earl

"[A mirage is] a distorted scene of distant objects resulting from the passage of light through a nonuniform medium. In a uniform atmosphere light would travel in straight lines and distant scenes would appear without distortion. Since the density of the air changes with height and with temperature, the atmosphere is not uniform and light rays follow curved paths."

—Robert Greenler, *McGraw-Hill Encyclopedia of Science and Technology*

"Each ray of sunshine is seven minutes old,"
Serge told me in New York one December night.

"So when I look at the sky, I see the past?"
"Yes, yes," he said, "especially on a clear day."

—Agha Shahid Ali, "Snow on the Desert"

1

I n the approaching weeks, after Doc breaks parole and Dead Earl becomes the centerpiece in Doc's waking dreams, hallucinations, visions—call them what you will—he will find himself beset by questions: Are the memories and lessons that dreams impart any less substantive than those left by actual experience? Is the imagined less real than the concrete if one is sufficiently convinced of its existence? And in the story of our lives, are we free to choose memories as we would stones pleasing to the eye, or is a harsher logic at work in this construction, and to what end?

Today, though, such concerns are as yet invisible. Dead Earl lurks, unseen, and it still feels possible to walk the straight and narrow.

Bike couriers and punks loiter by the Dupont Circle fountain. A tiny girl leans over the fountain's edge, poking the water with a stick. Sun-warmed bench slats press their heat through Doc's clothing. On other benches vagrants lie sleeping. Doc wonders how they got through the winter, vaguely comforted by their presence, as if they are a sign that spring has arrived.

The number of homeless wandering the streets or planted on corners is not something he anticipated. It is as if the human refuse of his old neighborhood has spread everywhere. He was prepared for something different when he got out, something cleaner and better, though this, he realizes, was foolish.

There is always something in sight that jars him—the openly gay couples of Dupont and Adams Morgan, the punks with their spiked mohawks and safety-pinned ears, people lined before cash machines that beep and spit out money, grocery registers that scan bar codes—always something near that keeps him nervous, keeps him from settling in. At first he found such novelty invigorating, but as he works and tries to fit in day by day, he's grown paranoid, afraid his unfamiliarity with this world will expose him as an aging, misplaced convict.

He pulls a comic from his duffel bag, absently gazing at the vivid colors of the cover—Spiderman swinging through a volley of exploding missiles. A man approaches, eyes bleary and crusted, his overcoat stained like the floor of a garage. Doc shakes his head before the man can speak, watches him continue his slow circuit of the benches, seeing in his walk something familiar, an image of Dead Earl surfacing. He tries to think of something else, but his mind perversely dredges up a host of details.

He's not surprised by the memory, just a little put-out. In the past months, images from his history continually float past, part of a glacial thaw deep in the skull. Dead Earl—Earl, then—was one of Doc's runners when he and Rebo were dealing heroin. He sighs as the freighted memories draw inexorably near. It's ironic, he thinks, that the penance paid for one's crimes has so little to do with ameliorating the guilt over them.

Earl had messed with a package but had banked on Doc doing nothing out of respect for Earl's father, a friend of Doc's. He was almost right.

Doc let it go. Told Earl it was okay, but that he wasn't going to get any more work from Doc. No work, no drugs. Two weeks later Earl appeared with his woman. When she finished talking Doc gave the pair a quarter-spoon of dope and a warning: "Pay me every month by the dime—I cannot allow for you to keep my drugs and you don't pay me. You know the law."

"Thanks, Doc, thanks," Earl said. He was the kind of fast talker who convinced nobody but himself. "I won't let you down, not after this kindness."

Doc watched Earl's woman. She kept her eyes downturned, focused on the ground, her gaunt face impassive. He didn't know her name.

Doc waved Earl away. "I ain't doing this for you, Earl. This is for your woman and your father, who got the shit luck to be in your life." He tried to meet the woman's eyes, but she turned with Earl and it was the last he saw of her.

Later, when Earl didn't pay what he owed, Doc wrestled him into the trunk of his car, duct tape binding Earl's wrists and covering his mouth. Doc drove through a section of Northeast D.C.—a part of the city dead even then—muttering and occasionally slamming a palm against the GM's steering wheel for emphasis, working himself into the necessary rage. His eyes did not stray to the rusted meat cleaver on the seat beside him as he stopped the car and turned off the engine. He stared out the windshield for a long moment, his hands gripped tight around the wheel.

Doc fit the haft of the cleaver into his belt. He pulled his loose jacket on—one of light cotton that he didn't like—and buttoned a single snap in the front, even as part of him wondered why he should bother to spare Earl the sight. He circled the car and pulled Earl from the trunk, surprised by the bird weight of the man. "You made this happen, not me!" he shouted into Earl's face. The duct tape and the man's skin seemed of a color.

"You think I'm weak, that you can use me? I ain't weak."

Earl tried to speak, to catch Doc's eyes, his voice little more than a moan. Distantly, traffic rushed along a highway overpass. Doc pushed Earl ahead, into an empty lot behind a collapsing warehouse. "I ain't weak," Doc repeated from behind him. "You, you're the one." The oil drum sat squat and dark in the center of the lot, the altar exactly as Doc had left it the day before.

Earl had not washed in a long time, the acrid scent of fear and sweat rising from him. Doc pushed him forward, fought the urge to gag.

Doc's left hand easily encircled Earl's thin, finely boned wrists. He forced them against the top of the oil drum, using his weight to jam Earl's left hand, the wrist crossed beneath that of the right, against the metal, bearing down until the clenched fingers splayed and the hand lay flat, palm down. Earl's view was partially blocked by Doc's left shoulder, and Doc was quick. Earl did not see the cleaver until he heard the hollow boom of the blade meeting the flat of the drum. At that instant, Earl jerked back, but too late, exposed bone flashing white. He tried to howl, the duct tape over his mouth blocking all but a violent choking noise. His hand sprayed blood on Doc as he scrabbled back, his face wet with sweat and snot. Doc left the cleaver beside the thumb and approached Earl, who shook his head back and forth. "Nnn—nnn—nnn."

Doc jerked him upright, his eyes fixed on the bloodied hand. Earl kicked and thrashed and bled. Doc lost his hold, his grip slick with sweat and blood. Earl fell before he'd run twenty feet. Doc faced him when he rose. His white eyes, rolling in their sockets, did not even seem to focus on Doc. Earl fell again when Doc hit him, did not resist when Doc pulled him to his feet. He shook his head left to right and back again.

When Doc held Earl's hands to the drum, Earl was still shaking his head, the motion empty of meaning, more a twitch than a negation of what was to come. Doc brought the cleaver down, leaving a deep wound, the blade skittering off bone. Earl jerked, weakly this time, without enough pull to loosen Doc's grip. It was then that their eyes met. Then that Doc saw Earl's hopelessness. No fear now, no pain, no recognition, just the dumb resignation of an animal in a slaughterhouse.

The next cut severed the remaining thumb, scoring the metal beneath.

A pigeon lands on the lip of the fountain, not far from where Doc sits in the morning sun. It shits a white smear onto the stone and flaps off, wings barely able to lift its heft.

He'd thought that was a historic play. Congratulating himself even while he finished throwing up. He wadded up his bloodied jacket and tossed it by Earl, who lay curled on the ground, perhaps conscious, perhaps not. He remembers thinking to himself that every time Earl picked anything up he would remember Doc. A historic play. Had he felt something else? He tries to recall, but cannot. For the first time he wonders if he would have taken the second thumb had he seen something else in Earl's eyes, anything but the resignation there.

He sighs, shivers. He rubs a hand over his face.

"I don't like Spiderman."

Doc blinks. The small girl from the fountain stands before him. Hands clasped behind her back, legs planted in an oddly formal stance. Doc smiles.

"You don't like spiders, I bet."

"Girls," she says. "I like girl heroes. Mary Jane's a wimp."

Doc leans back, reassessing this critic. "Girl heroes."

"Yes." She looks back over her shoulder. A breeze plays through her wispy blonde hair, raising a cowlick which she palms flat with a hand.

"Supergirl?"

She presses her lips together. "I don't think so." She keeps her hand on her head. "I'm not supposed to talk to you," she announces.

"I bet you ain't."

They stare at each other. She rubs a foot against the back of her other ankle.

Doc chuckles. "You look like you got a new dance all figured out. Mind you don't fall over."

She smiles and again looks over her shoulder. "I have to go."

"Okay."

"Storm," she says. "In *The X-Men*. She's not a wimp."

Doc watches her as she circles the fountain, the thick pillar supporting the fountain's dish obscuring her from view. A moment later she is at the edge of the park, hand in hand with a woman pushing a stroller.

Why you got to think about that fool Earl? Got enough on your mind without worrying about all the damn things you can't change.

"Out, out," Walker says, eager for their break, pushing Doc lightly through the doorway of the McDonald's and to the edge of the sidewalk where two posts anchor the entrance awning. The humid air seems luxuriously thick, softening the edges of D.C.'s business district. A blanket of clouds has settled, a fine mist suspended in the air that imparts a veiled, dreamy quality to the view. Doc wonders if he'll ever tire of being outdoors. It's as if he can't breathe enough indoors, no matter how many windows or doors are open. The wide glass doors and high, street-facing windows of the McDonald's sometimes make him feel as if he works in an aquarium or exhibit.

He sits on the edge of a large planter between the awning supports. Walker lights a cigarette, tries to blow a smoke ring. Doc finds the gesture endearing—he is glad that Walker doesn't know how young he looks when he smokes. The boy is tall and still a little gangly, muscle just beginning to sheath his teenaged frame, his expression perpetually startled.

"Supes ain't so tough," Doc says, resuming their debate.

"The Man of Steel? Who's gonna kick his ass? Bulletproof, heat-vision, superstrong. Sucker is invincible," Walker says.

"That's a shallow read."

"That's the facts," Walker says.

"Lex Luthor got none of that and he still gives Supes a run for the money. Know why? 'Cause he got brains, and brains get you through every time."

"Last I checked, Lex got his ass kicked by Mr. Kent," Walker says.

"That ain't his fault. Got a biased editorial staff is what it is. Comic companies need to make money. Can't have no villain winning the matchups 'cause then they got irate parents on their ass. Lawsuits, 'cause Little Billy got a negative role model."

Walker grinds his cigarette butt into the sidewalk. "Go ahead."

"What?"

"I know you started the whole damn conversation just so you can make your point about who the baddest-ass hero is and how I don't know a damn thing," Walker says.

Doc smiles. "I ain't got no agenda. Just passing time."

"Uh-huh."

"And it's a complex question. I ain't saying there's a right answer."

"You ain't."

"Fact is, anybody would say there's one hero stands out above all the others would have to be a bit of a fool," Doc says.

Walker grins and the sight of this feels to Doc like a reward. Doc likes this boy—likes that he reads *Cosmo* to learn more about the women he would date, likes that he studies the stock market though he has no money for it. The boy has aspirations. And there are other reasons for Doc's attraction, no less true for being obvious: Walker allows Doc to imagine his own son at the same age, to fill in this absence in his memory; to imagine, however indirectly, that he hasn't lost all connection to his son.

During lunch Doc keeps to the kitchen, cooking while Walker works the register and serves drinks. The heat by the fryers is intense, but nothing compared to a Tyburn cell. Perspiration soaks his collar, and his uniform chafes, but he thinks of each minute as a nickel, each hour as a few more dollars, and each paycheck as rent for his own place, food that doesn't come preheated in trays, clothes with no serial number—the list goes on.

And so what if his work is flipping burgers and packing french fries? He makes good fries, good burgers. Mindless work is nothing new and his shifts are bookended by everything that lies outside: the sight of women, of children, of families; the freedom to enjoy parks, to throw rocks in the river, to walk in the rain, to climb a tree. To stand in the night air and look up, past the city's glow, at the stars. It is almost overwhelming, reminiscent of those times he was released from the isolation of the Hole into general population, overcome by his keyed-up senses—by the noise and color and texture of the prison. The sensory range here is grand in comparison, too much and not enough, intoxicatingly rich.

He straightens at the sight of a lady in a deep-purple raincoat and long plaited hair who sweeps up to the register. She has high, angled cheekbones and lustrous skin the color of an exotic hardwood. Lust jolts through him like electricity.

The woman's eyes pass over him without registering, even as he smiles. She states her order, each word distinct, her cadence clipped, reading from the menu wall marquee without bothering to make eye contact with Walker.

Walker "yes ma'ams" her as he places her food on a tray. He rolls his eyes at Doc as she clicks to a table near the window. Doc joins Walker at the counter.

"One of them uptight Oreo bitches."

"I'm the man to eat her up," Doc says, watching.

Walker laughs. "You look like a walking heart attack, all bug-eyed and wobbly."

Doc draws himself up, slightly wounded by the barb. Women unbalance him in a way they haven't since he was fifteen. All that time looking at them in magazines and on the TV, and now they're real, they're everywhere, they're terrifying and fascinating. Bitch this and Bitch that for him and his cellmates for so many years, all that talk about fucking, all those glossy-magazine porno queens, all those fantasies, all that fronting, and yet he hasn't been able to hit on a woman in the half-year he's been out. *Like someone cut off your dick.* He swallows, his mouth dry.

"I don't know no CPR," Walker says.

Fuck this, Doc thinks. "Tell you what," he says. "You can hide back here with your dick all hard, but me? I'm a man of action." He puts on a smile and approaches the woman's table. His fingers tingle. "Afternoon, baby," he says.

She fixes him with a blank look. He leans forward solicitously. The rich scent of her perfume is a caress.

" 'Baby'?" she says.

"Baby," he confirms. "Someone who looks so fine got no business eating alone."

Her lips flatten as she eyes him up and down. "I have a rule against uniforms."

Doc deflates, suddenly conscious of the peaked cap balanced on his head and the way his work pants fit too tightly in the thighs. "This ain't nothing," he says. "I can be out of this in two seconds flat." His grin feels nailed in place.

No hint of a smile.

"Two seconds," he repeats hopefully. She just stares like she's still reading the menu marquee and has found nothing of interest. After a long silence he shrugs and retreats to the kitchen. *What the fuck does she know? Bitch got no taste, no humor, nothing.*

"Shut the fuck up," he says preemptively to Walker, annoyed by the boy's gleeful expression.

"I ain't said nothing. I'm just trying to process, you know? Take in the size of the wreckage. I'm thinking the *Titanic,* you know?"

"Ain't no accounting for taste," Doc says. "No accounting."

"You and Supes," Walker says, "both men of action and ain't either of you getting no respect."

Doc ties shut a garbage bag and pulls it from its casing, the clear plastic bag smeared with grease. As the back door to the alleyway closes he chucks the bag into the Dumpster and kicks at an emptied Thunderbird bottle, sending it skittering through a shallow puddle to shatter against the brick wall.

Got to relax, man. Stirling and them others? They'd give their left nut just to have a real woman in sight. Got to give it time, give it time.

It is a familiar refrain, *Give it time,* but it works, soothing him. He remembers Grippe's endlessly repeated refrain, that he hadn't changed in prison, that he wasn't going to. He's glad Grippe's not around to see just how wrong he proved to be.

In the bathroom, Doc sprays Windex on the mirrors, polishes the sink spigots. He is wringing the mop when a boy enters, his bald head gleaming as if buffed. Doc recognizes him as a regular, young and full of attitude, an exaggerated swagger to make up for his size, as if in his mind he's too big to fit through a doorway without turning sideways. *Young Blood,* he thinks. Definitely dealing.

The mop squelches wetly as Doc swings it before him in a wide arc. On the back of the boy's loose leather coat is a picture of a white sphere with a skull etched into it. Beneath this, block letters read CUE BALL.

The boy looks over his shoulder as he stands before a urinal. "Need me some damn privacy!" he says in a scratchy and surprisingly low voice.

"Your stage fright ain't nothing to me," Doc says. He continues mopping, digging the mop head into the grouted seams of the tiled floor.

"Feel like you going to grab my ass, the way you watching me, motherfucker."

Doc leans the mop against a stall. "I ain't got no beef with you. Faster you do your business the better." *Amazing these punks even make it to prison,* he thinks.

Cue Ball makes a show of zipping up. "You ain't getting nothing from me, you old faggot. Go back to making those limp-dick fries and leave me the fuck alone."

It is less the words than Cue Ball's expression that sets Doc off, in it a casual disrespect. A look that, real or imagined, has dogged Doc since release, evident in the face of his parole officer, in the face of the woman diner.

Didn't take no look like that in Tyburn, Kane.

A smile slips over Doc's face like a mask, his teeth bared, the almost-sexual promise of violence infusing his muscles with a hot, humming tension. Cue Ball's eyes widen as Doc grasps him by the shoulder of his jacket and spins him around, clamping him in a full nelson and forcing him against the sinks. It has been a long while since Doc's worked out. It is good to flex the muscle and find it strong. Cue Ball is surprisingly light.

"We was back in Disneyland and you'd be my bitch!" he booms. He has the boy bent over the sink, the mirror reflecting both their faces.

Cue Ball stares back with impressive composure, making little effort to resist; Doc realizes he's underestimated the boy. Outweighed by a hundred pounds, but you wouldn't know it to look at him. His eyes glint with an anger dense enough to have a specific gravity and Doc is caught in a gaze he hasn't seen since prison and one that he is unprepared to confront.

"You gonna show some respect!" Doc says. He pushes Cue Ball through the bathroom doorway and the restaurant, moving inexorably toward the restaurant's glass doors. The woman is still there, just finishing her meal, and her eyes widen with alarm. As Doc shoves by he feels a moment of satisfaction: *Ignore me now, bitch.*

"Next time you come in, you show some respect!" Doc shouts, oblivious to Eduardo and Walker's exclamations. He shoves Cue Ball onto the sidewalk.

Cue Ball grabs an awning support and swings to face Doc with his flat glare. He places an extended index finger to his cheekbone, thumb cocked, and motions as if to fire. Eduardo pulls Doc back from the doorway; Doc lets himself be led.

"In the office," Eduardo orders. He looks nervous and upset.

"Disrespect!" Doc says.

"Just sit," Eduardo says as they step into his office. He is low-slung and stocky, and his dark hair bristles from his head, quilled with gel.

Doc sinks into a chair and closes his eyes for a long moment, his heart hammering. Slowly the tension bleeds from his muscles. He half expects Eduardo to fire him.

Eduardo sits at his desk and fiddles with his tie pin, staring at Doc. "What if he had a gun? You think of that?"

"He didn't have no gun," Doc responds. And he knows this to be a fact—prison has taught him to pick out the man in a crowd carrying a shank; a gun is easy. Eduardo has thumbtacked photos to the wood paneling behind the desk, mainly yellowed postcards picturing a lake with an island in it. One reads *Santa Fe de la Laguna*. Several men balance in their tiny skiffs on the gleaming lake, silhouetted against the sun, arms spread wide, gauzy nets billowing around them. They look like butterflies.

"Maybe he breaks the windows tonight," Eduardo says.

"It's a busy street. Lots of people around—witnesses."

Eduardo raises an eyebrow.

"Okay, then. You got insurance?" Doc asks.

Eduardo runs a hand over his hair. "I don't want to think about it."

"Your call." Doc's eyes drift to the postcards.

"What did he do that you had to start with him!"

"In the bathroom. He was talking shit. Set me off," Doc states.

"This look like a nightclub to you, Kane? You do the fries, not security."

"All right." Doc keeps his voice even.

"People come to eat and you get paid to serve them, Kane. Service industry."

"I don't take disrespect."

"It's just words!" Eduardo exclaims.

"No," Doc says. "It ain't."

Eduardo glares but Doc does not look away.

"Situation like that, if you don't do nothing..." Doc realizes how he must sound, aware, too, of the irony of wanting to keep kids like Cue Ball out of the restaurant when he had been no different at that age. *You was never like them,* he thinks. *Had a code.* But then why feel this suffocating, disproportionate anger?

"Just stay in the kitchen."

"I can do that," Doc agrees.

"That's *all* you better do."

Doc points to the wall festooned with postcards. "Where's that place in the cards?"

"You don't earn no points with me tonight, Kane. Not like that."

"Just curious." Doc rises.

"Where I grew up. Mexico," Eduardo says as Doc opens the door. He pronounces it *"Meh-hee-co."* Doc leaves him staring moodily at the photos.

The street is poorly illuminated by the dim globes of the streetlights, the air still misted with rain. Doc's anger has faded and he is only weary, saying nothing as he accompanies Walker to the bus stop.

Walker, too, is subdued; Doc wonders if it's the thought of home, his ailing aunt, the kid brother he doesn't see enough.

Water beads on the Plexiglas enclosure, refracting the light of passing cars into constellations of white-and-red diamonds.

"You worried?" Walker asks.

"Ain't no punk-ass preschooler makes me nervous."

"Didn't figure you to snap like that."

"Just forget it," Doc says.

"They don't treat you right," Walker says bitterly. "See the uniform and figure they can bust on you." Doc understands his tone—the way it feels to dress for and perform this menial job when you know you're meant for more, for something better. When you have to watch young dealers come in, not yet old enough to drive, with thick wads of Jeffersons and ropes of gold around their necks.

Doc raises a hand to place on Walker's shoulder but drops it before completing the gesture. They watch the rain.

"Eduardo ought to remarket that place," Walker says. "Make it upscale. Like the McDonald's in France where you can buy wine.

Nicer uniforms, tablecloths, real music, comfortable seats, all that shit. Liquor license pays itself in a year, maybe two."

"Yeah?" Doc says halfheartedly.

"Yeah," Walker says, warming to the idea. "Right downtown? All sorts of lawyers working here. Wouldn't have to worry 'bout no trash coming in. Offer a special: the Three Martini Big Mac Lunch. For here or to go."

"That'd explain Ronald McDonald's red nose. The smile, too."

The walk home is a rush. Twenty-five minutes from downtown Northwest through the U Street–Cardozo area, away from the Square John trip at McDonald's and near the old neighborhood, then to his apartment. A feeling of muted danger pushes him up on the balls of his feet during these late-night walks, opens his eyes wide, cleans the fatigue from his system. He craves this walk, the edge of adrenaline clearing his muddled thoughts. The streets are slicked with water, though the rain has abated. A cold wind kicks up.

U Street and 14th Street Northwest used to be his haunt, back in the early sixties, long before Tyburn Penitentiary. Up around 18th and U the place is coming back to life, new shops and diners opening, but this time it's growing into a gentrified white neighborhood, one where he does not belong. And the rest, the black part, just makes him feel old, heightens his feeling of displacement. The area is beaten: listing townhouses, paint peeling, windows broken, streets cracked and pitted. Shops long since replaced by struggling liquor stores. Even worse than when it was the Valley of the Undead. *The Valley of the Dead,* he thinks as he circles a mildewed, collapsed couch that blocks the sidewalk.

Past the intersection of 14th and U he slows, the sign reading 15 ¾. Beneath this the green of the cross-street sign is blank. He hesitates, continues into streets empty even of parked cars. Farther, and the scene grows more desolate, the streets swept clean of garbage or any sign of people. He stops at a corner for his bearings, but the signs on the post rotate slowly like strange weathervanes, no longer true to the city grid. The wind washes against him wet and cold. From a stoop a disheveled figure rises, overcoat billowing like a sail, threatening to lift the man by his armpits.

Doc realizes that it's Dead Earl. Impossible or not, the man is there, right in front of him, falling into step beside Doc as he tries to hurry past. *You losing it, old man.* But Earl paces him, lingering in the periphery of Doc's vision, though Doc refuses to look directly at the apparition.

They walk in silence, beneath slowly wheeling signs, beneath stoplights blinking in syncopated flashes not meant for traffic, through empty streets, through urban arroyos banked by blind-eyed tenements, the flow of inhabitants long since departed, the asphalt bare and cracked as if from drought.

"Earl." Doc can partially see through Earl's profile, the skin a scrim revealing the fine lines of muscle and tendon and bone lit by some faint internal glow. "Earl," he repeats. "I got nothing to say. Tell me what you want. Tell me what to say to make you leave."

Earl continues walking even as Doc halts. "I'm tired of walking, you hear?" Doc says to Earl's back.

Dead Earl recedes and the light shifts again, the skyline wavering, blurring back to the familiar. It begins to rain again.

"I'm tired of walking," Doc repeats.

In his apartment he turns on his black-and-white TV. The reception is grainy and the images flutter and jerk, maddened by the confines of the small screen. Doc pulls a full fifth of Jack Daniel's from beneath his bed and lies back on his mattress. Dead Earl. It must have been a hallucination, had to have been. The whiskey spreads from the pit of his stomach, suffusing his limbs with a warm torpor. He feels as if he is floating. Outside, the rain intensifies.

The crackle of gunfire wakes him. Three shots, the sound of running. Through the parted slats of the blinds he sees lights blink on in the facing rowhouses. On the street there is no movement but the dark rush of water in the gutters. A broken row of parked cars snug against the sidewalk, a buzzing streetlamp mirrored by the wet pavement. Doc raises the bottle to his mouth, a warm trickle wetting his throat.

Soon the bottle falls from numb fingers. Light from the TV flickers over the bare walls.

2

Mike Franzen's slab-cheeked face is coarse and pocked, as if eroded by long years of hostile company. It is also, Doc notes, perpetually flushed. Somewhere in his sixties, Mike's large frame supports a body gone to fat. Doc can practically hear his PO's laboring heart.

"Fuck you, you little fuck!" Mike shouts.

Doc winces, queasy from the morning's hangover; the aspirin hasn't worked.

"You miss catching for your buddies back in Leavenworth? I know they miss you." Mike sets the phone's receiver on his desk and taps a cigarette from his pack, raising the butt burning in the full ashtray to light it. A tiny voice whines from the receiver. Mike grins at Doc, lifts the receiver. "Be here by three o'clock or you're a contender for Catcher Hall of Fame." He crushes the butt into the ashtray, mashing it into the cupped glass as if afraid it could start a brush fire. "Yeah, yeah, fuck you. Three o'clock." He hangs up.

The ceiling fan's motored hub whines steadily, powering the blades through the dense, cigarette-opaqued air.

"Early ain't much better than late." Smoke issues from Mike's mouth, the slight draft of the fan drawing it up in threads.

"Metro was running fast." Doc traces the cigarette smoke down to Mike's red face. He wonders if Mike is as hungover as he is.

The tip of Mike's cigarette brightens. "You got a woman yet?"

"That ain't no parole condition."

"Might put you in a better mood, you was to get some," Mike says.

"Ain't you got no work-related questions?"

"Just showing concern for your well-being, Kane. Regular sex is good for longevity, for your outlook. Take me and my wife—"

"I don't want to know nothing about it," Doc says, extending his hands palm-out.

"Just figured since you ain't getting any, maybe you want to hear—"

"I'm doing just fine. Question of priorities," Doc says stiffly.

Mike laughs at this. "Okay, Kane. So talk about the job."

"Same old. Forty a week at minimum wage plus a dime," Doc says, shrugging. "Two more months, maybe I get my big raise. Go from fry guy to cashier." He doesn't know how he means Mike to take this.

Mike nods and takes a drag from his cigarette. "That's sarcasm, right?"

"I don't know what you'd call it," Doc says. "I'm just voicing ambition, you know?"

Mike flips through a folder. "Like I thought," he says. "Nothing here about sarcasm." He smiles. "Now, I guess the question we got to consider is: Is this a sign of improvement or backsliding?"

"Sign of personality."

"You drinking?"

The question catches Doc off guard. He stifles the urge to deny it immediately, letting the moment linger. "Chocolate shakes."

Mike laughs again. "Not bad, Kane." He looks at a form with a grid on it, running his fingers down a column of numbers though it's clear to both that this is just for show. "Let's see, four more months of steady employment drops you three points." He looks up. "Brings you down from fourteen to eleven on your RPS, Kane. Progress. The lower the better, as you know."

Doc's face heats. At Tyburn, when he'd put together his release plan for the Parole Commission—setting up a three-month stay at a D.C. halfway house and a plan for a job search—he'd read all about the likely conditions of his pending parole as he had prior to every one of his hearings. The Risk Prediction Scale form, or RPS 80, is a guideline for parole conditions. Scored on a point system, a rating of fourteen is, for all practical purposes, identical to eleven—too high, firmly in upper risk category.

"That mean I go from maximum supervision to maximum supervision, right? High-activity supervision. Twice-monthly visits with parole supervisor; avoid association with former inmates of penal institutions and other individuals of bad character; refrain from the use of alcohol or narcotics; work at gainful employment—' "

" '—cooperate with your parole supervisor and the parole board,' " Mike says.

Don't vote. Let my apartment get searched with no warrant. Don't be black out at night. Allow PO to bust my ass whenever he wants and don't say shit, Doc thinks. Like now. Parole meetings never fail to piss him off.

"What's this attitude?"

Doc drops his eyes. His head hurts. "I don't know." *Just relax. Take a long run after this. Go out to them tracks and unwind, breathe that clean air.*

"Look," Mike says, "prison was harder than this, and you lasted through that. You been on parole before—maybe a long time ago, but this ain't nothing new. And eleven is better than fourteen. A move in the right direction."

Doc doesn't know what he resents more, the chastening note in Mike's voice or the pity that underlies it. He stares at the wall behind Mike. A steel bookcase sags beneath binders and stacked files, the bare patches of wall gouged and scuffed. Another run-down, government-issue room with another run-down, government-issue lackey giving him marching orders.

"Routine," Mike says. "I've been here twenty-four years and nothing's changed. That's what the Square John trip is all about. I'd guess prison's the same."

"This don't sound like therapeutic counseling to me," Doc says.

"Fuck. You spend all your time reading probation manuals, Kane?" Mike turns a page in Doc's folder. "Good memory and a high IQ ain't going to change a thing, so you can quit with the Mensa shit."

Doc crosses his forearms and rubs his biceps, as if cold. "Sorry," he says. "It's good being out, you know? It's just—I ain't a part of things." He feels naked at this utterance. Naked and distressed that Mike is the only one he can say this to.

Mike sits back, then tips his head back and sends a column of smoke eddying toward the fan. "You up on your bills?"

Fuck you, thinks Doc. *Fuck you, you motherfucker.* But he knows how it sounds, how it would sound to him: a manipulative bid. What, in fact, it would be in most any other circumstance. "You all put me on EM, maybe you ought to pay the phone bill. I ain't calling nobody."

"Shit, Kane, something did crawl up your ass. We got to keep tabs. Ain't like you got all that prison time as a reward for being a reliable, upstanding citizen."

"I served my time," Doc says.

Mike raises his eyebrows. "Not yet. Four years of good time is what got you out of Tyburn. And good time, as you know, is revocable. Exchangeable for prison time." He places his cigarette in the ashtray and drums his fingers on the table. "Regular work, no missed curfew check-ins, et cetera. Model parolee," he says. "You tell your boss you're a con?"

"Shit, you know how many jobs I got being clean about it?"

Mike laughs. "You got any more questions?" His eyes stray to his watch.

"How long I got to keep with this electronic monitoring? Sitting in that apartment every night, waiting for the computer to call . . ."

" 'Till the parole is up." Mike scratches his ear and his face settles serious. "It's that or Nevada. Simple." He stands.

Waiting for the metro at Judiciary Square, Doc wonders briefly about the drinking, about whether Mike cares, deciding he doesn't. Why the fuck would he? It's too much paperwork to send someone back in for boozing a little. Twenty-four years at the same job, a caseload of what—hundreds? In the same position Doc wouldn't care, either. He'd just wait for retirement.

In the metro car people sit evenly spaced in the seats, each seeking the insulation of one or more empty benches. A woman watches Doc, her sharp-featured face softened by dark crescents smudged beneath her eyes. He takes a good look, then eases back to stare out the window, his reflection revealed like the flip of a face card as the train reenters the darkened tunnel: thin, graying mustache framing a wide mouth, a raised scar angled across his chin. The patina of fine scratches on the window softens his skin and blurs the wrinkles. In the background the woman's reflection floats. The rejection of the previous day still stings.

The woman stands at the Gallery Place–Chinatown stop. She smiles but Doc turns his head and stares instead at the vaulted concrete bunker of the station. The metro always makes him feel as if he's entered a time warp and found himself fifty or a hundred years in the future. It's easy to imagine that the world outside has been laid waste and that these catacombs are all that remain, the sleep-deprived, pale faces of murmuring commuters giving the fiction an uncomfortable ring of truth. The metro, as with all of life on the outside after such a long absence, fascinates him even as it heightens his sense of dislocation.

Rising, the train glides over the Potomac, the river deep-brown and swollen from the previous night's rain. Water surges against an adjacent bridge, muddying the stone supports, pinning tangles of branches to them. Above, the sun melts through the clouds, the sky a blend of gray and blue. Doc savors the expanse of the vista, the size and scope of a world no longer interrupted: no bars to cut it into bands, no screens enmeshed in glass to break it into a grid.

A cut across the GW Parkway and he's running on wet turf. He winds under a wide bridge where the RF&P railway tracks cross, scales the fence to the railyard. The tracks stretch west over cinder and gravel, rails and ties a sharply delineated grid pressed into the earth. At the yard's edge rails rust and discarded ties lie in heaps, the wood rotted, dark with creosote, a jumbled mess against the backdrop of Arlington's glass-and-concrete skyline.

Gravel crunches beneath the metronomic strike of his feet. It feels good—*good!*—to run like this, run as far as he likes, alone. He passes between two defunct trains, the length of each hemming him in, the blind walls of rusted boxcars narrowing his view to that of the horizon point where the tracks converge. Dried weeds fill the gaps between the boxcars and beneath them, clinging to the iron disks of wheels that look as if they have fused with the rails on which they rest.

The cracking of metal on metal runs down a train like rapid-fire, sound sparking from between each car as it stretches its vertebrae and begins to move like a huge metal snake. In the gap between two boxcars to his right he sees the third train—this one unblemished by rust—jolt and start to roll and he's tempted: Climb on and ride it out. Roll into a new city. New name, new scam. And what? There was a time when this would have been enough. But now his wants are not so easily defined. They linger in the periphery of his vision, defying any direct stare—shadows that dissolve before the eye.

He fixes his eyes on the horizon point. Faster. The rails sing as if from the weight of a train. The stretch and release of his tendons strengthens; his feet beat a staccato. His sweat thins, oily beads now a clean drip that wicks up into his clothes, and then the sodden garments melt and run, exposing sleek skin with red and copper highlights, and he is naked but for the yellow radio collar bound to his ankle.

Behind him the sound of the train fades, the only noise the slap of his feet. The burn of the sun on his back abates as he closes on the horizon point, the sun sinking in the east, his shadow stretching far ahead. Morning light shifts diffuse and soft, returns to the glow of dawn, dissipates into the black of night. Moonlight coats the rails with its nacreous shine so that they appear as parallel seams of light. He is drawn smoothly forward.

It seems many hours have passed when the heat suffusing his muscles fades. Space has unfolded, revealing vast drifts of sand, humidity replaced by the arid edge of desert air. The moon floats, moored to the apex of its arc.

The rails disappear into the side of dune, and when he turns to where he's come from he sees their glow flicker and dim, the metal corroding with rust indistinguishable in color from that of the sand. Doc climbs a dune, sinking in a fine sand that rasps coldly against his feet. A wind erases his tracks. Eventually he sits and works his feet with his hands, forcing blood into his toes and that is when wind-scoured walls rise, solidify into a dim skyline. A jolt of recognition as the outline meshes with that of Doc's memory, the details of the abandoned lot locking into place, as vivid to him now as thirty years past. The wind blows over the ground, spindrift pricking his skin, seething against the upended oil drum planted in the center of the square.

He is not surprised to see the imprint of feet approach over the sand, not surprised to recognize the gait of the ethereal figure that coalesces above the footprints. He is only tired. Suddenly and terribly tired, the freedom and energy of the morning's run a dim memory. It is with great effort that he stands and holds his head up and offers his throat to the pair of hands that clumsily encircle his neck. Jagged nails dig into his skin, but the hands, each missing a thumb, cannot gain a grip. A sigh fades into the wind and he opens his eyes, his gaze traveling up forearms weak with ruptured veins, to meet the enervated, yellow eyes of Dead Earl.

Doc coughs. "There was times when I thought about you, Earl, when I said you could have my thumbs in restitution. But I guess you was never happy with what you was entitled to." He chuckles. "You want to try strangling me again?"

Dead Earl's downturned mouth opens. "Ever tried to use a spike with no thumbs? Try to hold your girl's hand? She got to hold your hand. And when you piss? Got to hold your dick like a cigarette." Dead Earl cocks his head and regards Doc. "You knew cutting me wouldn't make me quit no drugs."

"You right."

Dead Earl's eyes sparkle and tear. He squeezes Doc's throat desultorily.

"Go home, Earl," Doc says. "Ain't no justice for you here." He spreads Earl's forearms, draws the ghost to him in an almost tender gesture. "Don't think no more 'bout justice. You got more than you know."

But Dead Earl shakes his head and motions toward the ghostly city. "You got to follow me," he says.

Doc looks toward the dark walls and empty windows and shudders, dimly remembering when he last followed Earl into this city. "No," he says, "it ain't for me."

Dead Earl reaches for his hand, but Doc turns from him. The rails shine, arrowing toward the eastern horizon, and he is running, motion driving the cold and fatigue from his muscles, speed increasing, light growing as he aims for the rising sun.

He finds himself crouching by the tracks, a train rocking past. Shivering, he wonders how long he's been motionless, his knees aching.

Dead Earl. Shit. Plenty of the dead I want to see, but you ain't one of them.

At the steps of his apartment a Camaro speeds by, announced by the Doppler blare of its horn. It squeals around a corner. Doc waits for the sound of pursuit, then turns to the gate. His mailbox is stuffed with catalogues. He shifts his grocery bag. The address tags are unfamiliar or generic—CURRENT RESIDENT—but he is glad for the mail.

The house's yellow paint has flaked and cracks spider over the brick, the wider crevices poorly sutured with cement. On either side abandoned rowhouses lean in, windows sealed with cinderblock, fenced lawns an alluvium of matted weeds and garbage.

Angie Creal leans from the slot of her partially opened door. Graying hair curls in wisps from her knotted bun.

"Was that somebody honking for you?" she asks, her eyes narrowed. Her voice is high and raspy, her lips stained a deep purple from the Wild Irish Rose she drinks. He can't tell if her squint is curious or angry.

"No ma'am. Don't know who it was."

"You pay rent?"

Doc sighs. "Two weeks ago."

She attempts a smile, at the same time putting a hand to her neck, as if she might smooth away the wrinkles. "Why don't you never have no company?" She tucks an errant hair behind her ear, leaning farther out. Her face is slack with alcohol, her dark eyes framed with fine lines.

Doc coughs, trying to hide a smile, embarrassed for her. He fleetingly wonders if the woman at McDonald's had felt like this when he was hitting on her.

He hefts his bag of groceries, "I got to get upstairs, ma'am. I'm expecting a call."

Her face twists. "Don't think 'cause you was on time this month you can slide!" She slams the door.

Such interactions with Angie are routine. Doc reflects that it would be wise to shop early in the morning on his days off, while she is still asleep or hasn't yet had enough wine to bring a blush to her face. *Three months and you still ain't learned that.*

In his apartment he unpacks his groceries, leaving the cabinet doors open, as is his habit since release. He raises the blinds and opens the windows, letting in the evening's glow. The sky is soft green.

He sorts the mail on the table: lingerie and electronics catalogues. Sometimes he gets threatening collection notices addressed to past occupants—W-2 forms, a letter from the Census Bureau, sweepstakes announcements. Once he got a picture of a young couple at their prom, both posed before a ruffled curtain of pink satin, the boy wearing a startled expression, as if surprised to find himself there. There was no letter with it, nor any names, just the message *Thinking of you* scrawled on the back in an uneven hand. Doc keeps it on his refrigerator and studies it from time to time. He likes to imagine the lives of this couple—of their marriage, their children, of a divorce if his mood is foul.

He has a daughter who'd been close to the age of the girl in the photo when he'd first been sentenced to Tyburn. Mary had dropped out of high school to live with her useless husband, a boy not much older than she. Moises. Doc doesn't think of Mary often, at least he hasn't for the past few years, his mind avoiding such recollections because to recall them is to lance a boil of festering associations. He remembers the sight of Mary's bruised, discolored face. It was this sight—his daughter beaten, lips split and an eye swollen like a plum—that had sent him looking for Moises with a shotgun. And sixteen years served for the killing has never made him regret the act, just the repercussions. He'd felt a great satisfaction at seeing Moises dead on the ground, almost torn in two from the blast.

It's a sad irony that the effort to repair his family had had the opposite effect, as final as if Doc had put the gun to his own head, or to that of his wife or daughter or son. Even now he wonders what he could have done, what he would do if faced again with the same situation. Defend the honor of his family? Witness the inevitable downward trend of the beatings? *Catch-22*, he thinks. *Ain't nothing for it. Or for thinking on it.*

Mary wrote him during the first years of his sentence, but

sixteen years is a long time for a father to be dead and the letters stopped long ago. Does she now have children? A new last name? Where does she live? Has the passage of so many years weathered her? Made her heavy and given her lines about her neck? *Probably looks good. Got a man with a steady job. Children that say "yes ma'am."*

And his wife, Lydia? *Ain't going to get you nowhere, old man. Got to focus on the now.*

He flips through the lingerie catalogue first, wishing he could again order the host of porn magazines that he had in prison. But Angie has already questioned him about the comics that arrive weekly—his mail anything but private—and he needs to stay in her good graces. An eviction, however groundless, could threaten his parole.

The phone rings. Twice, three times, four. The ramifications of a missed phone call seem somehow distant. He considers ignoring it before lifting the receiver. "William Kane," he says. He pulls up his pantleg and presses a button on the electronic monitoring band strapped to his ankle, holding the receiver to it. A small speaker transmits a touch-tone number into the phone. He places the receiver to his ear again, verifying the connection, and in a moment hangs up. Out the window he sees a crow has alighted on a nearby telephone pole. It spreads its wings as a gust of wind hits. It caws once.

When he turns he sees Dead Earl sitting on the kitchen counter, huddled in his overcoat. "Twice in one day? Ain't you got no friends?" Doc asks as he sets two mugs on the kitchen table. He pulls a fifth of Bacardi from behind the refrigerator. Earl struggles to pull out a chair, tugging with both hands. He drinks with the mug clamped between his palms. The caramel liquid courses down his esophagus, just visible.

"Can't you do something about that?" Doc asks.

"You got a weak stomach?" Nonetheless, in a moment Dead Earl's figure firms, losing its translucence.

"Never thought I'd look forward to a visit from you."

"It ain't something I enjoy doing," Earl says.

"Well, I ain't the one that wandered into your house," Doc says.

"It just sort of happens," Earl confesses. He burps and pushes his cup forward. "I don't know why."

Doc studies the cup. "You remember that woman who was with you? The one that came with the sob story 'bout how you deserved another chance?"

"I remember."

"Who was she? What was her name?" Doc asks.

"I forget. I just told her she could have some dope if you went for the act." Dead Earl cocks his elbows out and raises his mug.

Doc chuckles. The rum heats his stomach. He drums his fingers, letting the silence lengthen. He hasn't eaten; already it seems that the room is unmoored at the edges of his vision.

"I took the thumbs," Earl says.

"What?"

"The thumbs," Earl says. "I took them. Time I walked to the hospital—"

"You couldn't get no ride?"

"How'm I gonna hitchhike?"

Doc laughs, shaking his head. "Sorry, I know it ain't funny." He laughs again.

"It ain't funny," Earl says emphatically. "Ain't no one going to pick up no bleeding nigger. Not where you left me."

"Not anywhere."

Earl coughs. "Time I got to the hospital they couldn't do nothing with them. Just wrapped my hands up like they was Q-Tips and gave me a bunch of shots."

Doc nods.

"Wouldn't let me keep the thumbs, neither," Earl adds. "Said they disposed of them 'in a manner consistent with hospital regulation.'"

"Well, what was you gonna do with them?" Doc raises his cup to his mouth.

"They was *mine*," Earl says, his voice aggrieved.

"You ain't much for conversation, Earl."

"Ain't nothing says I got to be friendly."

Doc contemplates Earl's churlish face. He feels himself tiring. "Why don't you go home, Earl?"

"This is home." Earl crosses his arms.

"I don't need this," Doc says. He pinches the bridge of his nose. "You ever see my family, Earl?"

"Family?"

"My wife." *Lydia. Where you at, woman? And what you like?*

"You got a wife?"

They have not communicated once since he was served the divorce papers in prison. Fourteen years. By then it had been a formality and, his wounded pride aside, he was only surprised that she had lasted through two previous jail sentences. She'd never been able to visit him all the way out in Nevada, but that was just as well. He was dead to her and she to him. The faster he could forget, the better. He'd thrown out her pictures, her letters. Of her face he remembers the glint of the hooped earrings she'd favored, the soft look in her eyes, her insistence that she have the right side of the bed.

The room darkens. Doc finds himself alone at the table, a full mug of rum set in front of an empty chair across from him. He goes to the window. A couple moves slowly past on the opposite side of the street. The musical laughter of the woman rises to his ears. He flicks a light switch, flooding the small kitchen with fluorescent glare, and opens the phone book. There are several listings for *Kane* and he runs his finger down the names, mouthing each entry. His index finger pauses: *M. Kane.* He twists and places the phone on the table and lets his hand rest on the receiver. Could she be unmarried? He dials.

"We're sorry, you have reached a number that has been disconnected or is no longer in service. If you—"

He closes the phone book, waits for the trembling to stop.

Later, in bed, the nocturnal noise of the city seeps in, ghostly, like faint voices bleeding through a bad connection. He relaxes into his mattress, hearing the slow, steady footfalls of a screw patrolling his cellblock and the somnolent, echoing breathing of prisoners escaped into sleep, as if his apartment has expanded to the cavernous dimensions of Cellblock B.

The phone rings, faint at first, then louder, dragging him from bed and into a slow stumble to the kitchen. He listens for a long moment to the ghostly voices seeping into the poor connection, still adrift and drunk, feeling warm from the Nevada light, then remembers to speak. "What?"

"Doc Kane, you still a grumpy motherfucker!"

"Do I know you?"

"Better than you think," Rebo says. "Better than you think."

Doc's breath catches. He glimpses his reflection in the darkened windowpane, the blinds still raised. He cannot tell if it is a smile or a grimace that greets him. Rebo. His partner in everything from dealing to armed robbery.

3

Doc empties a bag of precut fries into a cooking cage which he immerses in the deep fryer. The flaked ice pops in the heated vegetable oil. His station fills with the smell of cooking potatoes. Eduardo and Walker stand to his left, stationed at the front counter that bisects the room. Eduardo rises up on the balls of his feet as he yells at the tall boy.

"*Oyé*, Walker. You listening to me? Those registers is designed for idiots. So how come you keep fucking up?"

Doc closes his eyes at the sound of Eduardo's rapid-fire voice.

"I'm not an idiot," Walker says, looking down at Eduardo. His startled eyes belie the measured calm of his voice. "If I was, though, I guess I'd be able to use the damn register."

"I don't care what you are, *comprende*? I just want you to tell me that you can work the register without fucking up." Eduardo has his arms akimbo and his head juts forward on his thick neck; he resembles a bulldog straining at a leash.

"I can do it," Walker says.

"Yo, Mr. Morales," Doc says. Eduardo swings his head about. "What you want, Kane?"

"The fries," Doc says. "I need more bags."

"Then go to the freezer! What, you need a guide for that?"

Over Eduardo's shoulder Doc catches Walker's eye. Walker smiles.

"And you don't run out so fast if you don't pack each serving. Like those barbecues. I seen you giving them away. Don't give barbecues unless someone asks, and then only one."

Doc nods; he knows better than to argue with Eduardo. It's two weeks since he tossed Cue Ball from the restaurant and Eduardo hasn't forgotten. He wishes he hadn't acted as he did though he knows he had no real choice. The prison code is hardwired into him: the kid was disrespectful, the violence inevitable. But even so. Every day he enters the restaurant he wonders if he'll encounter Cue Ball, if the kid will pull a gun. Doc reads the paper daily. Crack is all the rage and there are thousands of Cue Balls careening through the streets with Glocks and attitude. Doc knows he was lucky in the bathroom.

"And I got complaints about the fries yesterday, Kane. No soft ones. You waiting for that timer to finish before you pull them out?"

"I make good fries. Ain't no one complained to me."

"You look in a mirror, Kane? Maybe people don't see you as Señor Friendly. You need to smile more. Service with a smile."

"Jiffy Lube," Doc says.

"What?"

" 'Service with a smile.' That ain't us. It's Jiffy Lube or someplace like it."

"You think I don't know what I'm talking about? I was the fry guy before you. Señor Papas, okay?" Eduardo smiles, relenting. "I like the rest of your work, though. Just no soft fries. Five months a long time to learn how to make fries."

" 'Señor Papas'?" Walker asks.

"Mr. Potato." He extends an arm, palm out. "Don't get no ideas."

Doc and Walker break before the dinner rush. Doc bites his Big Mac and a multicolored juice pools on the wax paper. Walker watches with distaste. "Big Macs, they're like oysters: Don't look like nothing you should eat."

"You don't eat oysters for the taste—but I guess you don't know 'bout that yet. That or food."

Walker grins. "That's right. I was forgetting 'bout your expertise in all things female." He pulls a fry from the pile tidily arranged in the lid of the Chicken McNuggets flip box. "These fries seem a little soft. Little bit, ah, flaccid."

"Death wish. You got a death wish."

Afterward Doc busies himself with the garbage. He tosses several bags into the back-alley Dumpster. The bags are smeared with grease and the vivid yellows and reds of mustard and ketchup, as if something has died wetly within. In the spring air he catches the scent of spoiled milk—another urban hint of warming weather. The air seems filmed with filth.

He removes his hat, rubs his forehead, works his pants down on his waist until they no longer ride up his crotch. His prison denims had never quite fit, either; too tight in the thighs and shoulders.

Still, he thinks, there were plenty of cons with him at the D.C. Department of Corrections halfway house who would be happy for this work. With no job there were no social passes, and without those, time began to drag, except the outside was right there, seen through the window, heard in the dark. So close that it was easy to walk out the door of the halfway house, breathe deep and decide that no, tonight you wouldn't be back before curfew. That there would be no more orders, no more locked doors, no paperwork, no caseworkers—no evidence of your history to impede your freedom. It was easy, he knew, to convince yourself that you were walking out into a new beginning even as the police came looking for you because of your past.

It isn't bad, this life. He's got most of what he dreamed about in prison on those long nights when all pretense was stripped: an apartment, a steady job, the freedom to roam through a park, space to be alone. But it's one thing to dream and another to attain that dream. Each day it is easier to disregard these gifts and harder to ignore other, pressing wants: a woman, respect, connection.

Again he thinks of Rebo, who's called him every few nights in the past weeks, the night before last at two or three in the morning, causing Doc to bolt from bed, thinking it an unscheduled check, perhaps requested by Mike, but hearing instead the somnolent sounds of a bar at closing time: the clink of glasses and bottles, the scrape of chairs, a slow, slurred voice repeating something unintelligible over and over.

He'd said nothing, just listening. It took a moment for Rebo to realize that the call had connected.

A throat cleared. "Doc?"

"I got to sleep, Rebo. Don't be calling this late."

"Why ain't we met?"

Doc had started to speak, paused, feeling that any explanation was be futile. "Shit," he said, "there ain't no easy answer for that. You ought to know."

"All I know is that you come here and you got old friends, booze, pussy, you name it. What you found better than that, nigger?"

"That ain't it. Got nothing to do with your sorry ass."

Rebo laughed, the deep rolling sound causing Doc to smile in the dark. "We ain't got much time to grow wool together, Doc. Best get over here."

"When I can," Doc said. "When I can."

The line had quieted, again the sound of the bar filtering through, and in the dim light of the kitchen it seemed not so much that the noise was borne through the phone line, but rather that its medium was somewhere less precisely situated; like a faintly falling snow, the sound sifted through the air around him, flakes of noise and association descending from out of the past.

"Soon," he mumbled to Rebo, "soon," before hanging up. But he knew what Rebo knew, what kept his old friend calling: that he was not out of the Life. That McDonald's and the Square John trip were tiring acts to play.

He wonders what Rebo looks like. It's been twenty years or more since he's seen his old partner. *Gonna find out tonight*, he thinks.

He steps back into the restaurant but pauses just inside the door. Through the hallway Cue Ball stands in profile at the counter with a pair of friends, one dressed in a sweatsuit that looks cut from an American flag. Cue Ball's friends are laughing at something. The one in the sweatsuit lightly pushes the other, who steps back into the diminutive Cue Ball, pushing the boy roughly against the counter. Cue Ball pushes back and curses, but what Doc notes is the way the boy reaches to the small of his back with one hand, reassuring himself that the gun beneath his jacket is still in place.

Doc stands motionless, wondering if he'll have to wait here until Cue Ball finishes with his meal, then breathes a sigh of relief as Walker hands over to-go bags of food to the trio. For much of the afternoon, though, he stays far back in the kitchen, telling himself that this is an act of prudence, not cowardice, that there is a difference.

By six o'clock people are spilling through the glass doors, pooling against the steel counter. The kitchen and dining areas are tiled, hard surfaces that reflect and magnify noise. In the din of voiced orders, of rush-hour traffic bleeding in from L Street, cashiers call for food and mill about, grabbing drinks, burgers, salads. Doc douses fries in hot oil, leaves a cage to drain. Sweat slicks his palms.

By ten the restaurant is silent. Doc mops, the smell of bleach in his clothes and on his hands. Several men sit nursing coffees, one sopping up ketchup with his fries. The Muzak is muted, a zydeco rendition of Beethoven's Ninth. Weekday nights the restaurant feels like a bar, but one where the bright lights and lack of alcohol keep the pain in view. No soft shadows, no smoke, no booze to hide behind. Just the aggressive glare of fluorescent lights.

The heat from the day's cooking has lingered in the kitchen. Doc slips into the walk-in freezer, leaning against the cool face of the door. The hum of the cooling motor vibrates through the metal. Boxes of hamburger patties and fish fillets rise in stacks.

Dead Earl clears his throat. The white cloud of his frosted breath seems to have more substance to it than the body from whence it issues. He sits perched on a stack of boxes.

"What the fuck, Earl," Doc says. "You got me on some high-rotation parole check of your own? Ain't enough to have Mike on my ass?" His anger wells up, heating his face.

"This ain't my idea of no vacation, neither."

"Can't you see I'm working?"

"You ain't working," Earl says.

"What does your sorry ass know about work?"

" 'Chi-ken fee-lay,' " Earl says, lingering over the sound as if he can taste it. He runs a finger over the print on a box. "I could never get no job at McDonald's. Not after—"

"Would you just shut up about your damn thumbs, Earl? It wasn't like you was on no fast track to success before that. I ain't to blame for your life."

"You ain't to blame."

"No, I ain't! And if I was to whip your ass right now, I wouldn't be to blame for that, neither!" Doc advances and Earl scrabbles back among the boxes.

"You ought to be civil to the dead." Earl pulls his overcoat around him and stands a bit straighter than usual.

"When you dead enough, I might be." Doc leans forward, arms braced on a box. "I don't got the time for this."

"This ain't about convenience."

Doc shakes his head. "I don't deserve this, hear? Not now, not ever. I served my time!" he shouts before turning and slamming the freezer door.

At shift's end, Doc and Walker, dressed in their street clothes, leave the kitchen gleaming and cool. Walker has been a little distant the past week, avoiding their after-shift walk by sneaking out a few minutes before closing.

"What's up with your brother?" Doc asks as they arrive at the bus stop. He wants to prolong the moment; with the exception of Rebo's phone calls, it seems as if he hasn't spoken to anybody in days. A week past, he'd been to Walker's for a poker game and he's wished every night since then that he could be back there with this boy and his young brother.

He remembers rapping at their gated door. Evan had appeared, regarding Doc through the bars with a solemn expression. Doc had smiled, wondering how such a thin neck supported such a big head. He hefted his bag of candy. "I brought cash."

"Gonna need it," Evan said.

At the poker table Doc and Walker waited for Evan to finish the serious business of arranging the Oreos, Gummi bears, and Skittles (25¢, 10¢, and 5¢, respectively) into neat piles. The walls of the house—kitchen included—were crowded with family photos, ranging from thumbtacked Polaroids to black-and-white formal shots, all of them featuring combinations of the two boys and a heavyset woman with a wide smile, as well as a much older woman gripping a cane. In the wall space between the photos the plaster had bubbled. Walker caught Doc studying the photos. "Momma and Aunt Ferney," he said.

"Aunt Ferney is in the hospital," Evan announced.

"You just shut up and deal the cards," Walker said.

They each anted with a Skittle as Evan dealt.

"She doing okay?" Doc asked.

Walker frowned at Evan.

"Nope," said Evan. "How much you want to bet?" He squirmed in his chair, unwittingly flashing his cards as he pulled at the sleeve of his oversized rugby.

Doc tossed out an Oreo. The kitchen was cramped, the refrigerator crowding Doc's left arm. In the living room he'd seen a foldout couch with bedpillows and sheets piled on top. It looked like Walker and Evan shared this space, the lone bedroom reserved for their ailing aunt.

"I see your Oreo and raise you three Gummi bears," Evan said.

"I'm just warning you," Doc said, "I got at least a pair and I saw you take four cards for that ace."

"You can rethink that bet, you want," Walker said.

Evan eyed them both cooly. "Okay. I raise your Oreo *six* Gummi bears."

Doc laughed and folded, happier than he'd been in a long time, wanting to hug them both.

"I heard you got yourself a woman," he said to Evan.

"Uh-uh," Evan said, staring at his cards.

"She got him," Walker said.

"Ain't got no time for that kid stuff," Evan said.

"You and your brother, both," Doc said.

"The hell—"

"I call the bet," Evan said.

"All right, James Bond," said Walker, laying out a pair of tens over sevens.

Evan spread out his flush and raked over the candy without breaking a smile. "Glad Momma ain't around to see you get whipped like this," he said.

"That's no way to talk," Walker said.

Even dropped his eyes. "You know what I mean."

After the game, Walker sent Evan to make the bed while he and Doc talked on the apartment's landing.

"Your aunt on Medicare?"

Walker nodded. "But the doctors ain't going to fix no lung cancer."

They watched a motorcycle shoot past, the whine of its engine scratching the silence of the evening.

"You tell me when the Social Security stops coming."

Walker shook his head. "Don't want to think about that."

"It ain't a request."

As they wait together for the bus Doc represses the desire to again offer his help, afraid that Walker will hear the need in his voice. Aunt Ferne was released from the hospital, he knows, but her condition has been evident in the strain in Walker's face.

"Evan's okay. Just got a job after school cleaning up and bagging at a corner market." Walker seems reluctant to talk about it.

"He getting any time with you?"

"I try."

Doc looks down the street. No cars in sight.

"You don't have to stick around." Walker's ears fan out from his head, angled by the hatband of his white baseball cap.

"You going home?" Doc asks.

Walker shakes his head. "Domino's."

"You got a thing for polyester uniforms I don't know about?"

"Need the money."

The bus arrives. Doc feels bad for making the joke. "You need help, you let me know," he says, wondering if he means this—no matter that he'd like to. The bus swings wide around a corner and disappears. As Doc walks to the next corner he sees an obsidian Cadillac idling curbside. Right on time. Rebo rolls down the window.

"You need a ride, old man?"

Doc suppresses a grin. He glances quickly about.

Rebo pushes open the passenger door and Doc hesitates the barest moment. Rebo grins lopsidedly—something amiss in his face, teeth flashing beneath the dome light. "Doc Kane, motherfucker," he whispers, gripping Doc's neck and pulling him into an awkward hug. "Motherfucker!" The car smells of cigars and the pine scent of the air freshener hanging from the rearview mirror.

"We going to get that drink?" Doc asks.

Rebo chuckles. "You was never the juicy type."

Doc grins and briefly closes his eyes. Rebo driving, the murmur of the engine running up his back—it could be twenty, thirty years ago. He lingers in this space a moment or two. Rebo. He's finally in the company of somebody with whom he can talk, to whom he has to explain so little. He thinks of Mike. *Fuck you, you motherfucker.* He can't see Rebo well in the dark, though the profile is familiar. His eyes stray to the dashboard—digital clock, accelerator readout, molded plastic. He hasn't been in a car other than a taxi since his release. The seat has wonderful lower-back support.

At 13th and T they park in front of Odessa's, the bar still operating amid the listing buildings and gapped lots. It takes Doc a moment to recognize the bar. It is central to the same neighborhood he avoids on his morning runs. The windows of the sag-roofed second story are boarded and a few women loiter near the entrance in clothes far too abbreviated for the temperature. He lags a bit behind Rebo as they enter, getting a long look at the prostitutes.

The unfamiliarity of the bar's interior shocks him. Walls have been knocked out, doors and windows bricked in. The bar itself resembles the original, though it fronts a different wall. He experiences a moment of dislocation like so many others since release, aware that this unfamiliar space was also his adolescent home. He doesn't know what he feels, sitting here after so much time, facing the unfamiliarity that still manages to evoke so many memories. How many owners between Odessa and Rebo?

In his early teens he'd spent several years working for Odessa, cleaning and peeling potatoes, washing dishes, anything she wanted in return for an upstairs spare room and three squares. Small, with a high forehead and arched eyebrows and jet-black skin, when Odessa smiled she was the center of attention. She'd filled him with adolescent fantasies, and he'd always hoped that her maternal love was in fact a different sort of affection, that it was just a matter of time—when he became a man—until their relationship changed. She'd known his father, though he never knew how well.

The first time his stepgrandfather kicked him out of the house was at twelve. He caught Doc—then, Billy—trying to steal his gold retirement watch. He'd been a porter at Union Station and took great pride in the watch, occasionally dangling it before his stepgrandson to illustrate the importance of discipline and a good work ethic. "You work hard and people respect you, reward you," he'd say, his eyes squinched up and almost lost in a face wrinkled like the contour map of rough terrain. "Your father ain't got one of these," he'd once added.

He'd been furious when he'd caught Doc with the watch, attempting simultaneously to hold the boy and strip his own belt free, yelling all the while about character. But even at twelve Doc was heavyset. Doc, resentful and embarrassed, called the watch a reward for being a house nigger, and that night had found the door barred to him. The exile didn't last long, but long enough for Doc to spend a little time at Odessa's bar. At fourteen, when his step-grandfather died, Doc had moved to Odessa's for good. She'd forced him to go to the funeral.

It is this time of his life that encompasses his fondest memories, the world just opening for him as he settled in with a loose family of his own choosing. Odessa had taken him for crabs from time to time, though it was only later, in retrospect, that he realized she did it more for her sake than for his, the outings creating as they did the brief, illusory image of mother and child. He remembers her many hats, remembers that she would let him sit in her bedroom and open her hatboxes for her as she searched for the best match before going out.

As he thinks of her he realizes with a jolt that she—his first, if unrequited love—is likely long dead. And alive or dead, he has no idea where he would find her.

Rebo greets the small, boisterous crowd gathered in the bar, waving to a few of the players at the pool tables, nodding at the bartender before ushering Doc into his office, a small, bare cube with a one-way window that looks out on the main room. He toasts Doc from behind his desk, then begins pulling small sheaves of bills from a drawer, stacking them. The light cast from a lamp fully reveals Rebo's face. A scar jags from his left temple, drops to follow the ridge of his cheekbone before descending to disappear below his ear. The nerves seem to be severed, the left side of Rebo's face hanging slack even when he smiles. He appears to wear two expressions at once: one half animated, smiling in welcome; the other sagging, impassive, the mouth's edge downturned, the dark left eye glittering from its socket, unreadable.

"You feeling generous in all your nostalgia?" Doc asks, growing annoyed. It is just like Rebo to try and pull rank like this.

"Just a little business. Got some things to take care of later, after we talk."

"You going to stay behind that desk and you might as well get started with your errands now. I came to drink with an old friend, not drink in front of some motherfucker with a desk."

Rebo laughs and rises, leaving the money on the table. "Just sit a minute. I got to piss."

Doc motions with his chin at the money. "Who the fuck you think you dealing with? You think you gonna test me with that bullshit? Like I some punk? Like we got no history?"

Rebo's chuckle is unconvincing.

"Stop embarrassing us both." Rebo has always been able to irritate him like nobody else.

"What you want to drink?" Rebo says at length.

"You got no call to distrust me," Doc says quietly.

Rebo steps up to him and in a quick move embraces Doc. "Good to have you back," he says.

At the bar they drink and talk as the night deepens.

"And now you out, just like that," Doc says as Rebo finishes detailing an eight-year bit at Leavenworth. More armed robbery.

"Yeah, just like that," Rebo says. "Been a year now."

"Don't lie to me, nigger! Repeat offender like you, you got to be on a short leash. They put you in a halfway house? You on parole? Got an EM band?"

"None of that shit," Rebo says.

"So what, you just walk out the halfway house?"

"They ain't got no business telling a man when he got to eat or go to sleep!"

"Hah. You never had the sense to know it on your own," Doc says.

Rebo watches the bartender lean over to get a beer. "The Man ain't come looking for some old con. Got more important things. Things that require less paperwork."

"Shit. You know him that well, how come you got caught in the first place?"

"Still a motherfucker. All this time and you still a motherfucker," Rebo continues. "Ain't too stupid to be doing just fine now I got out the system. Matter of fact, I got a few packages with the name 'Doc Kane' on 'em. Few bills, too."

"I ain't having this conversation," Doc says.

"I owe you."

"What do you owe me? Revoked parole?"

"Don't be belittling my debt!" Rebo says.

Doc has a flash of holding Rebo in the back of a speeding car, cinching a belt tightly around his friend's thigh, blood from a gunshot smeared up his arms and staining gray money bags, Rebo crying, "Doc, Doc..." A bank robbery that resulted in the second of three sentences, five years and then some, a primer for the sixteen that followed a few years after that.

Doc sighs. "Ain't you thought 'bout what happens if you go back to the joint?"

"Yeah, and I think 'bout getting hit by a car, too. And tornadoes, earthquakes, and fucking locusts, man—I'm all in knots about that shit." He drinks. "Worry all the time... That ain't no kind of life."

Doc rolls his shotglass between his palms. "So what you got going?"

"Hah! I knew you ain't been beat!"

Doc straightens but says nothing. His eyes stray to a low-slung woman farther down the bar, her braided hair gleaming brassily, the smooth skin of her shoulders glowing in the dim light. She smiles and his gaze skitters off as his heart jumps.

Rebo claps him on the back. "You sit and enjoy yourself. I got a few phone calls and then I'll be back." He disappears back into his office, leaving Doc to contemplate the reflections in the backbar mirror. The walleyed bartender sets a shot of Jim Beam before him. "Courtesy of Rebo," he says. "You drink for free tonight. Anything you want, you just yell for Flash."

"Flash like the comic book?"

The bartender squints at him, one eye on target, the other aimed at the ceiling. "What's that?"

"Like the comic book? The guy in the red suit?"

"One and the same." Flash moves off at a slow limp.

Doc chuckles. As he raises his glass to drink, the woman from down the bar sidles up beside him, bracelets jangling musically. The blurred light mutes the tired set of her face. She looks very young. Her jaw works on a piece of gum.

"What you drinking?" he asks.

She smiles. "White Russian."

Her eyes follow his hand to his front pocket as he pulls out his wallet and he laughs at himself, knowing she's ordered a hard drink both to get drunk and so she can see the size of his money wad. But she's young and ripe and he doesn't care that she's a whore because here, at last, is a fine-looking woman who is focused on him. Paying Flash for the drink, he sees their reflection, her proud face in profile.

Flash takes a good five minutes with the drink, during which the woman introduces herself as Blondelle. She puts her hand to his arm, leaning near, smelling of a sweet, fruity perfume and acrid sweat.

"How old are you, honey?" he asks.

"Old as you want me to be," she says. She pops her gum like a punctuation mark.

He drinks from his whiskey, hoping to slow the rise of his erection.

"Blondelle, get your ass back on the street!" Rebo says, joining them. "Ain't paying you to sling no pussy with my friends."

"He didn't say nothing about it!" she flares.

Rebo's hand snakes out, reptile-quick, catching her cheek with a clean snap. "What did I say?"

She swallows her drink, motion deliberate and slow but not too slow.

"See you learned how to treat women," Doc says quietly.

"Bitch needs to be earning me money," Rebo says as he stares after her.

"She cuts your dick off and don't come bleeding to me," Doc says.

"I got to go," Rebo says. "You coming?" He stands without waiting for an answer and walks toward the exit. Though Rebo does not look back, Doc knows that he would like to. In a moment Doc follows, feeling with his first step that he's locked himself into a groove from which there is no disengaging.

They drive down an alley of demolished rowhouses and into the interior of a weed-matted block cluttered with the hulks of derelict cars. Several windows of a low warehouse glow with feeble light. Rebo cuts the headlights. They are both a little drunk.

"What kind of errand you on?" The hair on Doc's forearm prickles.

"Got to pay the rent." A silhouette appears at one of the windows.

"Rent," Doc says. "So you got an employee base, or are you part of one?"

"I'm the man," Rebo says without much conviction. He pulls a paper bag from beneath his seat. Inside are several stacks of bills. He counts them, then puts all but two back in the bag. He looks at Doc, his face is sheened with sweat. He places the last two stacks of money with the rest.

"Don't bring what you gonna keep," Doc says. It tires him to realize that Rebo hasn't changed—makes what he is seem sadder and smaller. Doc feels a surge of pity for his expansive friend. "You need me in there?"

Rebo taps the steering wheel, not looking at Doc. "Naw. I got it."

"You make the call."

"You don't need to do shit but sit tight." Rebo breathes deep and opens the door.

"Rebo—"

"In a minute, my man." Rebo strides to the building and for a moment is framed by the panel of light as the door swings open, a second silhouette visible beyond him.

Doc wipes his forehead. Rebo has left the keys in the ignition. He climbs into the driver's seat. *Goddamn you, Rebo.* He smiles wanly as he shakes his head. Nervous. But also flushed, alive, reminded of the old B-More Crew, the noise and the swaggering, the thrills. Because even sixteen years hasn't negated the fact that robbing banks and jewelry stores—the whole game—was fun. You could look at your haul a week, two weeks later and catch a shiver from the memory of the deed. You could be getting dressed in clothes you bought with the stolen money and break into a smile or a fit of laughter on seeing yourself in the mirror. You could sit around drinking with your crew and utter one word about the crime and everyone would bust out laughing because you had all shared in it and understood the euphoria. You had been in it together and were in it together still. Always.

Shit.

One minute stretches to ten. Doc feels he's being watched, but sees no faces in the surrounding cars. Most of the warehouse windows are dark. He studies each in turn, the opaqued glass revealing nothing.

Doc opens the car door, approaches a window that reveals a basketball court–sized room poorly lit with standing lamps and a few fluorescent lights. Rebo stands with a group of young men about a crude desk—sawhorses, a door with a knob atop these. He's nodding vigorously and gesturing in an exaggerated manner, like a bad actor.

As Doc debates whether to knock or return to the car, the group breaks apart. The door swings wide and Rebo exits, stiff-legged and walking fast, motioning to Doc to get in the car. After a few minutes of driving he turns on the radio. He looks quickly at Doc from time to time, but the two do not speak until they arrive at Doc's apartment.

"Doc, I—"

Doc holds up a hand. "You don't need to say nothing, Rebo. I understand." *We all want to be more than what we is,* he thinks. He wonders who Rebo pays so that he can stay in business.

4

The angled bar of light from the bedroom window slides over the floor and up the opposing wall. The window's glass is old and slightly warped, the edges of the square of light on the wall limned the colors of the spectrum. Three raps on the door. Doc makes no move to rise. He's been awake for an hour, knowing he needs to get up soon to make his parole meeting but unable to rise. He recalls the previous night as if it's a bad dream embellished with more detail than he cares to remember.

A key rattles in the door's lock. "William?" Angie calls querulously.

What the fuck?

She shuffles to his bedroom just as he's rolled to his side and reached an arm down to slide an empty Seagram's bottle beneath the bed. She holds a bowl of soup.

"I didn't mean to intrude," she says. "I know it ain't right to come in. I just thought..."

Doc sits up, feeling dizzy. "I ain't feeling real—"

"I shouldn't have pushed in like this." She lifts the bowl. "I'll leave it on the table." A slight smile that wavers, flattens as she turns, the uncertainty of it eliciting in Doc a pang of tenderness.

"Thanks for the soup," Doc calls. But really he wishes he were in a position to demand the spare key she keeps. *Now she got another excuse to visit,* he thinks, knowing she'll come back for the bowl.

The door quietly closes. The soup, he has to admit, is not too bad, though he has scant time to appreciate it as he rushes to get ready to meet with Mike.

"You got a woman yet?" asks Mike as Doc takes his seat before the desk, breathing easily from the run between metro stop and the office.

"You got to start every meeting with that?"

"Okay, you drinking?"

"Shit," Doc says. "You think I gonna trade three-and-a-half years at Bone Hill for a fifth of Seagram's?" He wonders if it's that obvious. The hair on his forearms prickles.

A skid and the flat report of an impact jerks them from their chairs. They peer through the blinds. On the street, a red coupe faces toward oncoming traffic, crimped where a brown station wagon has struck. Glass glitters on the pavement. "You work to-day?" Mike asks.

"Work every day," Doc says, studying the wreck. His work routine has, in fact, acquired the same rhythm as the routine he ran in Tyburn, the patterns and movements at McDonald's a slight variation on the years spent standing in front of the sewing machines in prison industries, the nightly influx of diners a predictable ebb and flow, the sweeping, mopping, and scrubbing of tables and bathrooms a series of set movements, the end of each shift followed by cool evening air, the walk to clear his head, the two flights of stairs to his room, dinner, drink, sleep, the morning run.

The man in the coupe struggles with his seat belt, squeezing out to brush glass from his pants. The other driver circles slowly, tentatively touching the bent metal if to assess the actuality of the wreck. Spectators gather, most pausing at points equidistant from the accident, afraid to break a fragile meniscus of space encircling the damage.

"You think they're all right?" Doc asks, stepping back from the window.

"Looks like it," Mike says, still studying the scene. Doc glances at an open folder on the top of Mike's desk, does a doubletake, recognizing the name: Woodrow Pleddy. Bunt. *Got to be out,* he thinks, thrilled, his mood shifting from paranoia to euphoria. The address is Southeast D.C., 7th and L Streets. Not far from Walker.

Mike turns from the window. "So work ain't changed? I can call your boss, check that out?"

"Yeah." Doc sits. "Then, after you all have your heart-to-heart, he can fire my ass for lying 'bout my record on my employment application."

Mike lights a cigarette. "You give me a discount if I come by for lunch?"

"Depends. You going to pay the phone bill for those EM calls?"

Mike settles in his chair, reveals nicotine-yellowed teeth in a grimace. "So no girlfriend."

"No friends," Doc replies. " 'Bout cut out the whole neighborhood when you say I can't associate with those that been in the joint or 'individuals of bad character.' Cut them out and there ain't no one interesting left." He wonders what kind of job Bunt has, what his life is like. Probably not more than a few weeks past.

Mike exhales a stream of smoke. "Guess that leaves you with a lot of time for reflection."

"Lot of time for this," Doc says, pumping a hand over his crotch.

Mike laughs. "Shit, I don't even want to know, Kane."

"I don't ask the questions."

The phone rings. "Yeah," Mike says. "Yeah, I got the tickets. No, they wouldn't give me the discount rate. No. So what's twenty dollars? Those beach-umbrella drinks down there are gonna cost more than that. Okay, sweetheart.

"Vacation plans," Mike explains after hanging up.

Doc rubs his eyes in the awkward silence. "Where you going?"

"Barbados. One week."

"Must be nice."

The fan squeaks steadily.

Mike clears his throat. "So you're having a hard time—what'd you say?" He pages through notes from their last meeting. "You 'ain't a part of things'?"

"I watch another episode of *Cheers* and I ain't responsible for what happens," Doc says.

"Hah."

"Look. I don't know what you want to hear. I'm just saying it like it is: Parole feels a lot like doing time, 'cept I got bills to pay. I ain't going to pretend to be all overjoyed." He wonders if he's overplaying his hand. *Just make it look like you struggling to tough it out.*

Mike looks amused. "That bad, is it?"

"In prison I had friends. Now I got cockroaches and the *Post*. That ain't no substitute."

"Depends on the friends, I guess." Mike offers Doc a cigarette, which Doc declines. "You know your penology, Kane?" He taps his cigarette against the lip of his ashtray. "What am I talking about? You practically quote the parole manual every time you show up."

"I know some," Doc says.

"You know silence used to be a condition for sentences, back in the 1800s? Silence all the time. Used to make 'em wear hoods when they left their cells. No talking to anyone, not even themselves."

A siren wails in approach. "Used to use whips and the stocks, too," Doc says.

Mike nods.

The siren cuts off. Doc stares at his hands, then at Mike. "You got a point?" Doc asks.

"Some things aren't likely to change. 'Do the crime, do the time,'" Mike says.

"Or just say no to drugs. Like Nancy Reagan or any of them other motherfuckers knows shit about it."

"What?"

"Ain't that simple. You say that shit like that explains it. Say that shit so you can pretend it's simple. So you can go home and forget about it," Doc says.

Mike stubs out his cigarette. "It may not feel that simple, but it is. No gray in the legal system. You fuck up, you pay. You do drugs, you pay."

Doc shakes his head. *Let it slide. Get a drink after this.* But he can't. "Maybe you could use a little 'reflection time' to clean your head of all that shit. We ain't living in no elementary school. Life, it got complications. And prison, most of y'all don't know what you sentencing someone to when you put them in the joint—rape, shankings, AIDS and TB. Don't tell me about doing time like you some damn expert."

Mike stares at Doc as he taps another cigarette from his pack. "Let's wrap this up."

At work that afternoon, nearing the end of an early shift, Doc scrubs a garbage casing, fighting back the nausea that comes from the smell of refuse and the thought of food. He breaks and heads into the kitchen for some water. Walker has arrived—they work staggered shifts on Tuesdays—and stands peeling a few hamburger patties from squares of waxed paper.

"You got on the wrong headgear," Doc says.

Walker pulls his off and looks at it. "Shit. Did Eduardo see?"

Doc laughs. "He don't care if you work at Domino's. Ain't like you signed a noncompete clause on no contract."

Walker stuffs the hat in his pocket. Doc laughs as an awkward silence settles. He doesn't push it, returning instead to the garbage casing to finish with the cleaning.

Eduardo wanders back with his lunch—a sandwich from Schlotzky's. "Hey, Kane."

"What?" Doc's voice resonates in the confines of the box. He works at a dried stain of spilled creamers and catsup.

"You ever get bored working here?"

"Nope."

"You don't have to give no bullshit answer," Eduardo says.

Doc pulls back from the garbage casing and stands. "Then ask a different question."

Eduardo motions for Doc to join him. "I get bored," he announces. "My mind goes places, you know? *Cada día un viaje fabuloso.*" He grins sardonically.

Doc sits with him.

"Where you think my mind goes?" Eduardo prompts.

"Shit, I don't know. What kind of question is that?"

"Mexico. Those cards in the office? My grandfather lived by that lake. *Un pescador.* Fisherman. When I'm remembering, I see him standing in his boat holding those nets with the sun in them like he's catching the light for our dinner."

Eduardo drinks his iced tea and grimaces, then adds several packets of sugar and lemon juice. "Five years here, but when I dream my mind never goes to time I spend at work. Never."

"Huh."

Eduardo turns a lemon packet in his fingers. "I dream about my grandfather. He's cooking fish he caught and he tells me to get a lemon from the tree in his yard. Sometimes I still smell that clean lemon on my hands, like I just cut it. My uncle, he's there, too. He plays guitar after we eat and I watch his hands. He don't play good, but the song is a good song."

"Yeah?"

"But it's what I think that's important. I hear the guitar and taste the food in my mouth and I think this is the only time it will be this way." Eduardo is leaning forward, shoulders hunched and face intense, as if proximity to Doc will communicate his point. "It's specific. Unique. Every one of those times was different. I got a whole group of them to go back to. *Claridad.*"

Doc waits.

Eduardo drinks from his tea. "Not like here. This restaurant don't have lemons. Got packs of catsup, precut fries. Fish don't look like fish. Don't see potatoes for fries, tomato for catsup, lemon for juice. Been made all the same. Same size, same weight, same taste. And the music? We don't know where nothing comes from here.

"I don't know." Eduardo shakes his head, looks at Doc. His face is sad and Doc is surprised by his empathy. "Five years and I don't got memories like what I just told. Every day here the same. Like all this time at work I been asleep without even dreaming," Eduardo says.

"Like a sixteen-year day," Doc says, staring steadily at his employer.

"That kid? With the bald head? He was in here earlier," Eduardo says.

"Guess you could say his self-preservation instincts ain't too strong."

"He got as much right to come in as you, Kane."

"We don't even belong in the same sentence. I ain't nothing like that little punk." Doc's voice has a climbed and he pauses, resuming in a lower tone. "You got to have standards," he explains. "That boy, he ain't no different from those others shooting up this town like it's some kind of Boot Hill. You ask for trouble every time he's in here. I see him and I ain't responsible—"

"*¡Basta!*" Eduardo interrupts. "You are responsible." He shakes his head in frustration. "I can't have you getting into it with some kid over words. Don't do this, okay? You lose this job and I know it's not easy to get another, *sabes*?"

Doc's face flushes. "What does that mean?"

"Your record," Eduardo says. "What do you think."

"Record?"

Eduardo sighs. "Your sixteen-year day. You think I don't notice how you walk? How you put your arm around your food when you eat, like someone wants to take it?"

Doc stares.

"It don't matter," Eduardo says. "We understand each other?"

"I understand," Doc says.

At the counter he squares off with Walker, who hasn't emerged from the kitchen since arriving. "So," Doc says. "Is you and your little bro going to come out for dinner tonight?" Earlier, Doc offered to treat them to a crab feast and Walker said he'd think about it—check in with his aunt, maybe meet Doc down on the Waterfront when his later shift ended for the day.

Walker shrugs uncomfortably. "I called home and Evan, he ain't feeling so good. Sick, you know?"

"Sick."

Walker tries to smile into the silence. "Shit," he says finally. "He ain't sick. It's just my aunt, Ferney? She don't want us out . . . with you."

"Well, what you been telling her 'bout me?"

"Nothing," Walker says. " 'Least not lately."

"What the fuck does that mean?"

"I might of said something when she came back from the hospital 'bout thinking you'd done some time. And Aunt Ferney, she got a good memory."

"You think I did time?"

Walker stares at him, embarrassed. "Me and Eduardo talked about it some. Don't seem like it's no secret, is all. Don't make no difference to me," he adds.

"I can see that," Doc says, more harshly than he intends.

After shift Doc heads directly on his own for a crab feast, in no mood to talk to anyone.

The woman working the counter sizes Doc up. "All you can eat?"

Doc nods.

She hands him a basket of crabs, newspaper, a wooden mallet. The restaurant is dimly lit and cramped, but there are picnic tables outside, and Doc sits at one of these. He weights the newspaper with the crabs, then steps indoors to retrieve his Coke and a shaker of Old Bay Seasoning.

Near him sit a mother and her son. The boy is hammering at

the crabs, his enthusiastic strikes kicking up a spray of shell fragments. He clamps his lips shut when his mother attempts to feed him a pinch of crabmeat.

"Come on now, baby."

"The guts are green!"

Doc finishes a crab, savoring the delicate taste. The air is rich with the swampy scent of the Potomac and the Waterfront. An afternoon rain has glazed the streets and sidewalks, but the clouds have cleared and the gold light of the setting sun now glances from the river, the water and wet building-facades shining like burnished copper. Traffic shushes over the raised length of the Dwight D. Eisenhower Freeway in an unbroken rhythm. Even with another lonely evening looming, the view improves Doc's mood. It is good to be out. Good to be able to sit and watch the sunset and enjoy the fresh seafood. He wishes Ellis and Stirling could join him.

As he reaches for the second crab it sluggishly crawls over the others in an attempt to escape. The others writhe agitatedly beneath it. Doc jerks back. One crab falls from the basket. Dead Earl reaches from across the table to drop it back with the others.

Doc sighs, relaxing. He pushes the mallet toward Dead Earl. "Hungry?" he asks.

The coppery light of the sun seems to infuse Dead Earl with weight and vitality, his form only faintly translucent at the edges.

"Got to eat," Doc says. "Way you always dragging, being dead must be hard work."

"It's a rough schedule, all right."

Doc takes the mallet and smacks a crab about to drop from the table. "You got other old men to bug? Got to guilt the Pope? Keep Bob Hope from feeling too alive?"

"Just you," Earl says.

Doc sucks the meat from a leg. "So what's it like?"

Dead Earl nods toward the mallet. "I can't hit with that. No grip."

"You go home to the Dead Earl Family? Got Dead Rex wagging his tail when you come in?"

"It ain't like that," Earl says, ignoring the provocation. He laces his fingers and leans forward. "It's more like things is hazy, like they is when you tired in the morning and just drift before waking. 'Course when I do wake up, it's always with you right there looking like you gonna cut off some other part of me."

"You was better company and maybe I would be, too."

Dead Earl plucks a crab from the lapel of his trench coat. "Don't joke about family. I don't say nothing about yours."

"Figure you already know most of 'em, you being dead and all."

"It ain't like that, either," Earl says.

"You going to eat these crabs?" Doc asks.

"I don't got much appetite for crabs."

Doc dismembers one. The meat is cooked and tender though the tiny eyes look disconcertingly sentient.

"I ain't Dead Earl," Dead Earl says.

"Well, calling you Partly Dead Earl takes too long to say, even if it is accurate."

"You don't even know my last name," Earl says.

The mother and child seated nearby have been staring at Doc for some time. She has drawn her boy close in a protective embrace. They flinch when he hammers at the crab, then hurriedly rise and depart, leaving their food.

"Earl Buendía Compson."

"Buendía," Doc says.

"I got Colombian blood."

"I like Dead Earl. Keeps things straight in my mind," Doc says.

" 'Doc' does the same for me."

"You don't never quit, do you? You ain't got to remind me of what I did," Doc says testily.

"Your old man give you that nickname?" Earl asks.

"My daddy didn't give me nothing but a pair of shoes."

The wind strengthens and the sunlight fades. Beneath the slowly hazing sky Doc speaks to Earl of his father, his single clear memory of the man, watching him come into Odessa's the year

Doc started shaving. They'd gone to lunch and then to shop, his father buying him a pair of white buck shoes. He can't remember the face of the man, just describes the smooth roll of his gait, interrupted by a slight bump every time he came up on his left leg. "I'm a rolling stone. I make no moss and don't answer to nobody," his father had said over hamburgers. True to this, Doc had never seen him again.

A week after the visit a drunk lost his money gaming at Odessa's and knocked out the bouncer before working his way behind the bar, where Odessa was scrabbling for a gun. It is a story that Doc has often told. But now, as he unfolds it for Earl as he had for the kid, it again acquires an unusual clarity, stripped of the obscuring patina that coats aged memories too often recalled.

"I was in the kitchen peeling potatoes. I hear this racket and walk out and see this big fella got Odessa laid out on the bar and he's shaking her and yelling in her face. 'Give me my money, you bitch. Give me my money.'"

He remembers the six steps to reach the bar, remembers how easily and unconsciously he shifted the potato knife in his hand so that when he landed on the man's back the knife had already buried itself to the hilt twice, puncturing muscle and scraping against bone.

"When I'm done—when I can see again, first thing I notice is blood on my shoes. Got drops staining the toe caps. Someone come up and take the knife out of my hand and I'm looking at Odessa. She smiles a kind of scared smile—all shook up, but grateful, you know?—and I hear someone say I worked him like a doctor. That," he says, "that is the start of my life. My old man got nothing to do with it."

But Dead Earl has faded with the light. He realizes he is speaking to himself. "Ain't never had a pair of shoes like that since. . . ."

He looks around, sees that the woman and her child have departed without bothering to clear their table. He wonders what they saw. An old man mumbling to himself as he laid about with his mallet? *They ain't gonna send you back to prison, old man, they gonna lock you up within some padded cell with all the other dings.*

* * *

At home, Angie knocks as he washes dishes. He opens the door a crack. She smiles uncertainly, lips crescenting, wavering, a bottle of wine in hand. *Here it comes,* he thinks.

"You find some glasses and let me do this," she says, moving toward the sink.

"I can't be drinking, ma'am. Got to work early," Doc says.

" 'Ma'am'? Why you getting so formal?" She begins washing dishes at a fantastic rate.

"Just being respectful."

"You got music?" she asks, looking at him over her shoulder.

"No." He watches her, bent over the sink, belatedly realizing the motivation for her offer has less to do with cleanliness than with the view of her behind. It's clumsily endearing. He checks his watch. His EM call is likely to arrive any minute. His eyes linger on her.

Angie dries her hands. "Who's this fine-looking couple?" she asks, pointing to the prom picture taped to the enameled door of the refrigerator. Doc's fictitious children stand before a pink back-drop, startled by the camera.

"My son and his girl," he lies. He rests a hand on the phone.

"Mmmm-hmmm," she nods. "That boy got your looks. What's he do?"

"Prison."

Angie faces him, arms akimbo. "Uh-huh."

"It's true. Got married and he found his wife with another man. Had a gun ..."

"He shot her?" Angie takes a step back.

"Everybody act like a fool from time to time," he says. "And you know everybody got a gun. Just a matter of time. ..."

"I got a gun and never shot nobody yet."

Great, thinks Doc as she stares at him. He is acutely aware of the EM band on his ankle, of the fact that he'll have to pick up the phone as soon as it rings. He glances again at his watch.

"You ain't never shot nobody, have you?" she asks.

He hands her the bottle. "I appreciate the sentiment and all, Miss Angie, but you got to go." He herds her toward the door as the phone begins ringing.

"But I thought—"

He forces the door to the frame and locks it before rushing to the phone.

After his check-in he considers descending to apologize, but he is relieved to be alone and glad to have avoided a scene. Crush or no, he doesn't think she'll keep him around more than a minute if she learns where he's been. He sits at the table and distractedly pages through the phone book, mind wandering, wondering what Bunt is up to, if he, too, has been hitting the bottle heavy. He has Rebo's number scrawled on a napkin but doesn't dial, still holding out the hope that, somehow, there will be a reward for his efforts at this life, some acknowledgment of his struggle to replace the indifference of strangers.

5

The Conductor sways, mumbles, "Gimme a ticket," in a deep rasp. Doc has nicknamed him the Conductor both for the Night Train he drinks and for his habit of holding his hand out to every passerby he encounters. The cashier places a bottle of Night Train in a bag on the counter. Behind her a security camera juts from between stacked cigarette cartons. There is no pinprick red light to mark it active; Doc wonders if they bother to keep it on.

The Conductor chucklecoughs at the sight of the wrapped bottle. He laboriously places quarters, dimes, and nickels side by side, aided in his arithmetic by the cashier's impatient fingers.

A half-pint of Seagram's gin and potato chips for Doc, who already has a bag of Taco Bell burritos in hand. He'd buy more booze, but has left most of his cash at home. To the cashier's left, attending a separate line, a man works the second register. The open drawer offers a glimpse of stacked $100 and $50 dollar bills. *$Checks$Cashed$Here$* reads a sign pasted to the register. The first of the month and business is brisk. The line of people waiting to cash their SSI and AFDC checks extends almost to the glass doors.

As Doc exits he notes a bullet hole in the glass that has been sealed with packing tape.

Two teenage girls strut past the storefront. The smaller girl wears a crop-top that exposes the chocolate skin of her toned midriff. Her friend, heavier and buxom, has thin braids that sway counterpoint to the roll of her hips. Doc's eyes widen. He thinks of Blondelle sitting beside him at Odessa's.

The old man steps between Doc and the girls, open bottle cradled in the crook of his arm, a deeply seamed hand extended. "Change. Got change." He shuffles slowly, like an exhausted tap dancer, eyes fixed on a distant point past Doc's right shoulder.

"You was to see me and not some mark and you might get some green," Doc says as he shoulders past, embarrassed that this lack of recognition has upset him.

The U Street traffic has thickened with the night. Car-stereo bass thrums beneath the patter of horns and squeaking brakes. The humid, gauzy air blurs the streetlamps and smudges the trails of passing headlights. Doc crosses the street just behind the girls and pauses by the stoplight as they continue on their easy and unhurried way. The stoplight's switching box clunks just above his head. A white sports coupe pulls an illegal U-turn amid a blare of horns, slowing to pace the girls. The driver's window rolls down. "Hey baby . . ."

A white Mercedes with bad brakes squeaks to a stop scant feet from Doc, unable to beat the red light. Doc glances distractedly from the girls to the car and back again, jerking his head for a double take. Cue Ball is squeezed into the passenger's seat along with a girl. Doc wants to look away before the boy sees him, but cannot. As the light shifts Cue Ball's eyes flick to him, catch. Dead eyes. The brake lights brighten, but the car is in the middle of the intersection and the surrounding cars honk until the Mercedes moves forward.

Doc exhales slowly, watching until the tanklike car disappears. Across the street someone is waving at him. Angie. He sighs again and waits as the lights again shift.

"Don't you got better things to do than be out in the street?" Angie says as she joins him. She cradles a small bag in her arms.

"You should be home, too. What you doing out so late?"

"Well, it ain't usual."

Doc nods, intent on getting home without being sighted again by Cue Ball. He wonders if they'll circle back. "Let's get to the house."

Angie smiles.

"I used to work for the National Gallery," she says. "You been there?"

Doc glances behind them but doesn't see the Mercedes.

"It's on the Mall," Angie adds.

"You paint for them?"

"Just with Windex. But you ought to see it." She brushes against him.

"Yeah?" Doc says.

"On account of the art."

"Huh."

"I just did janitorial stuff, but it was good benefits." She opens the entrance gate to the house and turns, her face inches from his. "And there was all sorts of beauty. All around." She kisses him quickly, the sweet hint of wine warming his mouth.

"Angie..."

"Hush." She kisses him again, then opens her door. "I ain't going to ask you in."

He stares and she smiles, softly shuts the door.

He mixes the Seagram's with ginger ale and ice, and eats, waiting for his EM call. Neither the food nor the liquor seems to cut the taste of Angie's kiss. And there's the disturbing fact of his erection. *Shit, she got to be sixty,* he thinks. *You just getting too desperate. If you was to be working it, you'd already have something else going. Wouldn't even be considering this.*

Later, after the call, he finds himself pleasantly drunk outside of Angie's door. He crouches; the bottom edge is wedged with light.

"You didn't say I couldn't come in," he says when she answers his knock. Her eyes drop a moment and she tucks her hair behind her ear.

Her apartment is warm and dark. The walls are crowded with framed sketches and watercolors, almost all portraits. The air is layered with smells—spiced food, perfume, the dusty scent of damp corners—a heavy mix that speaks of windows too rarely opened.

Doc peers at a painting. The subject is shaded with sere olive and brown. Wide, strong chin, domed forehead balding. The eyes have a penetrating glint.

"You do this?"

"That's Charlie," Angie says. She smiles wistfully. "My husband. He used to work at the National Gallery, too. Security. That's how we met."

"Yeah?"

"A good man, good husband. He'd sit for me all day, sometimes." Her voice trails off.

Doc clears his throat, listens to the drone of a fan. "You want me to go?"

Angie hugs her arms to her. "I don't know."

Doc reaches for her, lets her arms encircle his waist and her head rest on his shoulder. "Why do you get angry so easy?" he asks.

She stiffens. "I don't have to justify myself."

He moves to kiss her and she draws back hesitantly. Their lips meet in a lingering kiss and of the same accord they pull away. He regards her. Above her pendulous breasts wing the delicate shadows of her collarbones. Age has slackened the skin of her neck, and the weight of her face is apparent, the wrinkles like stress fractures before the shear. Belatedly he realizes he's staring. "I got to get to sleep," Doc says. He feels awkward and unsettled, a roiling in his stomach. He smiles.

Angie nods.

All that drink fucking up your judgment, he thinks as he climbs the stairwell.

That night, in the moments before the dark of sleep, in the moments when the ghostly images and echoes of Tyburn surface, Angie's face comes into full view, radiant and young in the warp of his mind's lens. A faint, sexual spark, a rush of heat in his loins.

He wakes from a headache, his mouth parched. A burp leaves the taste of bile. He sits up, his head throbbing. *Gin with Taco Bell. What the fuck was you thinking?* He stumbles to the bathroom and sits on the toilet, bleakly listening to the ominous rumblings of his gut. He holds his head, elbows propped on his thighs.

Dead Earl stands in the doorway in his stained overcoat, almost invisible in the dim light of the apartment.

"Can't a man get a little privacy!" Doc shouts. He leans forward and slams the door.

"Need to talk," Earl says, his voice muffled.

"And I need you out of my life. Go find some dead friends of yours—look up Joe Louis or James Brown or some other dead motherfucker—get in your quality time."

"James Brown ain't dead," Earl says.

"Might as well be. And that don't stop you nohow." Doc flushes, washes his face, feeling queasy. There is no more liquor in the house. His arms tremble when he presses the washcloth to his forehead. "Fuck." He decides to go on a liquor run.

When he opens the door, Dead Earl is still standing there. Doc brushes by, pulls on his pants and jams a few dollars into his pocket. He laces his boots. "I ain't talking."

He is quiet on the stairwell, though he knows full well that Angie—more thorough in her stocking of the liquor cabinet—is deaf to any noise he could make. For a moment he wishes that she'd keep her door unlocked so that he could grab a bottle of the Wild Irish Rose she drinks.

The buzzing arc light in front of Lost Weekend Liquors shines like a beacon on the darkened street. Earl walks in step with Doc. "You want anything? Twinkies? Detergent for that dirty-ass coat you wear?" Doc asks.

Dead Earl shakes his head, eyes liquid and sad.

"Shit," Doc says. "You starting to smell dead, even if you ain't. I'll get you some Aqua Velva." He wishes Dead Earl would speak. At the store he tells him to wait outside.

The same clerks are at the registers, both looking tired and pale under the fluorescent lights. They watch him without moving and Doc is suddenly aware of his appearance, of how they might be waiting to see if he pulls a gun from where his waistband touches the small of his back. Wouldn't be surprised if he did, that much is sure. He walks to a side shelf, fingers running over the bottles. The door jingles open. To his right the small Chinese woman's eyes widen.

"Shut up, bitch!" someone yells, although no one has spoken. A man and woman approach the counter, the man waving a long-barreled .45 that looks as if it hasn't been cleaned in a great while. Both thieves wear nylons over their heads that flatten their features, like wax models that have softened from too much heat. Doc raises his hands and the man swings the gun in his direction. "Get on the floor!"

Doc drops, bruising his knees. The cashiers also comply. He remembers the check-cashing line from earlier in the day—first of the month is a payday. *Of all the nights you got to fetch yourself a drink, you dumb motherfucker.*

"Not you!" the man yells to the cashiers.

"You just take it easy, honey," the woman says to her accomplice. "Now," she says to the half-crouched cashiers, "just stand up and do what I say. Just open this register," she taps the cash-checking register with a painted nail, "then the other."

The male cashier hits buttons as the register beeps, getting more panicked. Eventually the recalcitrant drawer slides open.

"You all got a bag?" the woman asks, her tone conversational.

The woman cashier hands her a duffel with LOST WEEKEND LIQUORS stenciled above a smiling bottle.

The concrete floor is cool on Doc's chest. He sees a quarter wedged into the crack where the shelf to his left meets the floor.

The man lowers his gun slightly, his skinny arm tiring from the weight. Doc checks the security camera above the registers. No indication that it's on. He wonders if either thief has noticed it.

The female cashier opens her register, hitting the keys slowly. She seems to have regained her bearings, her face no longer showing any shock. She takes her time, studying each of the robbers intently.

"I need cigarettes!" the man shouts. When neither cashier reacts he screams, "Now!" and brandishes the gun.

"What kind you want, baby?" his accomplice asks, raising a placating hand. With her other she picks at the nylon, which seems to be bothering her eye.

He thinks this over. "Lucky Strikes. Want a carton. Want two cartons."

Doc guesses that the panic button to the silent alarm has long since alerted the police. In any case, the pair has already lingered too long, allowing everyone to calm down and get a good look. Probably their first job—that or they learn slow. They haven't even bothered to check behind the counter for weapons. As they pack the money and cigarettes into the duffel, the door rings. The man wheels around with his gun. "On the floor!" he shouts.

"Change, need change," comes the reply.

"You ain't getting shit but on the floor, you crusty crackhead!"

There is some grumbling, a groan as someone lowers himself to the floor. "Got to have change."

The man grabs a handle bottle of Jim Beam as they rush from the store. Doc rises slowly. Outside a siren wails in approach. An engine revs, tires screech.

Doc makes a beeline for the exit, not wanting to stick around for any cops' questions. The Conductor still lies on the floor and looks like he might soon fall into a doze. Doc steps over him, opens the door to see a police cruiser fly past, closely followed by another that bounces over the curb and skids to a stop just in front of the store. Doc steps back, immediately lying on the floor in the hopes that they won't take him for one of the robbers. Two cops burst in, guns drawn. Doc closes his eyes tightly, face pressed to the floor, waits for the feel of a foot against his neck or a muzzle jammed against his ear.

"They gone?" The first cop is black, a little overweight, with a smooth face yellowed like old paper.

"All gone, Officer Greene," the woman says. "You want a description?" She sounds relieved, already a little bored.

"You all okay?"

Doc opens his eyes, realizes he's being addressed. "Yeah, fine."

He and the Conductor get up while the cops look around. The wino reaches for the door. "Stick around, old man. We need you for questioning," Greene says. He turns to the cashiers. "The perps'll be in custody soon, unless the getaway driver's Mario Andretti."

"Who?" the woman says.

"That security cam working yet?" he asks.

Greene's partner wanders down an aisle. "You want anything to drink?" he yells.

Doc has no ID, knows that he can't stick around for the questioning. If they find out he is on parole and in a liquor store in the middle of the night, a call to Mike will be inevitable. And that is one meeting he won't come back from. He studies the bell on the door. It is small, hangs from a string.

The partner passes Doc with a Coke in hand. "Get a few of those statement forms, Verne," Greene says.

"Yeah," Verne says. He pushes past the door, the bell jingling. Doc walks to the door as it swings shut, making a show of looking outside. He grasps the bell in his fist, muffling it, and jerks it free of the doorhandle. "Think they'll be here soon?" he asks over his shoulder.

The cop pauses questioning the cashiers, shrugs. "You in a hurry?"

"Just want some air," Doc says. "Mind if I stand out front?"

Officer Greene looks him up and down, as if noting him for the first time.

"Ain't used to having a gun in my face," Doc says. "Just need some air." His mouth is dry.

"You got change?" asks the Conductor.

Distracted, Greene says, "What? For what?" He turns his attention to the Conductor, who's thrust a hand at him, palm up. Doc slips out.

Dead Earl sits on the hood of the police cruiser. Officer Verne is in the driver's seat, an upturned Coke bottle to his lips. Doc waits for the man to finish drinking, not wanting to make an obvious run for it. He catches Verne's eye. He points to his abdomen, makes to cross his legs. Verne sticks his head out the window. "You fucking with me?"

"Piss," Doc says. "I got to piss."

"Go inside," Verne says.

"They won't let me use it," Doc says. "You mind if I go out back?"

"That's a misdemeanor."

Doc looks at him, conjuring up a face that is as miserable as he feels. Earl stands. Officer Verne looks right through Earl, sighs. "All right. Come back here when you finish. Got to fill out a volunteer witness statement."

"Yessir." In thirty seconds Doc is two blocks away, heart hammering. Behind him Dead Earl labors to keep up. Doc ducks into an alley and crouches behind a derelict car for a few moments to catch his breath. He wonders if they'll bother to look for him, weighing the risk of waiting versus that of sprinting to his apartment. He sprints, making it to the house, fumbling with his keys, feeling the blessed wash of relief as he closes the gate behind him.

"You going to do it, ain't you?" Dead Earl pants as Doc strips out of his sweat-drenched shirt.

"What?"

"Go back to what you was," Dead Earl says.

"I ain't never going to be who I was, Earl." He stares hard at the apparition. "But there's times when I wish I could." He walks to the kitchen and pulls a knife from the dishrack, presses it against his EM band. Earl says nothing. *You gonna break it one way or another,* thinks Doc. And he is certain of this. Whether by chance and poor luck or decision, breaking parole seems inevitable. He is too ill adjusted and uncertain—of this world, of himself—to navigate such waters. All these months of struggle and no one to even notice, much less care. He stares at the knife, the edge just cutting into the band. *And what you gonna do? Get played or be a player.* He sets down the knife, regards Dead Earl. "Go home, Earl," he barks. "Ain't nothing for you here."

6

t is a pleasant afternoon, a slight breeze stirring the early-summer air. Doc and Rebo sit on the stoop of the rowhouse beside Odessa's. Doc is sure that Rebo knows just how much it bothers him to be out like this. He's just finished introducing Doc to the others in his set, who stand and sit about, engaged in conversation or simply enjoying the afternoon. Doc notes a quiet watchfulness to the group: frequent glances across the street to the crackhouse, any car or pedestrian carefully tracked. And the customers seem equally aware in spite of their need, shoulders hunched as if in anticipation of some blow. Other sharp-boned addicts lurk, hungry eyes roving, following the movements of those escorted to the safe house. Doc wonders what has happened to Rebo and his crew in the past few months. Too edgy. And the addicts. He stares hard at a few of them—they're not like the ones he once sold dope to. They've got a look to them like they're vibrating at a high frequency, like glass about to shatter.

The defunct cars parked curbside are bullet-pocked. It occurs to Doc that the cars weren't simply abandoned in front of the house by chance, but rather to provide cover. And the refuse in the alley beside the house—old tires, an overturned Dumpster, even two cracked, concrete highway dividers—obstacles for any person or car in pursuit.

"Let's go in Odessa's," Doc says.

"Just relax," Rebo says. He hands Doc his wrapped quart of Colt .45. Doc takes a pull. His eyes stray to Kelvin, who leans against one of the cars, his German shepherd, T-Rex, stretched at his feet. Kelvin's body looks like it is comprised of crude blocks of bone and muscle, his wide back narrowing in a wedge to meet a squared waist, his angular haircut accenting the cube shape of his head. His brow is markedly heavy, hooding his eyes in shadow; the effect, combined with the corded mass of his body, is chilling. He holds a thick book the size of a heavy dictionary or manual. Maybe a Bible. "What's that boy reading?" Doc asks with a motion of his chin.

Rebo chuckles. "The dictionary, man. Kelvin, he likes two things. Word games is one of them. Likes to bet on his vocabulary. Considers himself a man of letters." He reaches for the beer.

Kelvin's reading to Bibby, a boy with angular limbs and big, clumsy hands who moves his lips when Kelvin pauses to point to words. Doc wonders what it is that keeps the kid so enthralled. To Kelvin's left three of Rebo's moneymen talk animatedly. One casts frequent glances down the street at Blondelle and another woman. Blondelle wears a short skirt of some iridescent material that shimmers and sparkles with each shift of her hips. The man watching her is sag-faced, his mouth agape even when he's not speaking. He reminds Doc of a fish—one entranced by the glittering lure wrapped about Blondelle's waist.

Doc studies the women. Blondelle has the compact curves he likes. He wonders what she charges. Rebo hasn't brought up women yet, but Doc knows he'll have to lie when it comes up. He can't explain why he hasn't been with one since getting out, but he knows paying for sex is something he doesn't want. He hasn't been able to think it through beyond this. All that time obsessing over women, though, all those fantasies—he doesn't know what sex will unlock and this scares him.

"You need to make contacts. This antisocial shit don't fly out here. Ain't like doing your time—"

Doc realizes that Rebo is addressing him. He reaches again for the beer.

"Look to me like the only contacts you going to make out here is with any cop that happens by. Can't believe you pulling this shit out in the open," Doc says.

Rebo sets the bottle between his bent knees. "Got to have a presence," he says. "You don't get no standing hiding like you afraid all the time. And I got a little grease to spread around the beat cops."

"Seem to me that sitting out here every night is like being a stationary target. Think I didn't notice all those holes in the cars? Think I don't read the paper? You got your whole crew sitting in a war zone."

"I'm here, ain't I?" Rebo says. "I got more time on the streets and in the joint than any three dealers. I keep to my territory and the money." Even his dead eye lights. "The money. Crack ain't like nothing you sold. Ain't no getting enough."

"Just cause you ain't dealing at the Strip don't mean you immune to violence. You thinking money is some kind of flak jacket?"

"I don't got to explain shit to you," Rebo says.

" 'Presence,' " Doc says sarcastically. "Ain't you remember why we never got caught with the rock stores? Didn't that teach you nothing?"

Rebo smiles at the mention of this. "Been telling Kelvin 'bout that."

Even then Rebo had been preoccupied with image, Doc reflects. Doc had insisted that Rebo wear a tie when he'd enter the jewelry stores, but was always forcing him to tone down the outfit. Rebo would maintain that if the tie was bright enough, the outfit flashy enough, any potential witness would be too preoccupied with the clothes to get a read on his face.

"Talk about yourself," Doc says. "I don't want to be associated with nothing that wasn't proved."

"Shit. Or what was, either."

Doc smiles, warming to the memory of him and Rebo as they had been.

Doc had made Rebo read a book on gems, and they would try to guess ahead of time the kind of stones that the target store was unlikely to have. Then Rebo would enter and make like he was looking for an engagement ring, stalling with his requests so that he could linger in the store while the clerks scurried to show what they had, his eyes all the while checking for wired cases, for exits, for inventory if he could get a look. In the meantime Doc would familiarize himself with the roads, the location of the police station, plotting an escape route. He'd also call to verify when the store closed, and a few hours afterward to see if anyone had lingered to work late.

The rest of it had always seemed too easy: cutting a hole in the roof with a pickax, then waiting with a rope while Rebo tossed up the cheaper jewelry from the cases with no alarms before moving on to the more expensive items. They were usually far out of town by the time the police arrived on the scene.

"Ain't no reason we can't be better than we was," Rebo declares, and Doc knows that he's been rehashing the same memories.

"Ain't clear to me that things is like they was." Doc motions vaguely at the bullet-riddled cars. "Wasn't no one taking potshots at us then."

A harried-looking woman in a floral-print summer dress joins the trio of moneymen at the car. The skin of her face is stretched too tightly over her features, as if it might split to reveal the bone beneath. Their conversation drops to murmurs and finally one of the men takes a bill from her and motions with his head to the kid sitting with Kelvin. "Bibby! Escort!"

Bibby jerks up from where he sits with Kelvin, his rise more an awkward unfolding of limbs. The boy approaches the woman, tentatively touching her shoulder, the gesture somehow courtly. As he steers her across the street, the man who'd called him scratches at his mustache. "Ten to one he trips 'fore he gets back."

His friends laugh. The fish-faced one pulls a five from his pocket. "You on, Satchel."

Satchel grins. "Wait 'till he hits the stairs."

Kelvin has folded shut his book and risen to stand near the men. He stretches his arms over his head, yawns, but Doc sees something else at work—a tension in his stance.

Across the street, Bibby opens the door for the woman and enters with her. Doc guesses that the pitcher is somewhere indoors with the drugs—Bibby seems too relaxed to be holding. In a few moments he exits, descending the steps two at a time, his foot catching on the last. But he doesn't fall, just catches himself with a quick step.

"That's a trip!" Satchel says. "You saw it!"

"Wasn't no trip," the other says. "Got to fall when you trip."

"Was a stupid bet for you to take," Satchel says. "That nigger would fall over even if he had a kickstand screwed to his leg."

The others break into laughter. Kelvin steps forward and effortlessly lifts Satchel by the front of his jean jacket. Satchel knows better than to resist. "Shit, I ain't—"

Kelvin shakes his head. "You should learn to be more tolerant," he says, "or I will kill you."

Satchel says nothing.

Rebo nudges Doc. "Said there's two things he likes. Words and what you see there. Call him the Kelvinator cause he got the freeze. He likes control. Or as he says it, 'imposing my worldview.' He got some German word for it."

"Why don't you offer Bibby an apology?" The Kelvinator says. He lowers Satchel.

Rebo chuckles. "That boy, he gonna do well."

"So what the fuck he doing here?" Doc asks.

"Fuck you," Rebo says. "Cousin," he adds. He drinks and stares moodily at Doc. "And don't you be worrying 'bout me getting shot up."

"I ain't worried about you," Doc says.

Doc's memory of his final encounter with Byron Cripps hovers in the periphery of his mind's eye. He rubs a hand over his stomach, reaching up under his shirt, feeling the two raised knife scars on his stomach, hearing the sound of Cornelius's shovel splitting bone. He swallows, looks at his feet.

"Okay. So who you paying rent to over at that warehouse?"

"Don't matter as long as the rent gets paid." Rebo lights a cigarette.

Doc rolls his eyes.

"I got it under control," Rebo says, flashing his unsettling half-smile, the expression both animate and flat.

Rebo stands and enters the house. Doc stares at Kelvin and the others, not really seeing them, eyes moving slowly up the block, tracing the contours of the bricked-up or burnt-out rowhouses. He thinks of his parole hearing in Tyburn, of Herrig's voice asking him how he planned to cope with life outside, how he'd thought back to when and where he'd started dealing. The reality before him seems no different from that mental image. *Shit. What did you expect? Acting like prison turned you into some fucked-up idealist.*

Rebo returns with another Colt 45. He takes the bag from the empty and wraps the new, handing it to Doc. Rebo motions for Kelvin.

"What you got there," Doc says.

"Volume of the *Oxford English Dictionary*," Kelvin says, hefting the book.

"You get women with that act?"

Kelvin grins. " 'Nadir,' " he says.

"What?"

" 'Nadir.' What's it mean?"

"Shit," Doc says. "I ain't stupid, that's what you thinking." He lifts his beer, thinks. " 'Low point.' "

Rebo laughs.

Kelvin nods respectfully.

"You always like this?" Doc asks.

Kelvin shrugs, deltoids bunching. He's younger than Doc first thought: twenty, twenty-one.

"So you bet on the words?"

"Passes the time," Kelvin says.

Doc flips a few of the onionskin pages carefully, squinting to read the fine print. " 'Transubstantiate.' "

Kelvin thinks, shakes his head. "Damn."

"That puts me ahead," Doc says.

Rebo claps Doc on the shoulder before rising. "Kelvin got debt markers from just about everybody I know. Maybe you gonna be the one to even the scales." He rises and Doc follows him to the Caddy.

Evening fades, a red smear over the blocky silhouette of the D.C. skyline, clouds massing to the east. The air smells of rain. Doc stamps on the accelerator, his pulse jumping with the surge of the Cadillac, as it has for over an hour. Rebo waves his cigar. "Slow down, nigger! This ain't no Tonka Toy you can bust up in your sandbox!"

Doc accelerates again on a straight, eases off as they drop to the Rock Creek Expressway. The thrill of driving has not worn off all afternoon. The dusky light fades, the overarching trees hemming the parkway shielding them from the oppressive darkness of the incoming clouds. Rebo puffs his cigar. The air is clouded with smoke.

"Let's go to Odessa's," Rebo says. His seat is angled back so that Doc can't see his face, only the languid rise of his gesturing arm, hand tipped by the glowing coal of the cigar.

Doc turns up the radio, buoyed by the solid beat of the music, tapping his fingers on the steering wheel as he tracks the bass line.

"And no tickets," Rebo says. "You get us a ticket and I'll beat your ass for the cops."

"Only one thing you could beat," Doc says, motioning to his crotch.

"Fuck you, you childish motherfucker."

The headlights bore a tunnel into the night, the car following, engine humming throatily. Soon they are back in Northeast. The streets are buckled and pitted, rowhouses askew like rotted teeth, city blocks little more than scarred wreckage. As if the neighborhoods burnt in the chaotic wake of Martin Luther King's assassination have been burnt again and again. The car rocks over a decaying mattress that's been thrown in a deep pothole as an attempt at urban renewal. Near a stop sign two young boys dance about a swaying wino. Doc realizes they are kicking him—jump kicks, spin kicks, side kicks, crescent kicks—the old man a live practice dummy. The wino seems only vaguely aware of his tormentors and divorced of outrage, registering this attack as one would cold rain or an ugly wind, an inevitable fact of his surroundings.

"You see that," Doc says. He hasn't ventured this far into Northeast since getting out of Tyburn. It's hard to believe that what surrounds him isn't some twisted mirage.

Rebo nods, having lapsed into silence.

"What the fuck is all this?" Doc asks, still watching the kids kick at the wino. It doesn't look like he'll keep on his feet for much longer. "Broken," Doc adds, gesturing helplessly. "Windows, houses, streets, people."

Rebo laughs harshly. "You think all crack money comes from nowhere? Think those crackheads just suddenly appear? This is it, man. This is the market, the source. And all you got to do is open your eyes to know it ain't gonna last. Few more years and there ain't gonna be nobody around to smoke no crack."

Doc turns the corner, the headlamps sweeping past an overturned Dumpster half in the street. "It don't bother you?"

"Shit," Rebo says. "I ain't the one who made it like this. Don't go judging me. Whole city was falling apart *before* I got out. I just want to keep a part of what was for myself. Think Odessa's would be around without me?" he asks. "I want my home. My life. And if other parts of the city, other fuckups, if they got to go, then so be it."

"You don't make no goddamn sense," Doc says.

"You just ain't figured out how it is." Rebo waves his cigar. "You wait. See ruthless little motherfuckers, ten, eleven years old, strapped and looking to kill your ass—see what those crackheads will do for a hit—see all that and you'll grab what you can."

Doc shakes his head.

"You don't know, Doc. This ain't no place for no code. Ain't no morality here." Cigar smoke uncoils from his nostrils. "If you can't see that then stay the fuck out and the fuck away from me."

Doc is unable to respond. There is little comfort in knowing that Rebo feels equally misplaced and embattled.

They park at the far corner of the block where Odessa's sits. Next to Odessa's, Rebo's set still sprawls over the stoop of their rowhouse, light from an open door spilling over the dark figures. People mill about. One person dances in the middle of the street as those watching holler and clap. There is a steady influx of customers, noticeable for the speed and focus with which they walk to the moneymen, to the opposing crackhouse. Thunder rumbles distantly.

Odessa's is half-full, dense with noise and humid heat. Light from an outside arc lamp breaks through the blue and green glass beads that shield the windows, spangling the bar with cool spots of color: entering is like diving into the waters of a fecund swamp.

Doc and Rebo sit at the bar, watching the men and women at the pool tables, listening to the white noise of conversations and music. The crowd is a disparate lot, tending toward late middle age, clothes running from the grimy and tattered to a few sharp suits complete with tie pins and vests.

"So," Rebo says, "you going accept what I owe."

"You don't owe me a damn thing."

"You got dumb since you got out, nigger?"

"Can't you forget that shit? Spent the last thirty years running your mouth about something made me sorry I ever done it. This ain't no western," he says, frowning. "And it ain't like no numbers slip you got to pay, hear? You got shot, I put you in a car. End of story." Yet he knows that this is not true. Even as he attempts to dismiss it he recalls the sticky heat of Rebo's blood, hears his young, terrified voice—*Shit, Doc, I got blood leaking everywhere, Doc, Doc*—remembers Rebo's face, imploring eyes fixed on him as he cinched the belt tight above the leg's wound.

"No forgetting it," Rebo says, shaking his head. "It or what happened between then and now. Wouldn't be no now, wasn't for you."

"Hah. All that happen 'tween then and now is we spent too long in prison. You going to thank me for that?"

"That's different." He drinks, motions for more. "How you gonna get by? Shaking those fries? Running your mouth on some corner? Rapping some sorry story to whitey to get chump change? You a fucking convict. Ain't no way to explain all those years away. And you wouldn't be coming around here, you didn't want to get back in the Life."

The alcohol in Doc's stomach sits like a hot rock. Flash sets down whiskey shots.

Rebo's voice softens. "Best take what I'm offering, Doc. Got to stick with your people."

Doc drinks in one long swallow, bangs the glass on the bartop. "My people? I got family is my people!"

"Yeah." Rebo nods slowly. The right side of his mouth hints at a half-smile. "You seen 'em?"

"Fuck you!"

The smile is definite now. "Okay," Rebo says, tone reasonable, "then what you here for?"

"Who you paying rent to?" Doc asks.

Rebo reaches into his pocket, peels several bills from a roll and slaps them on the bar. "I knew you had heart," he says. "I knew you hadn't gone and changed on me."

Doc is sad that his friend believes this, sad but not surprised. Sad, too, that he finds himself believing it. He takes the money, walks to the bathroom. *Don't go blaming nothing on Rebo. You can pretend all you want, but you made the decision to come out here. Ain't no one responsible but you.* The smell of bleach and hum of the fluorescent light reminds him of McDonald's. He leans over the sink, studying his face in the metal mirror. He is tired and has to leave to answer his EM call. He splashes water over his face, wiping his eyes clear to see Dead Earl over the right shoulder of his reflection. In the bright light Earl's jaundiced skin is shown to good effect: He looks more corpselike than usual. Doc does not turn. "Damn, Earl." Doc attempts a smile. "What is it with you and the bathroom? There something you ain't telling me? Some animal attraction that leaves you powerless?"

Dead Earl stares. His face is skull-like but for the lack of a grin. Water burbles in the sink's drain.

Doc shakes his head and lets out a dry laugh. "Go home, Earl. This ain't for you." He pulls his sleeve over his left hand and rubs the mirror as if to remove a smudge, Earl's sad reflection fading with each pass.

In the main room Rebo stands with his arm around Blondelle, kissing her on the neck. She tries to push away halfheartedly, then gives in, waiting for him to tire.

Doc lingers, watching the crowd: the slow circling of the pool players; the back-slapping; Flash moving right and left in the slot behind the bar; people swaying before the jukebox to a dolorous song. Doc's eyes pull again to Blondelle and he can almost taste her, can almost feel her beneath his hands, feel the perfect curves of her flaring waist.

It is nearing ten o'clock. He motions for Rebo as he crosses the bar, trying not to look at Blondelle. Rebo walks him up the steps and outdoors. The wind is gusting, laden with rain. Doc decides to walk. "You going to answer my question? About the rent?" he asks Rebo.

Rebo nods and waits a beat. "Cripps," he says. "Levonne Cripps. That's who runs it all." The wind shivers between them. "What? You know the nigger?"

"I got to go," Doc says. "Got my parole check in twenty minutes."

Rebo laughs, the dark, metallic blue of his warm-ups shifting black beneath the faint globe of the streetlamp. He raises a hand. "You know where to find me."

Throughout the walk home Doc tries to shake the image of the kid in his last moments, the flat-eyed stare out in the prison yard as he jabbed with his shank. He wonders if Byron's brother, Levonne, has those same eyes.

7

At work, Doc finishes with refilling the cup dispensers and joins Walker in the back of the kitchen. It is evening and long after the dinner rush, the restaurant as empty as the streets of the surrounding business district. Walker cleans the grill with a spatula while staring balefully up at a speaker. The Muzak is a version of "In the Hall of the Mountain King" played at double speed with what sounds like kazoos. Walker seems unaware that he's scraping the spatula against the grill in time. When the music abruptly ends, he gives a little cheer. Eduardo emerges from his office, smiling. Salsa rhythms begin pattering from the speakers.

If it's gonna be hot . . . Eduardo shuffles his feet and spins on the tiled floor fronting the counter, dancing with an invisible partner.

Doc moves to the counter for a better look, stocking shelves with McNuggets sauce, packets of lemon juice, take-out bags, and napkins, pausing between trips to the storage room to watch Eduardo. Eduardo dances with his eyes closed, shoes scuffing the tiled floor. He smiles faintly. Doc wonders who it is he's dancing with, realizing how little he knows of the man and, with a sudden weight, how long it's been since he himself has danced. Decades since he last moved with a woman over the floor of a dance hall—who had it been? Not Lydia, his ex. And though he cannot remember the face or name of this distant partner, other details are markedly crisp: his open palm pressed flat to the small of her back; the smooth curve of a neck, fine tendrils of hair loose just behind her ear; the intoxicating scent of perfume and sweet breath. *Damn,* he thinks. *Damn damn damn.* He sometimes hears music wafting from Angie's apartment. It's surprisingly easy to picture himself dancing with her.

Eduardo continues to shuffle as the music fades, for a moment dancing in silence. Doc sees Walker watching. Their eyes meet and they look guiltily from one another, as if caught in an indecent, voyeuristic act. They turn to their work. Soon Eduardo desists.

Doc's been working hard—six days a week with some double shifts thrown in, on time and patient for the duration of his last three parole meetings, and yet it seems more and more an act, duties performed with a sense of remove, as if watching himself from behind a pane of glass. Still working, still jogging, still meeting with Mike, each day, each hour, each transition mentally rehearsed as if the days are a kind of dance that must be precisely choreographed if they are to be performed at all. And a performance is what it is: As if, done well enough, it will convince him that he will not begin working for Rebo in a mere two days.

He fills the mop bucket with hot water and wheels it to the bathroom. The reek of piss slaps him as he opens the door. Urine is puddled in the seams of the tiles. Drawn on the mirror above the sink is a large circle around two crossed guns topped by a wide-mouthed skull with narrowed eyes. Doc punches at the mirror with the mop head until the image smears before working on the floor. He hasn't seen Cue Ball in the restaurant this shift but knows the boy must have slipped in for just this. Doc had hoped that the boy had been a casualty he'd missed in the *Post,* but it's more likely that there was other mayhem to commit before returning here—an old man at McDonald's can't be high on the boy's list of priorities.

He mops, thinking about the boy eyefucking him from the window of the Mercedes, about the fact that a little hoodlum is stalking him, eager to add to his street rep. The boy will keep coming in, and sooner or later it will come back to a replay of the first confrontation. There is something to this moment, ineffable and binding, as if the two of them are paired. An underlying aggregate of circumstance, character, and past freighted with momentum, as if the man and boy were aimed at one another long before they had ever met, powerless to prevent collision. He rinses the mop and cleans the mirror in earnest. When he is done he stares at his reflection, his pulse accelerating. *Twenty years as a heavy in the D.C. Blacks. Cue Ball is nothing. Boy ain't shit.*

He knows his conflict with this boy cannot end well, has thought of this often in the past weeks. Of the possible outcomes, a lost job seems the best to hope for, even though this will threaten his parole. A familiar ache coalesces in his stomach. What if Cue Ball uses his gun? There's Walker and Eduardo to think about. The next time Cue Ball shows, he and Doc will both do what they must. *May as well kiss this job good-bye and pack for Tyburn.* But there is a final option, and no matter the specter of Levonne Cripps and his dead brother Byron, he is thankful that Rebo found him, that he has somewhere to go.

"Got to make your own options," he says to the mirror. "Take the initiative. Square John trip ain't nothing but an act." He's struck by the set of his face. The lines etched in his forehead and framing his mouth make it look as if he's wearing a mask, each a seam connecting an assemblage of aged features. "Time for the street," he says. "For respect."

Before shift ends he visits Eduardo in his office, knocking softly at the door.

"What do you need, Kane?" Eduardo asks.

Doc clears his throat. He pulls out an envelope containing four $1,000 postal orders made out to Walker, a combination of his savings and money Rebo has loaned him interest-free against future earnings. "I want you to give this to Walker."

Eduardo eyes the envelope for a moment after Doc sets it on his desk.

"You quitting?"

Doc shakes his head. "He won't take it from me, is all. Too proud."

"Too proud?"

"His aunt ain't right. Lung cancer. He tell you that?"

Eduardo shakes his head.

"I don't got to tell you he got a brother to watch and a second job."

"I seen the Domino's hat."

"He going to need this sometime," Doc says with a nod to the envelope. "I don't trust myself to hold on to it—had a problem gambling in the past," he half lies, thinking of Grippe at his parole hearing. "You just make sure he gets it down the line. Few months from now. Call it a tax refund or something—just make him take it and don't tell him where it come from."

Eduardo leans back in his chair. "You trust me with your money?"

"You know what's right," Doc says. "And you like the boy. As much as me."

Eduardo nods.

"He need someone to watch out for him. That's us," Doc says. "That's what this is."

Eduardo takes the envelope and places it in a drawer. "You do a good job here, Kane."

"I know it," Doc says. But the compliment feels empty.

The following morning Angie opens the door as Doc pulls his shirt on.

"Lord, you look like you rolled in some barbed wire," she says.

"Ought to wait when you knock."

"Least you ain't got tattoos."

"Don't start on art again, okay? Let's just wait until we get to wherever we going," Doc says.

Angie hums as they walk to the metro, grasps his arm when they cross intersections. Such close proximity is vaguely claustrophobic, though Doc is also glad for her company—a day off with no thought to the specter of Cue Ball is something he needs. She's brought an old calendar with her that features a sampling of painters and she opens this, pointing to one of the works being shown at the National Gallery.

"Edward Hopper," she says, "now, he got soul, but it's white soul."

"White soul," Doc says. "Hah! That's like white rhythm."

Angie laughs. "No, you just got to look for a while and then you see it start to come out of the painting, real clean and somberlike. Lonely, kind of restrained." She shows him the painting *Nighthawks*, the elements of the evening café scene immediately familiar to Doc, who remembers seeing something like it in someone's cell.

"See those colors? Like that green and gray? What does that make you feel?" Angie asks.

"Ain't Elvis supposed to be in this as the soda jerk?"

"There ain't no Elvis here. Now what do you think?"

Doc shrugs. He touches a finger to the dark face of the street behind the diner. "Cold."

Angie nods.

"You got others in there?" Doc asks. As she flips through the calendar Doc surreptitiously examines her face. The fluorescent lights reveal the topography of her wrinkles and pores in unforgiving detail. Her makeup has been carefully applied, though a border of lightly colored base contrasts with the natural, slightly darker hue of her skin where it hasn't been blended near her hairline. He doesn't know why it seems so easy to focus on the flaws in her appearance. She glances at him and smiles almost coquettishly, her hand unconsciously moving to her hair.

She moves on to the next, Gauguin's *Where do we come from?*

What are we? Where are we going? Bright Tahitian nudes burst from the page.

Doc chuckles at the title. "He ain't the first to get philosophical around naked women."

Angie gives him a look. "That ain't the point of it."

They first visit the East Wing of the National Gallery, the stone of the blank facade glowing cleanly in the sunlight. Clustered tourists clot the airy entranceway. Angie, recognizing someone, pulls Doc toward the coat-check, introducing him to a friend from her days as an employee. During the course of the conversation a museum guard joins them. The sight of a uniform puts Doc on edge. He stands at the periphery of the conversation, eyes roving over the influx of visitors who sidle past to leave light coats, satchels, and backpacks at the coat-check counter. As he and Angie walk through the museum she says, "You got to work on your manners."

Doc veers off at the foot stairwell they've descended toward the moving sidewalk that connects the East Wing to the main building. Two kids jump on and turn to walk against the movement of the track, bent forward as if in the face of a great wind. Their mother shakes her head.

"C'mon." Doc pulls Angie by the arm.

"We ain't finished here." But she follows him onto the moving sidewalk. Doc tests his walk, liking the added speed. He stumbles as he gets off, grins.

"What you so happy about?"

Doc shrugs.

Angie stares. "Ain't you never been on one of these?"

"Lots of times," Doc lies.

Angie soon begins to riff about the first painting that catches her interest. Doc listens with half an ear, wondering how long the tour will take. He's not much for museums—this is, in fact, the first he can remember visiting—but he is glad for Angie's company. When she isn't drinking she isn't too bad. A little uptight, but friendly. He thinks back to kissing her. Was it just the liquor acting? She's been overly friendly since. He checks her out. Full-figured, but old. *You could do better.* He admits, though, that he liked it a little when she linked arms with him—it felt courtly. And it's nice, anticipating the train ride home, walking together to the same house. It's suggestive of something larger—of a wife, a home, a companion.

Tied up with this, though, is the issue of renting from her, of leverage, of having to be pleasant. Though he realizes he's already done more than enough to warrant a parole violation, if Angie threw him out it would mean more difficulties with Mike. There's no way to fake your way through an eviction, not with the ten P.M. phone check.

Before heading home they settle on the lower slope of the sweeping hill from which the Washington Monument juts. Frisbees fly. They watch an informal soccer match.

Angie rolls on her stomach and props her chin on her folded arms, studying him. "You want a back rub?"

"I'm fine."

"Well." Angie turns over, stares up at the sky. "You ain't telling me something."

Here we go. "What ain't I telling you?"

"Why didn't you stay that night you was in my apartment?"

Doc shrugs. "You wasn't that enthusiastic, as I remember."

She watches him. "I just thought you'd take charge. You came down there. Seems like you always pulling away, like..."

"Like what?" Doc asks.

"I don't know. There something physical you can't talk about? I seen all those scars...."

"I work just fine."

But he can't deny how uncomfortable the scrutiny makes him. Masturbation has a rote quality to it, something done more out of the comfort of habit than out of need and he knows something in his head isn't right. During his first years in prison he'd think of his ex-wife, Lydia, or past girlfriends for the duration of a fantasy. But as these faces faded he found he had less control, the images of other cons or guards appearing unbidden, the fantasy storyline acquiring a brutal, violent quality centered on power and control. And so for a long time it's been pornography that gets him by; feeling safe among the vaguely abstract images of airbrushed women, feeling safe among fantasies guided by penned storylines that confine his imagination to the secure, sanctioned corridors of his consciousness.

Angie takes his hand, squeezing it. "I don't mean anything bad, William. I'm curious, you know?"

"Like I said, everything works fine."

She continues to lie on her back, her hand on his, and he lets her hold it, ignoring his reservations. *William.* He likes the formality of it, the unfamiliar ring.

"Did you like the gallery?" she asks.

Doc grunts.

"If you wanted, I could get you an interview. For a job."

"I got a job," Doc says. "And I make damn good fries." It's a little embarrassing to hear himself say this; he's surprised to realize that the job feels important, that it has become a source of pride even though he's decided to leave it. "Ain't nothing wrong with restaurant work," he adds belatedly.

"But a government job," she says, "you can get some real security with it. Even comes with health insurance and a pension plan. I still know people in Building Maintenance."

Security, he thinks. *Health insurance. A pension plan. You got no references. And how you gonna lie about your record? The government, they gonna know you for what you is as soon as they run your Social Security number.* "I appreciate it. But I'm happy where I'm at," he says without enthusiasm. *More like you gone as high as you gonna get.* He is filled with disgust and his pleasure with the morning abruptly dissipates. He can pretend, but this is no more than a few hours with his alcoholic landlady. Nothing more can come of it.

8

The tinfoil package is taped exactly where Rebo said it would be. Doc peels it from the porcelain toiletback. It is bigger than he expected. He opens the foil, his hands trembling slightly, revealing the heroin wrapped in tiny, waxed-paper envelopes. Standing there, the drugs in his palm, he's struck by the moment. In prison he'd imagined himself in all sorts of situations out in the real world—going to dinner and a movie, dating, fucking, just catching a cab or jogging through a park; but this moment, it was never even a possibility to be entertained. Not once did he dream of this. He'd changed, right? All that shit, the dealing, the violence, it was behind him no matter what Grippe said, no matter how many times the parole board sent him back to his cell. He closes the package and jams it in his windbreaker's pocket, then washes his face and tries to focus on his new haircut. Through the door he hears a few of the barbers chatting with their customers and the chatter of a baseball game from a TV.

You in the shit now. Possession of narcotics on top of all the rest.

On the way out he nods to the man who cut his hair, eyes settling on Kelvin's Jeep, which has just pulled up outside the front window. Right on time. The sunshine glows through the Jeep's clouded plastic windows. The air is very dry, giving the view of the city a singular clarity; such sharp focus brings to mind the rarefied Nevada atmosphere, and Doc realizes with a start that he's missed the cool crispness of morning desert air. In the back, behind Kelvin's German shepherd, T-Rex, Doc has an iced six of beer and several sandwiches in a cooler. That and a cheap fishing rod and folding deck chair.

"'Selachian,'" Kelvin says.

"Shit," Doc says. "You got to at least ask words that get used. Adjective?"

"Yeah."

"You get the point, but under protest."

"You want the definition?" Kelvin asks.

"I ain't never going to hear it again, so no."

"Not even curious?"

"Not even. Now keep quiet. I got to clear my head, get ready for fishing," Doc says.

"You bring sunblock?"

"Brought comic books. 'Lycanthropy'?"

"Too easy," Kelvin says.

They pull onto Ohio Drive and then into the lot of the unassuming National Park Service Headquarters. The lot is usually close to empty, and while much of the traffic into East Potomac Park passes through this area, few linger, most visitors intent on reaching Hains Point or the golf course. Kelvin leaves his jeep aimed in the direction of 395, which heads over the river into Virginia. If they need to, they can get out of the District in less than a minute. Doc unfolds his chair in the shade of Long Bridge, looking out across the Potomac. A freight train rocks overhead, the weight of it shivering down the bridge supports and through the cement of the sidewalk, vibrations emphasizing the steady rhythm of the clicking wheels.

Thick girders crisscross the underside of the bridge, the spiderwebs spun between them popping into view when light mirrored by the river glances up to illuminate their geometric lacing.

Once gunmetal gray, Long Bridge is now virescent, the narrow band of painted metal mirroring the spectrum of the green river and slate sky. Rust streaks trail from the sides, discoloring the ochre stone supports that rise from the Potomac.

Doc leans back in his deck chair and casts his rod, the lure spinning out in an arc and plunking into the still water. A few men dot the bank, desultorily casting their rods. Leaving the rod leaning against the sidewalk railing Doc tries to relax, glancing once to his left. Kelvin has finished walking T-Rex, at the same time having planted several packets, which he's placed in magnetized key cases: one stuck to the inside of the lip of a covered garbage can in front of the headquarters walk, another to the underside of a nearby bench, another to the metal railing where it faces the river—Doc guesses Kelvin's set out five or six. Each time a customer comes by to pay Doc, he sends them up the walk to Kelvin, who directs them to their package. He doesn't think Kelvin likes working for Doc, given he's been with Rebo longer, but this arrangement does keep either of them from handling the drugs too often. In the cooler, Doc has an empty plastic ice pack with a slit cut into it where he stores the money.

As the first sales occur—the referred customers wary around him, but no trouble—he becomes marginally more comfortable, somewhat secure in the fact that this dealing setup seems to be working for Rebo in other spots.

Kelvin joins him for lunch, the pair studying the polished expanse of the river. It is warm and the beer makes Doc feel pleasantly lethargic. T-Rex licks Doc's ear, then makes a grab for Doc's sandwich.

"Shit, keep that damn dog away!" Doc says.

" 'Salivate,' " Kelvin says. " 'Lachrymate.' "

"Crocodile tears," Doc says.

Something catches Doc's lure, and Kelvin lunges forward, grabbing the rod. He starts to play the fish, but lets Doc take the rod from him. Doc jerks sharply, then again, the line abruptly going slack. He smiles. "I hate fish."

"You ever sail?" Kelvin asks. "Go out on the Chesapeake or the Atlantic?"

"I ain't much for water," Doc says. "Take the desert any day."

"You get used to it at Tyburn?"

Doc ponders this, wondering how much of Doc's life Rebo has relayed to Kelvin. "A little," he says. "Hard to spend so much time in a place without it leaving a deep mark."

Across the river, planes angle down or rise from the tarmac of National Airport, the repetition of landing patterns comforting.

He remembers seeing TV coverage from a plane crash on the 14th Street Bridge when he was in prison. A low-bellied plane caught on the bridge, fracturing into chunks of wreckage. A few years past, maybe '83? He pictures the slab of the Potomac, the white of ice, and above this the haze of falling snow. While at the D.C. Community Treatment Center, two months after his release, it had snowed. Wide flakes had fallen, languorous in descent, piling thick on the ground. Hackneyed or not, he'd marked that day as the start of something new, a day notable for a purity and reflective silence, qualities evidenced by the thick blanket of snow that damped the spasmodic city noise and glowed a clean white. He'd stood, face upturned, the feather-soft brush of snowflakes touching his skin and melting, overwhelmed with a vibrant optimism that has since faded. Now he has Dead Earl. A bad dream that isn't content to reside in the confines of his head. And Kelvin—a young dealer eager to hear Doc start war-storying, like the mess of his past is something to crow over.

He studies Kelvin's blocky profile, wonders what he's gotten himself into. He remembers the drive with Rebo, thinks of the daily *Post* articles describing the violent frenzy that surrounds the crack trade. Rebo's plan to keep small, isolated cells around the city—areas distant from the bustle of Malcolm X Park or the O Street Market—areas where modest sales can be made a few days a week in anonymity—seems to Doc as insubstantial as the high offered by the drugs he sells. He's glad to be selling heroin, a drug he understands.

"No continuity, no order," Rebo has said. "They just like the

Pepsi Generation in the joint. Hell, they are the Pepsi Generation in the joint. Got no respect for no order. No motherfucking respect." Doc wonders what run-ins Rebo has already had with the street powers-that-be—particularly with Levonne. Or Byron before him. *You in the world of Byron Cripps,* he thinks. *You the new fish out here and this ain't gonna be no easier than getting by in Tyburn.* All that advice wasted on the kid and now it turns out he's the one who needs it most.

He pictures Byron Cripps on that first day in Tyburn, trying to superimpose the image of the scared boy in his cell with that of his face out in the prison yard, the knife in hand; it is difficult to mesh the two, even now. *And now you working for the motherfucker's brother.*

At the end of the afternoon he leaves Kelvin with the day's take. "Need me a walk," he says after loading his cooler and chair into the Jeep. "See you back at Odessa's."

Farther along East Potomac Park picnicking families sit on blankets beneath the cherry trees. Cars cruise Ohio Drive, guys leaning out of the passenger windows to chat up the groups of girls walking along the road's edge. Some boys have parked their cars and opened the doors, filling the air with the rhythmic pulse of reggae, rap, hip-hop. Girls pause at these stops, laughing while guys look up from where they stand polishing their cars to try lines on them, pass the time.

At Hains Point, where the spit of land wedges into the confluence of the Potomac and Anacostia Rivers, Doc wanders onto the grass, lying back to a view of the slow, smooth progression of the scintillant water. Several yards away sits a family of five. The smallest child balances on his seated father's shoulders, burying his tiny hands in his dad's dreadlocks to keep his place, face screwing up with laughter each time his father shifts.

Doc does not think of his family often. He cannot clearly recall the face of his ex-wife, of his daughter, of his son, nor what they might look like now. But for a moment this does not prevent him from trying. Lydia. Mary. Willie.

Willie should be twenty-two by now, likely heavyset and short, like Doc. At twenty-two Doc was enjoying a few years at liberty before his second sentence in Lorton for robbing a bank with Rebo. He hears the voice of his grandfather rumbling a bedside story, sees the image of himself looking at his son as Willie's breathing settles in the wake of the story he has told. A long moment of silence in the dark. His son's small hand in his.

He sits and watches the river, the riverlight rippling and blurring into patterns both random and ordered.

He hasn't been swimming since his release. He imagines walking into the sluggish water, the weight of it pressing against his chest, his arms buoyantly rising from his sides. He soon drifts to sleep, and in his half-waking dream he sees the Potomac rise, sees it spread up the grassy plain of the park, pooling around him, lapping at his feet, lifting him in a swirling mix of warm and cold, in a spectrum of prismatic light, and then he is floating with the currents, spinning, bobbing, now fast, now slow, twisting and rolling as the water rises and rises, pressing against the windows of cars and office buildings, bowing the glass inward until it fractures with sudden crazings, glass shards suspended for a moment before falling slowly in glittering sheets, the old city slowly dissolving. In the water he sees others from his past—Stirling, Odessa, Ellis—moving in a lazy, dreamy drift. Soon, though, he is alone again and growing tired, tired and warm, legs and arms and eyes heavy, feeling placid as he spirals down, sinking to the muddy bottom of a vast well where seaweed matted on yellowed bones waves in the currents.

The blue-and-green glass curtain covering the front windows of Odessa's prisms and splinters the light into an aqueous shade. Two men circling a pool table give Doc a once-over before returning to the game. Feet shift on the tile floor. Billiard balls click. The video games lining the far wall are silent, screens blank. The TV is on but Doc doesn't see Flash around. He steps behind the bar and finds Flash stretched out on the floor mats.

"You all right?" Doc asks.

Flash laboriously gets up. "Just stretching."

"Why they call you Flash, anyway?"

"Fell down some stairs; my legs ain't been right since." Flash's hair is peppered gray and his skin, stippled with moles, is of a match, the light brown of it gray in the light.

"I won't use it, you don't want," Doc offers. It doesn't seem fair to ridicule an injury with the name.

"Been twenty years," Flash says. "Don't know what else I'd go by."

"What's your real name?"

"Grover."

"I hear you," Doc says. The front door bangs open and Blondelle descends the abbreviated staircase slowly, letting her eyes adjust before moving to the mirrored bar. She snaps her gum and winks at Doc. "A drink for the lady, Flash," Doc says. "White Russian, right?" he asks.

Blondelle nods. "You been working with Rebo," she says. Her bracelets jangle musically as she plants her forearms on the bar.

Doc shrugs.

Blondelle waits for Flash to set down her drink and return to the far edge of the bar. She turns to Doc. "I'm working right now, you know."

Doc's mouth is dry.

"You got a rock? I'll suck your dick for a rock."

"I ain't dealing crack," Doc says. "And I don't got nothing on me."

She stares at him, cracks her gum, now chewing more slowly. "You got money?"

Doc finds himself nodding.

The narrow hallway at the back of the bar is as he remembers it. Doc is sure that if he peeled away the cracking paint above the lintel of the rear entrance he'd find the initials he carved there at fifteen. His eyes drop to Blondelle, to the sway of her hips. She leads him into a windowless side room that is overly bright with the light of three bulbs set into a bare ceiling fixture.

"So you and Rebo is old friends," she says.

"You ain't got to pretend to be interested," he says.

"Long as you don't go on war-storying about life back in the day, I'll be interested. Rebo, he don't never tire of that shit." A double snap of the gum.

Without preamble she slips off her ribbed top, revealing her generous breasts. One nipple points toward the ceiling, the other toward the floor. She eyes him disinterestedly, a little impatiently. "You ready?"

He is not. The room was once Odessa's, though the window and side bathroom have been bricked shut. It seems somehow indecent that this is where Rebo's whores take their johns, no matter that Odessa was in the same business.

He stares at her, rooted in place, unsure of how to begin.

"You ain't forgot, has you?" she asks.

"You going to take that gum out of your mouth?"

"I ain't kissing you, that what you asking," she says. "I don't do that."

Her bossiness and confidence annoy him. He reaches out to touch her face and instead draws her roughly to him, forcing her to her knees, wrapping one hand in her hair tight enough that she cries out. "Go to it, bitch," he says, deepening his voice, trying to edge it with threat. It sounds to him as if someone else is speaking, and he closes his eyes.

Her mouth is soft and warm, but it is the sound of her cry replaying in his head that makes him hard. He roughly pushes into her mouth, his breath coming in pants before abruptly pulling away. She looks up at him and he nods toward the bed. He sees that she's rolled a condom onto his penis.

He loosens his belt and drops his pants, kicks out of his sneakers, feeling the grit from the floor on his soles. She sits on the sagging mattress watching, her gum popping intermittently. Her eyes pull to the yellow band of his EM device without much apparent surprise.

Doc inhales, the warm air sour and musty with the scent of unwashed sheets, sex, air freshener. Blondelle pops her gum.

"Get on your stomach," Doc barks.

She sighs.

Doc pushes up her skirt and roughly pulls aside her underwear, forcing himself into her, thrusting hard, his hands bearing down on her shoulders, driving her into the mattress. Moving faster and feeling her move back, automatically crying out an uninspired, Yeah, baby, oh yeah, come on baby, yeah.

His anger drives him to push harder. 'Oh baby, yeah, baby.'

He pulls out. "Don't call me that," he says hoarsely.

She tries to look back at him. "What?"

" 'Baby.' Don't call me that. Call me Doc, you hear? I ain't your baby and I ain't no john like all the others." He forces his dick into her ass. "Doc! You gonna call me Doc!" Sweating, panting, thrusting, repeating Doc, Doc, Doc, dimly aware that she is saying the same in tandem, and then a final contraction, a choking exhalation, an orgasm immobilizing him for a blind, ecstatic moment.

He rolls to his side. Footsteps sound in the hallway. A door slams.

Blondelle sits up, tilts her head to get a better look at him; he won't meet her eyes. He strips off the condom and tosses it in a wastebasket beside the bed.

"You okay, baby?" she asks.

"Just shut the fuck up," he whispers. *Can't even handle no teenage whore,* he thinks.

A knock at the door. "Let's go, Doc! I got appointments!" Rebo's voice.

Doc dresses quickly, thankful for the interruption. He pulls out his wallet. "How much?"

"Fifty."

He hands her the bills, his eyes focused just beyond her left shoulder.

"You ain't got to feel guilty," she says with a hint of something genuine. "Everyone got needs."

In his stomach a growing, nauseal ache makes him want to double over as it constricts his breathing.

"Just shut up," he says. "Shut up." He won't trust himself to look at her. It's in everybody's eyes, he knows—indifference or pity or contempt. No one sees him as he is. He turns and exits quickly.

In the car with Rebo his mood worsens as his friend fidgets with the radio volume. "Leave off with that shit," he says. The last of the light evaporates into the night sky.

"Most people relax when they get laid."

"I don't want to talk about it," Doc says.

"How about work, think you can talk about that?"

Doc shrugs.

"How you do today?"

Doc shrugs again. "Lot of nervous white folk."

"They'll get used to your ugly face, don't worry," Rebo says.

"Where the fuck we going?" Doc says.

"Noplace you ain't been before," Rebo says. "And you don't have to do shit but stay in the car."

"What, like your biggest worry is that your car gonna get stole?"

Rebo turns up the volume of the radio. "You ain't no good for conversation nohow," he says.

"Levonne Cripps," Doc says, the anger from the night welling out. "That nigger ain't nothing. A zero just like his brother. Fear that little motherfucker and it just shows how small you is."

"What do you know about the Cripps brothers?" Rebo says. "Like you some *Dragnet* motherfucker."

"I *know*," Doc says. "Byron Cripps I *know*."

Rebo turns off the radio. "Stop talking shit."

"I *know*," Doc repeats. "Pull the car over," he says, and when Rebo does not immediately comply he jerks the wheel.

"Fuck, Doc," Rebo says, "relax."

Doc turns on the dome light and pulls up his shirt—the scars from Byron's shank are still pink and raised. "Byron Cripps, this was the best he could do. And in the end, I'm here, and that punk, he's underground." His breath comes with a ragged edge as he glares at his friend. "And I'll tell you something else, you and all those you got scrabbling to make you money"—he punches his finger into Rebo's shoulder—"you *soft*. You soft if a Cripps brother got the juice to run your streets."

Rebo stares at his friend and gradually Doc's breathing eases. He starts to chuckle. "Doc Kane. You always thought you was something." He pulls back on the road.

Doc already regrets his outburst. He hasn't felt this much anger in a long while, and though there is something invigorating to the intensity of it, he knows he should have kept it bottled up. That he was involved with Byron's death is a fact best kept secret.

Rebo continues. "Listening to you, it's like listening to some fish, first time in the joint, fronting like he knows it all." He holds up a palm to forestall Doc's response. "They got a different language out here. A different code. And unless you want to end up how Byron did then you better take the time to learn it." He pulls into the backlot with the warehouse they've visited before—Levonne's turf. Rebo gets out of the car, a paper sack filled with money in hand. When Doc opens his door and stands, Rebo stares hard at him. "You ready to learn?"

Doc nods curtly. He'd really like to stay in the car, no matter his talk.

The warehouse door parts to reveal a cavernous room with a bare cement floor. Doc recognizes Levonne immediately—he's slimmer than his brother, but with the same finely carved features and light-colored skin. He sits slumped on a new couch still sheathed in plastic, one of several that line the half-court where a basketball rim with an electronic shot clock has been set up. He's dressed in a loose pair of white sweats and an oversized Georgetown sweatshirt, a mess of magazines at his feet. On the arm of the same couch perches a chubby-faced kid whose eyes are the only hard thing about him.

A piercing, extended scream echoes through the largely empty warehouse amid a clamor of exclamations. On the far side of the warehouse a group of five sits watching a big-screen TV. The screaming dies off gradually, replaced by the mechanical buzz of a hand tool amplified by the stereo speakers on either side of the TV. Paint cans are stacked against two walls.

Rebo smiles and reaches to shake with Levonne, who places a pamphlet in his hand.

"What's this?" Rebo asks.

"Who's this nigger?" Levonne asks.

"Doc," Rebo says. "He's working with me."

"Do I know you?" Levonne says. He looks sleepy, his eyes half-lidded, his speech just barely slurred.

Doc shakes his head.

"Then why you staring?" Levonne says.

"Doc and me go way back," Rebo says. "He just got out the joint."

Levonne tilts his head. "Where you do your time?" he asks.

"Leavenworth," Doc lies.

"Old heads," Levonne says to himself, chuckling and shaking his head. "Ain't you motherfuckers never heard of retirement? Social Security and all that?" He blinks, a slow lidding of the eyes. "So you a old-school con, that right? Like Rebo here?"

Doc nods.

"And that's like a qualification, right? Like I'm supposed to be impressed that you got caught and thrown in jail for shit you done." He glances at his friend on the couch, then again at Doc. " 'Course, you do your job right and you don't do time. Leavenworth, that's just proof you fucked up."

Doc shrugs.

"What does that mean?" Levonne asks.

"Whatever you want it to," Doc says. "Ain't nothing to me what you think about the time I done."

Levonne smiles at this. "Let's have it," he says, motioning for the bag in Rebo's hand. He opens the bag and perfunctorily scans the bills. "That's a real-estate brochure you got," he says to Rebo. "Got listings for houses up in Georgetown. You see the prices they charging for a house?"

Rebo thumbs through it.

"A half million dollars and that don't even mean you get a pool," Levonne says. "No lawn, no garage, even."

Doc studies Levonne. Everything about him seems intentionally slowed, his gestures paced as if underwater. But his eyes don't miss a thing. Doc's eyes glance from his as Levonne looks up.

"No lawn, no garage," Levonne repeats. "You got on-street parking on your block, ain't you?"

Rebo grins, nods.

"That's what I'm talking about," Levonne says. "Got your parking, got a prime retail outlet. Any nigger can drive right up, just like McDonald's. You got commercial zoning is what it is," Levonne says.

The pudgy kid nods. Doc guesses him to be sixteen or so. He wonders how many in Levonne's crew are even old enough to get sentenced as adults. The kid glares, using his best eyefuck, his hand moving unconsciously to the waist of his light jacket. *Little punk-ass gonna shoot me for looking at him wrong,* thinks Doc. He abruptly looks away. *Staring contests. Shit.* He might as well be trying to upstage Cue Ball in the bathroom of the McDonald's over who has the biggest dick—it doesn't make a damn bit of difference. *Everyone so damned concerned with respect they'll do anything for it. Bust a cap in your ass. Throw you through the front doors of a restaurant. You ain't no different from the rest, old man.* More screaming erupts from the TV.

"How many years you do?" Levonne asks, uplifting his chin in Doc's direction.

"Sixteen," Doc says.

"That's a good number," Levonne says. "What you think, Rebo? You like that number?"

Rebo nods uncertainly, the right side of his face as dead as the scarred left.

"I need to make me some capital improvements," Levonne says, gesturing vaguely about him. "Get me some track lighting and shit." He nods to himself. "Next time you come, I want what's in here plus sixteen percent."

"Shit," Rebo says. "I ain't doing no more business than before. I can't pay that."

Levonne addresses Doc. "Did I ask him a question?"

Presence, thinks Doc. No different than his brother. Doc shakes his head.

"That's *right,*" Levonne says. He motions with his head toward the door. Rebo and Doc take their leave.

9

Mike lights the third cigarette of the interview. *Five minutes a cigarette,* thinks Doc. *Got twenty minutes left.* Doc wonders when Bunt's scheduled to come in. Knowing that his old friend has been sitting in the same folding chair and enduring the same stupid meeting makes it easier to bear. He's thought about looking Bunt up, though he entertains this in much the way he entertains other daydreams—it's one thing to break your own parole, but another to compromise that of a friend. He wonders if Bunt still wears his trademark bandanna. Some cons like to advertise where they've been when they're out—the exaggerated pimp roll and the convict-style clothes. Others go the opposite direction, everything from suits to self-consciously dropping any slang or prison cadences they picked up.

"I think they're gonna take it next year," Mike says.

"Maybe," Doc says, trying to feign interest. It isn't the first time Mike has killed time talking about the Redskins rather than letting Doc leave early. Never mind that the season hasn't even begun.

"Darrell Green? Art Monk, Gary Clark, Joe Jacoby? Dallas is going to get the hurt put on them. And the fuckers deserve it. The fuckers always deserve it."

Doc has never been a Redskins fan. Growing up it was the Baltimore Colts, but like everything, they've left. Indianapolis. "I got a shot at a new job," Doc says.

Jets of smoke issue from Mike's nose. "Let me guess: Burger King."

Doc keeps his expression neutral. "My landlady, she knows people at the National Gallery. Building Maintenance."

Mike nods. "So you're telling me we're going to have the same employer."

"I'm saying I got a shot at a new job," Doc says. "One that beats making fries."

"Your record," Mike says.

"That's why I ain't applied yet," Doc says.

"Not much I can say. But I'm guessing the odds of them hiring a convicted bank robber to work in a place where they got paintings worth millions . . . well, let's just say a letter of recommendation from me ain't likely to help much," Mike says.

"Ain't there no law about discrimination?"

Mike exhales and leans back in his chair. "We all make decisions with consequences, Kane. Getting married, going to school, robbing banks—they all put you on paths."

It would be easy to break this man, Doc reflects. To pulp his face in such a way that his smug expression wouldn't be likely to show again. " 'Paths,' " says Doc, holding his voice steady. " 'Paths.' And I'm on the fry-guy path, is that it? Got to know my place like a good nigger?"

"Relax, Kane. This ain't about race. And I ain't the one to get mad at. You put yourself in this position. You made the decision to become a repeat offender, a career criminal. Don't go crying about it now."

Doc stands. "I'm bigger than what you want me to be, you hear? I ain't no short-order cook, no cleaning boy, no beaten-down con."

"I got no problem with that," Mike says, a slight smile on his face that infuriates Doc. "Join the Redskins, wear a dress—be whatever you want, just so long as you meet your parole requirements."

When Doc exits the building he is still shaking with anger. Across the street Dead Earl leans against a streetlamp. A slight breeze brushes open his tattered overcoat, exposing dark pants that drape loosely over his thin legs. *You lucky you got a street between us, Earl.*

By the time he gets to Georgetown his mood has smoothed. It is, after all, a day he's looked forward to: He will spend the afternoon with Walker and Walker's younger brother, Evan, whose birthday it is. Doc has offered to treat them to a lunch and an afternoon out—for Evan this means an afternoon at the Time Out Arcade.

He finds the brothers lingering outside the arcade, Walker staring at a window display. He smiles at Doc and nods toward the mannequin in the window. "Check it out," he says.

Doc peers at a mannequin outfitted in a charcoal double-breasted suit. A cobalt-blue silk tie is knotted about its neck, the cloth shimmering in the light.

"That," Walker says, "is what it's all about."

"Suits?" Doc asks.

Walker nods, face serious. Doc addresses Evan. "What you think, little man? That what it's about?"

Evan shrugs, eyes fixed on the arcade's entrance. "We got to get to the arcade."

"In a minute," Walker says, looking again at the display mannequin. "Suit like that is a work of art. Look how it hangs just right. Suit like that makes people take you serious. Says you have something to *say*."

Doc laughs, the tension in him easing.

"Suit ain't nothing but icing," Doc says. "Character is what it's about."

Walker rolls his eyes, "I don't know where you been, but you go out for a night on the town in a McDonald's uniform, and you can forget about dancing. Forget about everything but funny looks."

The trio enters the recesses of Time Out. The sound of electronic mayhem is deafening. Doc and Walker let Evan pull them to a tank game.

A few humiliating losses later Doc and Walker retreat while Evan takes on new challengers.

"You sure this ain't going to give your Aunt Ferney no heart attack, you consorting with a known felon?" asks Doc. He means it as a joke, but the hurt in his voice bleeds through. Since Ferney's return he hasn't been out with the boys once. Almost three months.

Walker shrugs, though Doc knows that this disinterest belies the truth. "Ferney don't have to know everything," Walker says.

Nearby two teens in metallic-looking sweatsuits and thick gold chains stand side by side at a game.

"Check it out," Walker says.

Doc looks them over.

"What you think those chains and rings is worth?"

Doc shrugs.

"A thousand, easy," Walker says. "Add the shoes, suits, shades—say, fifteen hundred." He shakes his head.

"You got a point?"

"A waste."

"Shit. What was you just whining about upstairs? What's a good suit run?" Doc asks.

"Just stupid, is all. You know they been dealing for that kind of gear, risking prison and all that shit, and all they can think to do is buy flash threads."

"It's a street suit," Doc says. "Business attire."

"I could take that money and make money with it," Walker says. "Easy."

"Yeah?"

"Technology stocks," Walker says.

"Hah. What you know 'bout technology? Just saw your little bro whip you at a video game."

"I read *The Wall Street Journal*," Walker says. "I ain't talking out of my ass. Had some working capital and—"

"They got drugs for working capital," Doc says. "Entrepreneurs just like you want to be. Just ain't no Dow Jones for them."

"The world is bigger than a crackhouse."

Doc studies the boy. He likes Walker's smart mouth, his big ideas, seeing in them something of himself and something, too, of his son Willie. He hasn't seen Willie since he was shipped to Tyburn, but even at age six the child was precocious and cocky. Big plans and an active imagination, wild stories of what his life would be like and where he would go. Stories that had made Doc swell with pride even while he wondered if he should indulge the child's fantasies—how did you pretend away the hard fact of circumstance, of poverty, of race?

"How's he doing in school?" Doc asks, with a tilt of the head toward Evan.

"Okay," Walker says. His face falls slightly.

"He ain't having problems?"

"Everyone got problems at his school," says Walker. "Just a question of how big."

Doc waits.

"I ain't never around, is all," Walker explains. "Two jobs, you know."

"Need to get you something that pays better. A job that lets you have some time with Little Man." Doc hesitates before stumbling on, the idea only half formed in his head. "I been talking to this woman I know. She used to work at the National Gallery. You been there?"

"Uh-uh," Walker says.

"You take a look around on your day off. That way you can impress her. She talks to her friends and maybe you get a job checking coats or in janitorial. Easy work, good benefits."

Walker scratches his ear, his eyes downcast.

"So you interested? Or you think you got to stick around, refine your burger-flipping technique, your kitchen mope?"

Walker's mouth tightens. Doc knows that the boy thinks he's meant for better—he knows exactly how this feels and he knows, too, that Walker is right to think this. The boy is better than his circumstances allow. "It's a step," Doc says. "Put you on firmer ground. We ain't talking no job you got to hold 'till the end of your days."

Walker's expression doesn't change and Doc wonders what it is that he's missing. "Look," he says. "There ain't no catch to this. I know someone, that's all. It ain't no tycoon position, but it's something."

"Why you doing this? I ain't done nothing for you."

It depresses Doc to see the awkwardness and suspicion in Walker's face.

"I want to do it," Doc says. "And you need it." He pauses. "Shit, maybe I need it. Might make me feel better, seeing you in a real job."

"I don't mope," Walker says. "I never said nothing 'bout any of that."

"People is easier to read than you think," Doc says. "That's one thing you learn in the joint. And what you going to do when your aunt's checks stop?"

"Why'd you get sent to prison?"

"Son-in-law beat my daughter. I shot him." Doc holds Walker's eyes. "All you got to say is yes or no. You don't want to take my help and I'll leave you be."

Walker nods uncertainly.

They watch Evan shift in his seat as he maneuvers his tank, intent on the game.

Where you at, Willie? thinks Doc, wishing his son were present to accept some money, some attention, to accept a gesture to make up for a part, however small, of a father's unforgivable absence.

Across the arcade, Dead Earl stands watching. *Don't say nothing, Earl. This ain't about you and me.* And he knows that this is true. There is no way to play father to these boys. Other choices have precluded this. With a depressing certainty he knows that if he has family, it is the likes of Cue Ball and Dead Earl that comprise it.

But he turns back to these boys. For the moment he will pretend. Ignore their aunt's suspicions, ignore Dead Earl, ignore his frustrations with parole and the fact of his new employment. He puts a hand to Walker's shoulder. "You all eat yet?"

10

Doc closes his eyes and leans his head back as Blondelle increases the pace of her sucking. He exhales with a grunt to the rhythmic, wet sound and feel of her mouth. She stands, her hand trailing along his leg to his waist and winks at him before popping her gum. It is early morning at Odessa's, the most private time he can think of for this.

"How do you do that?" he asks. In the past weeks he's come to rely on sex with Blondelle, the humiliation of having to pay for it curbed by the calm that settles on him in the wake of these moments. He's no longer so embarrassed that he can't talk with her. And for her part, while it remains all business, there are small gestures from time to time, like now, with her small hand at his bare waist, her sharp fingernails tickling the skin.

"Practice," she says. "That and natural talent."

"I mean the gum," he says.

"I got fine motor control," she says. She's dropped some weight in the past weeks and even in the smudged light of the dimly lit room her face is acquiring harder angles. Doc wonders how many times a day she's getting high.

She holds out her hand and he reaches for his pants, paying

her, as has been his habit, more than she charges. It's easy to do, especially with the money rolling in and so little to spend it on—he's never been much for clothes and there's only so much he can drink at the bar, especially with Flash giving him free drinks. Most of his cash has gone into the pile of money orders made out to Walker that Eduardo keeps for him.

He leaves the bar and ventures out to McDonald's for an afternoon shift. Rebo wants him out on the street more than the four days a week he's been doing in the wake of reducing his schedule at the restaurant, but Doc can't let go of the job, even without parole in mind. Work gives him an excuse to spend time with Walker. The two jobs leave him tired and anxious, but this is better than feeling empty.

But the McDonald's is closed. The windows have been shot open, the shatter-resistant glass sagging inward in glittering sheets, police tape is Xed over each rectangle. The front doors are still intact, though Cue Ball's tag—the skull inside a circle—grins in Day-Glo green on the glass. Doc lingers across the street, his stomach knotted.

Eduardo emerges from the restaurant with a suited man and woman, each of whom carries a clipboard. Doc guesses they have something to do with insurance. Eduardo motions at one of the windows, careful not to step where the glass gleams on the sidewalk. At one point in his conversation he looks in Doc's direction. Doc pushes himself from the wall he's been leaning against and tentatively raises a hand. Even from across the street he sees Eduardo's compact body go tight with rage. Doc drops his hand. Turning away, he wonders if Eduardo will track down Mike, if he's already placed a call to the parole office. His last link with the Square John trip is broken. He doesn't even want to risk returning home to pack his things—the chance that Mike might be there is slight, but it would mean four more years in prison. *You was going to quit anyway,* he thinks, trying to convince himself that the home he's headed to is the one he wants, that Eduardo's anger and the loss of more hours with Walker doesn't matter.

* * *

That afternoon Doc sits at East Potomac Park. Dealing here has worked well, and yet now that it is all he has, it seems as limiting as McDonald's, just in different ways. He's about more than this, yet can't express how this is the case, or why he believes it. *More than half a century and you still ain't figured out who you is.*

"Ajax?"

Doc leans back in his lawn chair, studying his latest customer. She is short, her blonde hair in a ponytail. She is too nervous to crouch by him, instead her eyes jumping from him to the river and back again. Rebo, to his credit, has limited Doc's customers. Most tend toward the seedily respectable, many of them white suburbanites—with only one or two smelling and looking unwashed, their habit having eclipsed any call for hygiene.

"Don't tell me black folks make you nervous," he says.

She shakes her head too quickly. Doc sighs. "How much you need?" he asks. The past month has featured Dr. Livingston ("Dr. Livingston, I presume?"), Trojan Horse, and Ajax, the brands stamped on the wax paper; Rebo wouldn't go for Lotus Eater ("Just the same as calling it her'on."). Kelvin's been on a kick about Homer, having just finished the *Odyssey* and now at work on the *Iliad.*

Doc takes her money, sends her to Kelvin. He watches the entire transaction, tracking her to the bench where she pulls the magnetized key case from beneath it and removes the drugs, his eyes on her until she is lost from sight. The cops haven't yet bothered, or even seemed to notice him, and he's gained enough confidence that he's even done a few drops for Rebo solo, muling the product himself. It feels strange today, though, to realize that this has become his entire life, that at best he'll have a room in the back of Odessa's for the night, listening to Rebo's whores and the drunken rumble of the bar. He'd like to send one of Rebo's crew to pick up his stuff at Angie's, but what kind of message would convince her to open up the apartment? It's just as well that he's out of her life, he reflects. There's nothing good that could have come of the two of them, not with his past. *Shit. Or your present.*

The water of the Potomac slides past silently. The fish aren't biting. The previous day he'd actually caught one—catfish—which Kelvin had insisted he keep; the cooler still reeks of it and gives, or so he thinks, the beer a fishy flavor. The sky has a leaden cast, though there are no clouds. Rain is predicted.

By noon Doc has finished half of the six-pack, one beer short of killing his appetite, and in such a state he is more attentive to the meal than is usual. Kelvin has picked up Burger King. He ignores Doc's critique of the woeful state of the fries.

"You was so concerned about your health, you'd stay sober. Surprised you can stay awake drinking all that beer."

"There's lots of parts of this job that ain't easy," Doc comments. Behind Kelvin a black Mercedes with tinted windows glides slowly past.

" 'Antipathy.' "

"Take that dog," Doc says. "Ain't no way to slobber that much 'less he got some gland problem. Ought to tape a cup to his jaw. Or a big-ass sponge."

" 'Enmity.' "

Doc ignores Kelvin, the appeal of the game having worn thin. T-Rex tries to lick him and he pushes the dog's face away. It begins to rain lightly and the pair move to beneath the bridge.

"Check this out," Kelvin says. "This is Ajax at work: 'The spear struck Archelochus, son of Antenor, for heaven counseled his destruction. It struck him where the head springs from the neck at the top joint of the spine, and severed both the tendons at the back of the head. His head, mouth and nostrils reached the ground long before his legs and knees could do so.' "

"Ain't no difference between that and watching the nightly news. What's with you and all this shit, anyway?"

"Know thine enemy."

"Hah. Your enemy gonna be some little punk-ass nigger with

a Tec-9. That or a cop. Ain't either one of them ever heard of Homer. What you think, that you gonna do battle with some Georgetown professor?"

"Call it home-schooling," Kelvin says. He motions around them with a spiraling of his finger. "There's a bigger world than this nickel-and-dime racket."

"Everyone's a fucking entrepreneur."

"Not you," Kelvin says.

" 'Ajax'—what the fuck kind of brand name is that? Make it sound like we're selling oven cleaner. That ain't no entrepreneurial concept."

Kelvin's beeper sounds. He checks the code. "Rebo," he says. He walks off to use the pay phone near the tennis courts. Doc leans on the riverside railing, watching the water. If the rain worsens they'll have to close for the day.

"You was at Tyburn, not Leavenworth."

Doc straightens slowly and turns to face Levonne. The boy stands a good six inches taller, a .22 steady in his hand, the muzzle inches from Doc's head. The rush of adrenaline seems to calm him and he stares evenly at the boy, looking past the gun to the face. Levonne verges on gaunt, his heavy-lidded eyes open wide and sparkling beneath the hood of his jacket. For a moment he looks as if Dead Earl's face has been superimposed upon his own. Doc shakes his head. Rebo, he knows, has sold him out. He fights the perverse desire to grin—maybe Rebo has what it takes to make it after all. He's underestimated his old partner.

"Ain't you got nothing to say?"

Doc forces his shoulders to unknot. "Ain't nothing going to change the past."

"You a piece of work, old head," Levonne says. He tilts his head and studies Doc. "Byron, he wrote me letters. Said you was always talking too much. Called it the 'granpa routine.' "

Rain sifts down around them, a slight breeze wafting a fine spray of droplets to where they stand beneath the bridge supports, imparting the moment with a ghostly, faded quality.

"Well?" Levonne asks impatiently.

"What?"

"Why you did it. I want to know why you did it."

The rain increases. The roar of a plane shivers overhead.

"You going to shoot me," Doc states.

Levonne nods.

The moment stretches. Doc feels somehow unable to get his mind around it, as if he's watching some reflection of himself face this boy with the gun. And what, really, is there for him to say? The patterns of this violence are what they are, no different from those that set him in conflict with Cue Ball, an ineluctable cycle of violence, pride, revenge, and desire for an ephemeral respect. "I don't have to tell you a damn thing," he says, catching a quick movement out of the corner of his eye.

He feels himself knocked back by the report of the gun, wakes to the world seesawing, visible through one eye, the other stinging and wet. He lies on his side on the cement walk with a hot wetness spreading out beneath his head. Kelvin kneels several feet away, arms pistoning his fists downward, each strike punctuated by a grunt, the blurred sight and sound eerily sexual. Kelvin pauses and then twists and half rises to a wet sound followed by a cracking. Doc inhales and tries to push himself up on all fours. Blood runs into his mouth and drips from his nose. The world whirls.

Within moments Kelvin has him stumbling into the Jeep.

"I'm shot," Doc says, pawing at the visor to get at the mirror. He blots at his left temple with a rag from the floorboard. Blood flows freely from the side of his scalp though he can feel no pain, but there is no hole in his skull, the bullet having ripped open his scalp from his left temple to well behind his ear. "Take me up to Bethesda or Reston, leave me at a hospital." A hospital far from D.C. is safest. With no ID, they won't know who to call and it will take time if they decide to run a check on his prints.

T-Rex paces the backseat and barks at the scent of the blood.

Doc feels nauseous. He fumbles with his wallet, dropping it to the floorboards. "Leave me out front of the emergency room." He struggles to deepen his breathing.

"You gonna be fine," Kelvin says.

"I got shot," Doc says. "In the head."

"You gonna be fine," Kelvin repeats.

Doc's mouth is dry and it is difficult to keep the view of the road from angling crazily. He closes his eyes. "My EM band," he says. "You got to cut it."

Kelvin stops the Jeep in the parking lot of the Reston Medical Center. Doc is vaguely aware of Kelvin bracing his foot against the dashboard. Kelvin pulls up the cuff of Doc's pants and works the blade of his buck knife between Doc's ankle and the yellow band. The plastic parts grudgingly. Doc envisions a signal flashing out, in an instant his status shifting from paroled convict to fugitive, the moment the closing of another chapter in his life that hasn't ended as he'd hoped.

"You killed Levonne," Doc says. It is difficult to speak.

Kelvin stares at him, then reaches across to open the passenger door.

"Why ain't you killed me? Why you doing this?"

Kelvin gives him a hard smile, but there is something genuine to it in spite of this. "You don't fit out here," he says. "This way, you go back to where you belong while me and Rebo sort it all out. Keep your mouth shut and maybe you'll be back in a few years. Maybe you'll have the sense to stay away from all this." With a thrust of his powerful arm, he pushes Doc onto the asphalt.

Doc falls and doesn't have the balance to rise to his feet. "You ain't no different from them," he says. "Not you or Rebo." Kelvin tosses the EM band after him. The dizzying whirl in Doc's head accelerates. He sees the wet tread of a tire and then nothing.

Rain beats on the roof like tired fingers drumming on a tabletop. It pools in the roof's declivities, flows over the slick tarpaper, gathering momentum, rushing down the gutters, spraying onto the sodden turf behind the Reston Medical Center. Doc awakes, eyes wide. Not ten feet away a cop dozes in a chair, her red hair loose over one eye. As Doc sits up, the pain and a dizzying head rush drive him back to the mattress. When his head clears he feels the pull of the handcuff locked to the bedframe. Fuck. The memories of Kelvin and Levonne wash over him. He's been printed and IDed—any gunshot wound gets reported to the police and they probably found his severed EM band. A surge of adrenaline sharpens his vision. His fingers are black with ink. His free hand tentatively explores the bandages about his skull. The left side is swollen and frighteningly numb. The cop has not moved. The other bed in the room is empty.

He stands and braces the bedside cuff with a hand to silence it as he begins twisting the chain. It's an awkward process. His wrist is bleeding freely when a link gives.

Outside, water seeps through topsoil, through underlying layers of clay where a fuel pipeline rests, the metal sleeve machined smooth and seamless. Furrows score the topside steel, rustflakes vibrating to the muted rumble of the fuel pressurized at six hundred pounds per square inch. In one furrow a final rustflake loosens, the steel beneath bowing outward, a jet of fuel spraying forth. The metal splits in a ragged gash, fuel erupting through the topsoil and up a hundred feet.

The initial boom of the exploding fuel line is dulled by the blanketing earth, a groan that jolts those inside from their troubled dreams. The cop wakes and stares without focus at Doc. He leaps, pinning her arm before she can reach for her gun. She yells as they roll on the floor, biting at Doc's hand as he forces the edge of it into her mouth.

"Fuck!" he exclaims as her teeth break the flesh. He pushes hard with the weight of his torso behind his arm, snapping her head against the tiled floor. Her mouth slackens and he palms her face, slapping her head to the floor several times until she stops moving. He takes her gun and radio and sprints down the hall, knocking a nurse to the floor. The air is cool against the open back of his papery gown.

As the door of the stairwell's base swings wide the blare of the alarm lances into his skull. He drops the gun and radio and breaks into a stumbling run over wet grass, then comes up short just in front of a geyser. From the exploded pipeline kerosene sprays upward in a twenty-foot column. The parking-lot sodium floodlights backlight it, the electric white lighting the geyser brilliantly in the predawn gray. Kerosene rains on him, stinging his eyes and igniting a line of pain along the cut on his head and around his ripped wrist. He jerks into a run, tripping, falling, up again and moving. The alarm fades as he reaches a dark line of trees.

The woods are silent, as if gravity has borne down unnaturally hard, bowing branches and smothering sound, bending even the predawn light until the trees blur and waver, near collapse. The underbrush slices at his skin and rips at the soles of his feet. He emerges from the trees, slides into Sugarland Run Creek. He tries to keep his mouth clear of the water. The current catches and spins him.

As he nears a bank something grabs at his head. It is Dead Earl, his callused hands holding tight. Their limbs tangle in a mesh of roots that hang from a collapsed riverbank.

Doc pushes his forearm between the hands at his neck and twists, clawing with his other hand for purchase among the roots. His fingers close on a thick root and he jerks himself out, pulling now with both hands, the weight of Dead Earl on his back. Earl's broken nails rip into skin as they loosen. Doc collapses at the top of the riverbank, coughing, retching, arms up to protect his head from Earl's strikes. Then he is crawling, grasping a branch and twisting over onto his back, the branch accelerating with his arm into a backhand blow that lands solidly on Earl's neck. Earl falls back, then lunges for Doc, who has gained his feet. Doc grapples with him, pins him, punching until the hands scrabbling for his face weaken. He places his thumbs on the convexities of Earl's eyes. "You ain't gonna find me again, Earl. Never."

He presses hard with his thumbs, yelling with Dead Earl.

Capital Pipeline Company detects a drop in pressure at five A.M. and shuts off the flow, reducing the geyser to a bubbling spring of heavy water. Fumes warp the weak dawn light. The nearby woods waver like a desert mirage. Four hundred thousand gallons have spilled, a quarter of this into Sugarland Run, and thence to the muddy rapids of the Potomac.

Doc staggers to a pay phone in an empty strip mall, barely able to enunciate clearly enough to get a collect call through to Walker. *Please be there. Got to be there.* He presses himself against the wall as a pack of police cars and several ambulances pass in a whirl of light and earsplitting sirens.

"Yeah?" Walker's voice is sleep-fogged.

"You got to come get me," Doc chatters.

"Doc? You all right?"

"No." He misses Walker's next comment as a violent fit of shivering shifts the receiver away from his ear. "You got to come get me," he repeats.

"What's happened?"

"Just get me!" Doc shouts. The wind rushes over him.

"I don't have a car," Walker says.

"Get one, get me," Doc says. "And bring blankets." He gives the directions carefully, describing the strip mall, the location of the pay phone, the trees where he'll be hiding.

A white Pacer with a badly dented side shows about forty minutes later, slowing where Doc has spent the time crouched, watching the passing stream of police cars and fire engines. He scuttles toward the car, realizing as he does that he's so dizzy he can barely keep his stiffened legs under him. By now one hundred thousand gallons of fuel roil atop the Potomac, bound for the Chesapeake Bay and the Atlantic. Doc settles into the car, ignoring Walker's shocked look. "Drive," he says.

Walker jerks the car into gear and they lurch forward, almost stalling, Doc's head exploding with pain from the motion. "Drive the motherfucking car!" he shouts, bracing his arm against the dashboard. He ignores the boy's angry, terrified face.

Crossing the river his head begins to clear. He's wrapped a blanket around his shoulders and his head like a shawl.

"What am I doing?" Walker asks softly, breaking the silence.

"Trying to drive," Doc says.

"No," Walker says. "I mean, what am I doing? What did you do that you got that bandage on your head, that you need to hide in the bushes, that you smell like a gas station? Why is there a handcuff on your wrist?"

Doc says nothing.

"You got me committing a crime and I want to know," Walker says, his voice rising.

Doc winces at the volume. "You don't know enough to be doing no crime," he says. "Keep it that way."

"Aunt Ferney, she got your number. Wouldn't be in this if I listened to her. You been trying to play me all along." His voice quivers.

"I never tried to play you," says Doc. He doesn't know where to go. Mike will know about the cut EM band, about his gunshot wound, his stay at the hospital, and by now—likely—his escape. Angie's is out.

"I ain't going to prison for you!" Walker shouts, his hands white-knuckling the steering wheel.

"You ain't done nothing wrong," Doc says soothingly, though he doesn't know that this is true.

But Walker isn't listening. "You don't care nothing about Evan or me! You just playing us! Like that talk about that job."

"Walker."

"Just shut up!" Walker yells. He stops the car at 7th and L Southeast. "I got you where you want to go," he says.

"Walker," Doc says again. "Don't do me like this." He doesn't want it to end like this: D.C. closed to him, on the run, his one attempt at kindness suspect and rejected. "I wanted something good for you," he says. "And the rest . . ." His voice trails off.

"I got to go," Walker says, his hands clenched to the steering wheel, staring out the windshield.

"At least look at me," Doc says.

Walker will not. Doc opens the door and steps out. Walker drives away and Doc does not see him look back.

Doc turns back to the houses, walking to one that juts from the end of the block, the sidewalk skirting one sidewall, the wreckage of the adjacent house piled against the other. He pulls an envelope from the mailslot. *W. Pleddy.*

Bunt cracks the door some time after Doc knocks, his face a mask of distrust, wrinkled forehead covered by a blue bandanna. "I ain't got what you need," he says.

Doc pushes the blanket back to reveal his face.

Bunt's face collapses. "Doc. What kind of shit you got yourself into?" he says softly.

Doc ducks his head in humiliation. "I'm sorry, man." He pulls closer to his shoulders. "I—I ain't asking you for nothing you can't give."

Bunt unchains the door. "Shit. There's not asking and not asking."

The stutter of Porky Pig glances from the bare walls of the living room, the flashing TV screen the only color in the room. A few pillows and a single mattress furnish it.

"It ain't that I ain't happy to see you."

"Ain't no good circumstances for seeing each other," Doc agrees. He smiles wanly at his old Tyburn friend. "I just need a day or two. Long enough to figure where to go." He tentatively touches his temple. "I know what you risking."

"Don't have no choice nohow." Bunt's voice is sour. "Goddamn, nigger! How the fuck you get so stupid?"

Doc stares steadily at his old friend. Sad and scared, comforted and guilty. "There wasn't no choice. Not when it came down to it. Like when you opened that door even though you wanted to shut it in my face."

"Shit."

Their understanding brings with it no comfort, just a crushing weight.

A faint, overripe smell fills Doc's nostrils and he shivers, recalling the sensation of Earl's eyes puncturing beneath his thumbs. "Earl?" Doc's voice is hoarse from sleep. On the wall above the mattress the outline of a cross glows from the sooty posterboard. He imagines a huddled form nested in the shadows of the far corner. "I didn't mean it, Earl."

But there is no Earl, just bunched shadows. There is no Dead Earl just as there was no Earl hours earlier when he was jolted from sleep by the imagined feel of hands about his throat. Though early, Bunt has long since left for *The Washington Times,* where he places inserts in the papers as they come off the press. On the floor beside the mattress sits the ice pack Bunt retrieved the previous day, still smelling of fish. A lucky break that Kelvin had forgotten the cooler, that whoever had found it had dumped the contents like garbage. Doc sits up and works the bills free of the opaque plastic. He counts fifteen hundred dollars.

The day looms before Doc, empty and hollow. No work, no Walker, no Angie. No Eduardo, no McDonald's, no parole. No nothing. He pictures Angie answering Mike's questions, maybe watching a few cops search Doc's apartment for clues to his whereabouts. He sees her framed in the doorway as they leave, turning to face Doc's apartment: the prom photo of the strangers he claimed were his kids, his comics stacked by his bedside. All left for her to pack.

What else is there for her to find? He chuckles, remembering the porn magazines, but the laughter belies the ache. He imagines her face, imagines her wandering through his empty apartment. She will find the letters, he realizes. Letters from his daughter, a few drawings from when Willie was six, seven, eight, the clearest record he has of his past. He sees her sitting on his bed, the letters open before her, as if examining these will give her some insight into the man who's disappeared. The letters are a painful loss, the last proof of his family. Without them it feels as if the memories are un- moored, as if they will drift, mixing with his dreams and leaving him somehow unsure of their veracity. He looks around Bunt's empty apartment. Other than the money and a set of sweats and sneakers Bunt's picked up for him, he has nothing—less than when he was in prison.

Doc examines himself in the bathroom mirror. The stitches have held, though the skin is an ugly whitish color where the kerosene-soaked bandages have pressed against the raw edges of the wound. Doc takes Neosporin and rubs it over the cut, then rewraps his head and hides the bandages with one of Bunt's ban- dannas. Scrapes and cuts mark his arms and torso. His left wrist is swollen, maybe sprained, the welt from the handcuff ringing his wrist a vivid red. He has nothing to cut the remaining handcuff with and contents himself with taping it as high up on his forearm as he can slide it.

The parks seem to be the best place to hide for the day, empty and private as they are during work hours. Cyclists and joggers flash past in swatches of brightly colored Lycra along Rock Creek, but there are no cops on the trails. North of the zoo Doc sits on a flat rock by the creek, listening to the water rush over the humped shoulders of submerged boulders. Pools of light seem to collect where the water eddies, glistening, dappling the walled greenery to either side with reflected brilliance. A sight he'd like to share, a moment that smoothes the roil of his thoughts.

He thinks of Stirling, wondering whom he's found as a new adversary for the Risk game. He smiles at the thought of wanting to return to be with Ellis and Stirling, knowing that they must dream at times of sitting where he now finds himself—the air, the sun, the beauty. So different from the gray concrete. *Scenery ain't doing you a damn bit of good.* There is nowhere to go. Fifty-five, fifteen hundred to his name; a walk, talk and look straight out of Tyburn; his own town no place for him. Kelvin was right.

And more galling still is the certainty that these circumstances were inevitable. And had he not saved Odessa with the potato knife so long ago? Had he not felt such a thrill at riding armed with Rebo and the others, at seeing the bank come into view...?

You is who you is, old man. You was to have walked the straight and narrow and who would you be? Just another old man in the kitchen or behind the mop. Ain't no way to live. Square John trip is for suckers.... That and being a con, both.

He hucks a rock at a milk carton floating past.

There is nothing for him here. All that was familiar revolved around Rebo. Doc spits into the river. It makes dispiriting sense that he'd be set up. Either outcome—Doc dead and Rebo credited by Levonne for having provided a chance for payback, or Levonne dead and out of Rebo's way for good—works to his ex-partner's advantage. He wonders how much Kelvin knew going into it, thinking of the timing of the beeper, of Kelvin's convenient return. He tries to rationalize it—*You was using them, too*—but there's a difference he can't deny. It's difficult to process the betrayal. And this, he knows, is exactly why he will never make it on the streets.

That night he and Bunt talk over the noise of the TV, Coke bottles sweating in their hands.

"So you gonna talk to her?"

"Shit. I don't know. She's got it going on, you know, but every time I get ready to lay a line on her—shit, I picture me standing there in my birthday suit with this damn radio collar. Ain't no fashion accessory, know what I'm saying." Bunt absently picks at the plastic band where it shows beneath his pantcuff. He's lost weight and muscle tone since leaving Tyburn, his round body sadly deflated.

"It's just like Ellis said about you, Bunt: Life gonna pass you by 'cause you never involved."

"Don't want no involvement if my head gonna get fucked up like yours."

Doc toasts the riposte with a tip of his bottle.

"What about you?" Bunt asks. "You had a woman and you damn sure wouldn't be here."

"Ain't something I want to discuss," Doc says. He feels guilty about Angie even though he tells himself he has no reason to.

Bunt shrugs.

Doc wonders if Angie is sitting in her living room, painting. That or unpacking from Eastern Market. He reads Bunt's watch—Angie will make her nightly pass at Lost Weekend Liquors in a little more than an hour. "Marion?" he asks.

"What I said. Cornelius don't care. D.C. Black or not, that motherfucker scared me. Bet Stirling is just as relieved as the rest to have him out the way."

"He really did Ivory like that? In the middle of the cafeteria?"

"Kidney shot with the shank, then took his time. Didn't even look up when the hacks showed up."

Doc rolls the cool soda bottle between his palms. "I know what you mean about that band," he says.

"Yeah?"

"Humiliating is what it is. Like when they put a number on you in the joint."

Bunt nods.

"Angie, my landlady? She was all right. Been thinking about her a lot."

Bunt waits.

"Ain't no going back, though. Not there." Doc studies the bottle before him. "What you heard about Ellis?"

Bunt rises from the mattress to switch channels. "He doing okay. Older. The same."

"Stirling?"

The TV glows with static for a moment. Bunt clicks again. The evening news settles on screen. "Six weeks in solitary before I left."

"Six weeks."

"He ain't the same," Bunt says. "Or he wasn't when I got out. But it wears off. Sort of. You know how it is."

They stare at the TV. A commercial laugh track erupts.

It hurts, realizing how little joy reunion brings. The past is no place to hide. Doc's vision blurs. He rises and runs his hands over his face. "I got to get out for a bit."

Bunt shrugs, eyes the TV too intently.

At Lost Weekend Liquors the Conductor approaches. "Change. Got change."

Doc presses a five into his hand. The man's wiry, white beard crinkles around his mouth. A smile. "Heh." He touches his hand to his forehead, a formal, courtly gesture, then shuffles into the liquor store. Traffic on U Street is sparse. The neon of the smiling bottle sign buzzes intermittently, bathing the front wall in sickly yellow.

Forty minutes later Angie appears on the sidewalk. It irritates him that she's out so late, alone on the sidewalk and easy prey. Doc steps from the building, behind the cars parked in the side lot. She passes without noting him, her face strained, lines bunched in her forehead—her own version of the junkie's mission walk. The store door swings wide with a ring; Doc absently notes that the owners must have replaced the bell he ripped from it the night of the robbery. He can't say why he doesn't follow her inside or why his heart is beating so fast.

When she emerges, a wrapped bottle of what he knows is Wild

Irish Rose beneath her arm, he steps out in front of her. Angie jumps back and utters a startled cry which she quickly swallows. She backs toward the light of the store.

"Angie," Doc says softly. He pulls back the hood of his sweat-jacket. She stills.

"I wanted to see you," Doc says. She continues to stare and he knows she's taking in the glowing white of his swathed head. He feels his face flushing with embarrassment.

"Look at you," she says, sharply, shaking her head in disbelief. "The police," she says, "they were at my house." Her face is without the humor or softness he'd hoped to see.

Doc stares at her, shifting his weight from foot to foot. Even with her face so hard she looks pretty to him.

"Well," she says, "what do you want?"

He shakes his head. "To see you....I don't know."

"You want something," she says. "Wouldn't be skulking around here scaring old ladies otherwise."

But what he wants is too ridiculous to utter, can in fact only be entertained so long as it remains unuttered—to have a life free of prison and, in so many ways, free of his past. "You take care," he says, and turns away.

He spends several hours on the rooftop of a closed gas station, the lights of the city and the blurred, looming shapes of treetops around him. Warm summer breezes stir the leaves. In the dark he can content himself with the familiar sound and smell of the city— the swampy edge of the air and the ceaseless white noise of traffic—both no different despite the shifting topography of the buildings and streets. It is easy to linger here, though again and again his thoughts shift from Rebo to Angie, from Walker to Ellis, from Bunt to Grippe, and nowhere can he find the comfort of memory or clearly recall the fit that comes with belonging. He has to get out of here, out of this city and away from his past.

The sky is still black, the faintly dimming stars the only sign of impending morning, when he returns to Bunt's. He'd like to say good-bye before Bunt leaves for work, before Doc himself leaves.

He corners on to L Street, stalling at the blue-and-red flash of lights. At the far end of the street two police cruisers block the road, lights flashing. Doc stands transfixed, his pulse hammering in his ears.

"My friend. My friend," he whispers. He can't bear to see Bunt escorted out of the house, is blocks away and running at full sprint when this occurs.

12

A transport bus firms into view, matte black, windows darkened with steel mesh, its engine laboring through the Nevada heat en route from Las Vegas to Tyburn. Behind it, a taxicab accelerates, already moving at more than ninety, the scale of the surrounding desert plain so vast as to give this speed a static quality.

The cab swings wide into the left lane. Doc looks up at the windows of the bus. Faces pressed against the glass blur by. Doc catches the eye of a young man, craning his neck until the angle breaks the view, he himself filled with the same fear and desultory hope of escape written on the face of the con. Ahead, the road arrows through alkaline flats scabbed with crusted earth, through encroaching drifts of sand and fields of desiccated creosote. Doc's memories of seventeen years earlier unfold with the landscape. He can half hear the rattle of chains, smells the panic oozing from his pores, as if he is on the bus receding in the rearview mirror. His eyes search ahead and he exhales with a grunt, as if struck in the solar plexus, as Tyburn Penitentiary rises from the broad declivity of the desert, the wedged facade like the immense, weather-beaten prow of a ship westward-bound. He can't catch his breath: it is as if a band is tightening about his ribs. He remembers squeezing through the vents for Ellis, looking for the rats, the pressure of all that stone on him.

"You okay?" the cabby asks, a young white kid with a Fu Manchu mustache who's been nervous the entire drive.

Doc closes his eyes, the afterimage pulsing to his heartbeat. "Turn up the AC," he says, wiping his forehead.

The car slows before the prison, pulling into the wide graveled lot beside a line of parked staff cars. Doc regards the massive walls, the rusted lettering bolted to the lintel stone. Tyburn Federal Penitentiary.

He steps from the car. A hot, dry wind abrades his face. Dimly, the cacophony from the prison's interior filters through the long, vertical windows cut into the westward-facing wall. The wavering light of the reddening sun imparts a glow to the stone that makes it look as if it is a monstrous kiln. An evening of redness in the West. He holds his hand up, palm out.

The transport bus swings into the lot, the sally-port gates opening to admit it. The heavy steel panels slam shut with a clang of finality Doc remembers well. He shivers and returns to the cab. West of the prison they turn onto a smaller side road, this an unpaved stretch of washboards leading to the small town of Caliente. Doc studies the map he's brought and directs the driver.

"This is it," Doc says as they pull astride a slumped clapboard house with a peeling tar-paper roof and a porch that looks to have collapsed at one end.

The cabby looks back at Doc. "You want me to wait?"

Doc shakes his head and hands over four twenties. A few hunched elms shade a bare yard in the center of which a stubby-legged dog chained to a stake is stretched out on the hard-packed earth. Doc opens the fence gate and skirts the dog, who hardly raises his head. At the screened porch Doc pauses to listen. The tinny chords of a blues song waver through the open door. The interior of the house looks dark and cool and inviting. He slips in, smelling fried eggs and onion. The living room is neater than he'd expected; a khaki uniform draped over a chair, framed botanical prints on the walls, stacks of *National Geographic* and other magazines carefully filed on a low bookcase. Doc fingers the uniform. On the chair seat a polished truncheon rests atop a belt with holstered pepper spray and handcuffs. He touches the truncheon, a static charge jolting up his arm. The grip is wrapped tightly with an absorbent blue tape. He picks it up and tests the heft, remembering what it feels like to be prodded in the gut or kidney with one, to have it jammed under his jaw. The clash of dishes draws him to the hallway leading to the kitchen.

Grippe has his back to Doc, humming to the music while leaning over the stove. To his left, on the counter, is an open bottle of Jack Daniel's. Doc raps the truncheon against the open door. Grippe stills and in the slow moment before he turns, Doc idly wonders how often the man has imagined this scene: an ex-con come calling to settle old scores. In a T-shirt and an old pair of cargo pants Grippe looks diminished, nothing like the looming presence he plays in Doc's memories of Tyburn. He must be nearing sixty, his body more fat than muscle.

"You didn't knock," Grippe says. He holds the skillet in one hand, the eggs sizzling on the hot iron.

"Figure sixteen years makes us like family," Doc says. Grippe's yellow eyes follow the truncheon as Doc points it at him. "You can let go of that frying pan," he says. Grippe reluctantly sets it back on the stove. He looks scared, his breathing coming fast, afraid to blink. A moment to be savored, though Doc discovers he has no appetite for it, no matter how often he's dreamed of seeing his guard and tormentor like this.

The tape in the player winds to a stop and clicks off.

"Ain't you got nothing to say?" Doc asks. " 'Bout how you knew I'd be back?"

"I ain't got stupid since I last saw you, Kane," Grippe says.

Doc nods. "So if I put this down," he waves the truncheon, "we get a real conversation?"

Grippe waits. A drop of sweat inches down the ebony skin of his jawline.

"Quit looking like you going to shit your pants," Doc says. He steps forward and motions Grippe past him, toward the living room, reaching with his other hand for the bottle of Jack. He can't resist prodding the man lightly with the truncheon as he passes. Grippe stiffens. Doc shakes his head. "I wanted to throw down and it'd be over already," he says, growing angrier with each second. Grippe's fear is an affront, an insult. "What the fuck you think," he says, his voice booming, "that I came out here to kill you? Sixteen years of knowing me and that's all you can think?"

Grippe sinks onto the couch. "What did you come for?"

"That I'm going to get from you?" Doc sets the bottle on the coffee table and studies Grippe. "Less than I thought, that's sure." He smacks the truncheon against his open palm. "How many heads you bust with this?" Grippe's eyes glance from Doc's. Doc nods slowly. "That's right, you better not answer."

"Fuck you," Grippe says.

Doc smiles, glad to see Grippe's fear turning to anger. This is the man he'd hoped to meet. "I look rehabilitated to you?" he asks.

"What?"

"Rehabilitated. When I got out you said I wasn't rehabilitated, that I'd be back."

"I was right," Grippe says. He points to the truncheon. "You trespass in my house, threaten me with that—you think you've changed?"

Doc lifts the bottle and drinks then holds it out to Grippe. " 'Threaten'? Ain't no threatening going on just 'cause you scared."

"Don't fuck with me, Kane. Just tell me what you want."

"What I want?" Doc repeats. "What I want is for you to take a drink," he says at length. After Grippe holds the bottle to his lips, Doc adds, "What I want is a understanding."

"An understanding."

"You think I'm going to fuck you up," Doc says.

Grippe says nothing.

"I *ain't* going to fuck you up," Doc says. "You just expect that because you think you know me."

"Shit, not this again, Kane," Grippe says. "What's to know? I said you ain't changed and now you've gone and proved me right."

Doc twists his neck left and right forces his shoulders to loosen, surprised by his anger. "You better be glad you ain't right," he says quietly. "You was right and you wouldn't be in no position to say shit." He steps back and taps the truncheon against the glass pane of one of the botanical prints just hard enough to split the glass. "I am what you think," he says, realizing he'd like nothing more than to beat Grippe with the club. He looks directly at Grippe. "But that ain't *all* I am." He thinks briefly of Walker: not of their final moment in the car, but of Walker cashing those money orders one by one, of what they will mean to the boy and his brother. It is a small comfort, but comfort nonetheless.

Doc walks to the door and pauses there, holding up Grippe's truncheon. "You think about that the next time you go to use this on a con." He drops the club to the floor.

In an outlying Vegas motel room that night he deals a hand of solitaire, his mind wandering. A cricket chirps. Exhaustion suffuses his muscles with lethargy and gradually his playing slows, even the minimal motion of placing the cards too great an effort. He drifts, coyotes yipping outside, a sound he hasn't heard since leaving Tyburn, a sound which disturbs the silt of memory, images sifting up through the murky water of consciousness and into the shifting light of the moment, the smell of sweat and dust, the breathing of friends, the four of them—Ellis, Stirling, Bunt, and himself—sitting on a cell floor, each with a hand of cards.

"Don't flush the queen so fast," Stirling says to Bunt. "Got no sense of style, going for blood on the second trick."

"You just saying that 'cause you know you gonna eat the queen."

"You the one to eat the bitch twice already."

"Don't go confusing your momma with the game."

They are playing hearts, a game that they'd met regularly for over a period of a year or more. The evening light is peculiar, almost granular, tinted sepia, the motions of the players lazy, their speech faint.

Ellis takes the trick and leads with a high spade.

"He gonna shoot the moon," Bunt mutters.

Ellis glares. "Last I heard, we didn't pay you for no running commentary."

"Man can think, can't he?"

"Who you fooling, Bunt? Score is proof you ain't never had no thought," Stirling says.

"You stop him, then. I ain't gonna be no sacrificial martyr so's to block him."

"Sacrificial what?" Stirling asks.

"He went to one of those Nation of Islam meetings," Doc says. "Thinks it's gonna help with the parole board. He don't even know what it means."

"Five bucks," Bunt says.

"I'll take that bet," Stirling says. "Doc, get the dictionary."

Doc groans, not wanting to get up.

Outside the coyotes begin yipping, a gleeful sound, almost celebratory.

"Listen to those fuckers," Stirling says, head tilted to catch the sound, his clipped ear sharp, the scarred skin rimming it smooth enough to catch light from the overhead bulb.

"Your turn, Doc," Ellis says.

"You'd sound like that, too, you was on the outside," Bunt says.

Doc is reaching to place his card when the scuff of feet wakes him. An exhausted, wheezing cough sounds, as if from behind a wall. "Earl?"

In the bathroom he splashes water on his face, behind his neck, lets it run over his wrists and hands, the metal bracelet of the handcuff, watching his face in the mirror above the sink. He's lost weight. A soft layer of fat has melted away, like a mask removed. His features poke through angular, more defined than he remembers them. The old scar on his chin and the new line stitched from temple to ear seem to mesh with the hollowed cheeks and edged chin, not so much embellishments of a hard life as elements of his essential features.

Outside it is silent. He walks behind the motel lot, the lights of Las Vegas thickening eastward toward the city's center. The moon is full, swollen, a harvest moon, its face stained amber and red. Doc climbs a hillock, feet stirring a chalky dust. Stars speckle the sky, their light cold and bright and clear in the rarefied air.

"What do you see?" Dead Earl asks. He sits a few feet away.

"Earl," Doc says, finding it difficult to speak. And again: "Earl."

Dead Earl has his overcoat wrapped tightly about him, the collar pulled up so high as to largely obscure his profile.

Doc clears his throat. "I didn't expect to see you again." Earl looks thinner than ever—wasted and curled in on himself, more ancient than Old Man Ellis. "You okay?"

Earl shakes his head but makes no move to face Doc.

"I'm sorry, Earl," Doc says. "I know that don't excuse nothing."

"Sorry don't help no more than it did the first time." He turns to regard Doc with emptied sockets.

Doc shudders: Earl is skeletal, the skin of his face drawn taut over bone, lacking any fat or muscle underneath, the eye sockets a depthless black.

"What do you see?" Earl repeats.

Doc stares for a long moment, overcome. He reaches out with a hand and places it against Earl's cheek. The skin feels no different from his—not cold. He stays like that, not moving, letting Earl's hand come to rest against his own face. He closes his eyes and moves his hand over the contours of Earl's face. "There's a moon in the heavens. Yellow and big with the sky dark all around."

Acknowledgments

Thanks to Robert Boswell, my long-suffering friend and mentor, and to Thom Jones, Judith Grossman, Jim McPherson, and Fred Dillen for their advice and encouragement.

I'm grateful to my family—Mom and Dad, my bro, Mac, and Mimi—for their love and support. Thanks, too, to my misfit friends for their peculiar brand of abusive encouragement. Brü, Ad, Finkel, Johnny Mac, John Greenman, Brett Block, Slodish, Devin, Kath, Mark Baechtel, Ed Ungvarsky, Eric Gemmen, Levine, Ollie & Leslie, and the U of I Communications Crowd.

Finally, a high five to my excellent editor and fellow author, Sean Desmond, to my agent, Kim Witherspoon, and to the inestimable Jon Karp, *el hombre más macho de todo*.

I was fortunate to find Pete Earley's outstanding book, *The Hot House: Life Inside Leavenworth Prison* (Bantam, New York, 1992). The Big House may not be exactly as I've described it—this is fiction—but what is rendered here owes much to Mr. Earley's fine reporting.